To Brian, my real life hero,

husband, and soulmate.

I'm so grateful God put you in my path.

Acknowledgments

This book was a labor of love that would not have been possible without the support, encouragement, and belief of so many people. Although you know who you are, I still want to thank many of you right here.

A huge thank you to my editor Char Chaffin and all of those at Soul Mate Publishing for making my dream of being a published author a reality. Your belief in me and this book has changed my life in the best of ways.

To my Georgia Romance Writers Tribe. Your support and inspiration since I joined back in 2013 has changed me in profound ways beyond just writing. You are the most caring, giving, and wonderful group of women and men I have ever met. I will forever be indebted to your guidance, wisdom, and love.

To my Romance Writers of America Tribe. You have taught me that there is always room at the table for every writer to have success. You are my cheerleaders and not my competition. And you have also gifted me the ability to carve out my own path my own way and in my own time.

And to my dear friend and critique partner, Tanya. You have read every horrible early draft of every manuscript I've shown you and supported me through some truly painful events in my personal life while reading those words. I will forever be grateful for all of your wisdom, support, and encouragement along this journey.

To my friends, especially my G-400 sisters of over twenty years, and family members, who have known of this secret dream of mine to be a writer and encouraged me for decades. And for those of you who just found out and embraced me whole heartedly, your support has blown me away. Thank you.

And to the administrators at Holy Innocents' Episcopal School. I am so grateful to be supported and celebrated in this endeavor. And, to my principal, Theresa. Your unbridled excitement and joy when I told you I was offered a publishing contract on this book brought me to tears and meant the world to me. Thank you for being a fan from the first moment and for keeping my book a secret until I was ready to reveal it.

To my students that I have been lucky enough to teach and learn from these last twenty years. You inspire me in countless ways with your courage, resilience, and off the charts creativity. Keep reaching for the stars. I can't wait to watch you pluck them out of the sky.

To my Mom and Dad for igniting my lifelong love of books. You took me on countless trips to the library to check out handfuls of books that filled my imagination and my heart. You also taught me the importance of working hard for what you want and getting up and dusting yourself off again when you got knocked down. I love you.

To my grandmother, Joanne Meeker, who smuggled me my first romance novel at a terribly young age and always brought me more. You read every piece of writing I dared show you, and you always believed I would be a published writer one day. You hunted wild boar and could tell me the name of every type of cloud in the sky. I endeavor to someday be as brave and fearless as you. I miss you.

And to my husband, Brian, who encouraged me to join RWA and GRW in 2013 and share my writing with the world. Your belief in me helped me breathe life into this book and into a part of myself I was afraid to share. You've helped me learn how to become a heroine in my own life, and I love you beyond measure.

Prologue

Clun, England
February, 1839

Old Man Codger's frozen toe rolled across the floor toward the door.

"Lord above. Mind the corner, sister," Lucy muttered. She blew an errant curl from her cheek as they swung the man's stiff body onto the scarred wooden table in front of the hearth. The body landed with a thud.

Blast. Lucy scanned the floor. Nothing. *Where had it gone?* She lifted her skirts.

"There you are," she grumbled. The rogue digit rested between the scuffed heels of her old brown boots. Using the edge of one of the sleeves of her faded blue blouse, she leaned down and clutched the rather putrid, large hairy toe and placed it on the man's chest. Now she'd have to sew on a toe, too. A frozen toe.

Perfect.

Priscilla covered her mouth with the back of her hand and yielded a dry retch. Plugging her nose, she rolled her eyes. "There *has* to be another way."

Lucy eyed her pert younger sister and sighed. At thirteen, Cil was on the cusp of womanhood. There were so many things she would miss from their parents not being there to guide her. The guilt over the death of Mother and Father a month past stung like a barb under Lucy's skin. If only she'd arrived home at the cottage sooner instead of lingering about the forest to find her pet starling. She banished the thought away.

After tying back her hair, Lucy pushed up her sleeves to the elbow. "If there had been any other option, we'd have done it. It's either prep him for burial or starve. It's just us now, Cil."

The old man's time in the woods had not been kind to him, but at least the extreme cold had kept the insects at bay. A white milky maggot dropped from his nose to the table. Lucy shuddered. *Most of them.* She loathed insects, especially worms. Things that could move without legs weren't natural.

"Hand me the needle and thread." Lucy rested her hands on her hips. "I need to get this toe sewn back on when he thaws. I'll not be docked pay for him missing parts."

Chapter 1
The Caller

Clun, England
Ten Years Later

A knocking on the cottage door above stairs startled Lucy, and she poked her finger with the thick sewing needle she held.

"Thistles," she cursed, pressing her apron to her bleeding thumb. Evidently, repairing the tear at the hem of Becca's dress would have to wait.

Who would be calling at such an early hour? It was hardly half past nine.

"Enter," she called up from her root cellar.

She shuddered as the door squeaked open above her. She should oil the blasted hinges on the ancient door, but who had time for such nonsense? Her finger throbbed, but the blood had stopped. Shaking it in the air, she caught sight of the pale female form on her prepping table.

What am I complaining of?

Poor Becca. Lucy swallowed hard. Covering and repairing the girl's wounds would prove difficult, but she'd try. Becca was her friend. *Had* been her friend.

"I hear if I need a body prepped, you are the person to see." A deep rich baritone boomed against the cottage rafters.

The man's neatly clipped tones screamed *city*. Londoner, most likely. What would he want here in Shropshire? Nothing of much import ever happened here.

"I suppose," she offered. "Depends on who's asking." Lucy tiptoed over to the base of the root cellar staircase and peeked upstairs. The high shine of the man's black leather boots caught her eye. *Lord above*. A person could see their reflection in such a glimmer.

The fine, close cut of dark trousers and a gray waistcoat hugged the man's rigid frame, his white cravat starched and tied in precise lines as if it dared not be out of place. He *was* a gentleman. The man had means to be sure, so she supposed she was the person to see after all. She wiped her hands on her stained apron and ascended the stairs to the main floor.

The stranger stepped forward but stilled at her approach. His eyes widened as her face heated. Did the sight of her frighten him? She patted the side of her hair and cringed. *Blast*. It was as tangled as straw in a bird's nest. Perhaps a brush would have been in order this morning to tame her unruly locks. She'd try to remember such details in future.

Clearing his throat, Mr. Shiny Boots removed his hat and stepped forward, offering a small bow of greeting. On such days, Lucy missed her sense of smell. No doubt the man would have oozed of lingering shave cream, spicy cologne, or the subtle tang of wax and tallow.

"Miss, I am in need of your services." He flashed her a set of straight white teeth, a stark contrast to the olive of his skin and darkness of his hair and eyes.

Lord, he's handsome.

"Dead relative that needs preparations?"

"No. Not yet anyway." A smile tugged at his lips, and he ran his fingers about the thin rim of his black topper. "I require your services in looking *upon* a body."

Twisting her lips, she frowned. Men never paid for mere looking. She'd been a layer-out of the dead long enough to know that. Mr. Shiny Boots would offer up little in earnings this day. "I don't take your meaning, sir."

His gaze flitted about her face and landed on her right cheek.

"I . . ." He pulled a fine linen handkerchief from his pocket and offered it to her. "You seem to have a touch of . . ." He gestured to her cheek.

She accepted the handkerchief and wiped her face. Looking at the soiled material against the crisp cloth, she sighed. "Sorry, sir. A bit of flesh. It happens from time to time." Folding the material over upon itself, she attempted to return it.

He held up a gloved hand. "Do keep it."

"Thank you, sir." She tucked the expensive cloth into the pocket of her dress.

"As I was explaining, I require your skills and knowledge for an inquiry."

"*You* are an inquiry agent?" If she'd been but born a man, she'd have sought out just such a profession.

"Not quite. Constable, actually. Magistrate Kieran appointed me to Shropshire from London."

"Ah." She studied him. *Former* Constable Old Man Codger, rest his soul, would have been none too pleased to see a Londoner taking on his old post.

"I asked for a man who handled these sorts of dealings, and I was sent your way."

She shrugged. "I am the mistress of the dead, I suppose."

"I heard you additionally serve the living when needed."

She smiled, proud to also help those who still drew breath. "Yes. Stitches, mostly. Reattachments when I can."

"So I've heard." His gaze roved over her face in appreciation, and he paused. "The name they have for you is quite apt, now that I've seen you."

Confused, she shifted on her feet. "And what name would that be, sir?"

"At The Boar and Sable they call you Lovely Digits."

Lovely what?

Embarrassment heated her skin. No doubt she was as red as a boiled beet. She chewed on her lower lip. While she'd always hoped to attract customers through word of mouth, *Lovely Digits*? What a horrid name to pass along.

He stepped closer. "My apologies. I've upset you."

An awkward silence bloomed between them. His dark blue eyes lightened, and he released another brilliant smile. "I failed to introduce myself, miss. Let us begin anew. My name is Brodie. John Brodie."

She nodded. "And I am Lucy Wycliffe."

"Well, Miss Wycliffe, will you assist me in this case?"

"What exactly would such assistance require?" She rubbed her chin. "And earn?"

He laughed and faint lines crinkled around his eyes. "I see we shall get on well, Miss Wycliffe."

"Why is that, sir?"

"You say exactly what you mean."

"Is there time for anything else?"

"No." He placed his topper back on his head. "I suppose not. Shall we?" He gestured to the door.

"You meant now? This very moment?"

"Yes. I'd like to move the body within the hour. I fear the weather will turn soon. I'd like your thoughts on what you see as it is now."

She rubbed the inside of her palm with her thumb. "Isn't that most unusual? I've never heard of such before."

He tilted his head back and forth. "Perhaps. I was trained to analyze the body where it is discovered. As to wages, would a shilling an hour do? I daresay it may take two hours."

Lucy's throat dried. *Two shillings in a mere pair of hours?* That was equal to a quarter of what she earned for an entire body prepping, and her old arsenic jar held few shillings.

With Cil a widow of war with a young daughter and the loan to Fiske for this very cottage coming due in mere weeks, each shilling was precious. Who knew when someone would next need her services? But fortune didn't just fall in one's lap, did it? Lucy firmed her lips and squared her shoulders.

"Are you jesting with me, sir?"

He retrieved identification from his coat pocket. "Here are my papers, miss."

She reached for them and scanned the scribblings and official seal before returning them. Perhaps Mr. Shiny Boots *was* legitimate. "Where is the body?" Curiosity nibbled along her limbs. This would be the second body she'd seen within the last few days.

He chuckled and smiled. "Ah, I see I may have almost convinced you. She is but a bit south of Lake Summerland."

Lucy froze, and her pulse quickened. "Lake Summerland?"

"Yes. Is that of importance?" His eyes narrowed.

"It may be. The girl now resting upon my table below was also found dead not far from Summerland."

"The cause of her passing?" He inquired a hint above a whisper.

"By way of murder, sir."

Chapter 2
Lake Summerland

Bollocks. What had he done?

John pulled up on his butterscotch colored mount and readjusted his dark overcoat. As the black hackney he'd hired in town lurched to a start, John clicked his tongue and nudged his horse into a trot alongside it. He dared a glance into the oblong carriage window and admired the smooth strong profile of Miss Lucy Wycliffe.

Nothing could have prepared him for that first sight of her at the small cottage. The bright violet of her eyes against the pearl-like smoothness of her face and unruly cinnamon colored hair had gutted him. She was an absolute mirror of her mother.

Except she was alive.

An image of the girl's dead mother, lying prone on the floor of that same cottage almost a decade ago, flashed before him. After all those years of wondering what had become of the two girls, he thought he'd prepared himself. However, the beautiful Miss Lucy Wycliffe had almost brought him to his knees.

Guilt cleaved his chest. Despite the loss of her parents, the woman seemed resolute, clever, and strong. And she was a layer-out of the dead, no less. The horrors of the past hadn't defined her. Could he say the same?

Truth be told, he couldn't.

He tugged on the leather reins to match the driver's slower weaving along the pocked dirt road to the lake. Since that dark bloody night, John had fought to be a better man . . . and right every other wrong in the world to compensate for the one he couldn't.

Surely fate whispered in his ear to take this position to atone for his sins against this woman and her sister.

Sunlight skittered along the path as John emerged from the coverage of evergreens and glimpsed the lake's edge. The heady scents of damp earth and wild animals settled about him. He gathered a deep breath and released it. It would not be long now. The dead woman was just past the bend in the road. He needed to prepare himself for another encounter with Miss Wycliffe.

Studying the smooth pebbles dotting the lake's edge, he counted their gray heads one at a time to calm himself as he had as a boy. The hackney inched forward and came to a yawning stop, rocking back and forth once more before ceasing its movement. He guided his horse up alongside it.

The driver jumped down and opened the carriage door. John dismounted and approached.

"Miss Wycliffe?" John offered his arm. "'Tis just past the tree line."

She nodded and clutched his forearm without a word. Her silence unnerved him. He didn't know females to be so quiet. Perhaps this wasn't such a good idea.

Light reflected off the serene glass of the lake, and he tugged the brim of his topper to shade his eyes. The chill of the day was wreaking havoc on his bad leg, but he climbed over the half-frozen foliage, determined to see this through. For the sake of the woman on his arm and the woman resting on the earth ahead of them. This was his chance to right two wrongs, was it not?

Dark evergreens swayed in the budding wind, and he could see the woman's yellow dress fluttering like a flower petal. Miss Wycliffe's steps faltered, and she lurched to a stop.

"Miss Wycliffe?"

She brushed a wisp of hair from her cheek. "I . . ." She stared ahead. "I believe I have seen such a dress before. It may be Miriam. Miriam Cunningham. She always favored yellow."

John tensed. What *had* he done? Here he was, trying to make amends, and he was forcing the poor woman to stare upon a dead friend? In his selfish desire to right a wrong, he was exposing her to more pain. "I'm sorry. This was a bad idea on my part. I should have known you might be familiar with the victim."

She flinched on the *m* of victim.

He cringed. He was only making matters worse. "Let me have the driver return you. And I will pay for your time. My apologies. Truly."

Pulling her shoulders back, she poked up her chin. "I'm here and wish to be useful. Let us go on. If it is Miriam, she deserves what I can do for her." When she faced him, the determination in the firm set of her mouth and bright violet of her eyes seized him.

Once again, she surprised him.

"As you wish," he answered.

They carried on one step after another through the thickening brush, their boots crushing the crisp stalks of weeds and plants. He expected her to falter, to call quits to their advance, but the closer they came to the body, the stronger her steps fell. He eyed her. Was she gaining strength? He'd seen it before in battle, but only from the bravest of soldiers. Those who sacrificed themselves to save others. What had she sacrificed for those she loved?

He glanced before him. The dead woman rested in a twisted, unresolved *S* on the ground. No bonnet, no cloak, or gloves. Just boots and a mustard colored walking dress covered her petite form. The shock of her fair hair and pale frozen skin against the dark green of the ground created a contrast more beautiful than ghastly. The woman stared into the sky above as if she awaited the stars. One hand clutched the grass beneath while the other reached for something . . . or someone.

Miss Wycliffe stepped away from him and stooped down. She studied every part of the body. "Oh, Miriam," she murmured, resting on her haunches. "What's happened to you?"

John bent down next to her, though pain screamed along his thigh. The journey and damp weather had coiled his muscles into sinewy cords beneath his skin. But he needed to comfort her and find this poor woman's killer. His discomfort mattered little.

Breathing through his nose quelled the throbbing in his leg, and he mustered what he hoped was a soothing tone. "I'm sorry, Miss Wycliffe. Did you know her well?" He removed his hat.

Emotion flashed and flittered through her eyes when she met his gaze, and his chest tightened. She *had* known the victim. And known her well. Lucy's drawn features told him as much, and he loathed himself all the more for putting her in this position.

She nodded.

"Does her family reside here in Clun?"

"Yes." She stood, staring across the frozen lake. "Back toward town. Just a ways past my own cottage. We often walked to school together." She turned to him and offered a weak smile. "Miriam was fiercely talented with numbers. Far better than I."

John gained his feet stiffly. Placing his hat upon his head, he stood next to Lucy in silence. He dared not utter anything else to add to her misery.

"We were the same age, just seven and twenty. Her birthday was last month." She wiped a tear from her eye and chuckled. "We bemoaned our spinsterhood. Both of us had younger sisters who married, but we . . ." She paused and shrugged. "We had no luck with such matches."

A lump filled John's throat. Miss Wycliffe, a spinster? A widow perhaps, but he'd never thought her unmarried. How was she a spinster? If he were a man with anything to offer about these parts, he would have claimed her as his own. A beauty with strength and intelligence would have been a worthy match. Clun had to be made of fools. There was no other explanation.

"Mr. Brodie? Mr. Brodie?"

"Sorry. Yes?"

"What is it you wish me to take note of for you?"

He shifted on his feet. "You do not have to, Miss Wycliffe. I have no wish to cause you more sadness or distress."

"I wish to help you in any way I can in discovering what's become of her. I know I don't look like much, but I'm strong. I promise not to swoon before you."

The woman was an endearing blend of courage and fragility. He pulled a pencil and a small bound ledger from his inner coat pocket. Licking the tip of the pencil, he nodded to her. "Tell me if there is anything about her physically that has been altered."

"Sir?" A deep wrinkle creased her forehead.

"Any altering of her hair, hands, or face since your last meeting?"

She pressed her lips together and knelt beside the body. "May I touch her?"

"If it helps."

Turning, Miss Wycliffe guided the woman's blonde hair from her neck. A dark brown blotch the shape of an egg appeared at the base of her nape. "No changes to her hair or scalp. This is a scar she's had as long as I've known her. Not a birthmark, but a scar from when she was young. So young she did not remember how it came to be."

John sketched the scar on a blank page and jotted notes. "And the parents never gave an explanation as to the cause?"

"Household accident of some sort. I always thought it looked like a burn."

He nodded and she continued by studying the woman's hands. Miss Wycliffe nibbled her lower lip as she scanned each finger and glimpsed under the nails. John stopped jotting and watched her work. Her mind was succinct and agile, no doubt from her years as a prepper. The men at the inn said she'd worked in the trade for almost a decade. So many bodies those eyes and hands had studied. Such a life for a young woman, he could not imagine.

No doubt she understood the cruelty of fate. So did he.

"Miriam was fastidious about her appearance," she pointed out. "She never would have had soil under her nails. And the dirt is not from here. It's too dark. Could you smell it for me?"

"Can I *what*?"

A flush stained Miss Wycliffe's cheeks and she lowered her gaze. "I lost my sense of smell when I was younger. I had a bad fall, hit my head, and when I woke, I couldn't smell anything." She shrugged. "I always thought one day it might return, but it never did. So, I don't know if that dirt smells of lavender or manure. Could you tell me what you smell? It may help me guess where she was before she came here." She tugged at her gloved fingertips.

Of all the questions women had asked him throughout his life, this was a first. John knelt, swallowing the pain as it seized again upon his thigh. He'd need some whiskey tonight if he hoped for an ounce of sleep. His muscle would only tighten further as the cold enveloped him.

"So, is this sort of a gift how you have been able to prep bodies over the years?"

She released a tentative smile. "It does help. My poor sister Cil retched with every delivery to the cottage that first year. I finally placed a bucket under the table. It was easier than mopping up her sickness from the floor each night. Transforming our old root cellar to my prepping area also helped immensely. Keeps the bodies cool and allows me the time I need to prepare them for burial without further decay."

"If my smelling her hands will help you, then I will be your nose this day." He lifted Miriam's lifeless hand near his face and sniffed. He closed his eyes and breathed in once more. "Decomposition of earth, musk. Peat perhaps."

Miss Wycliffe sighed and frowned. "Peat?"

"Yes. You seem surprised."

"There are few peat bogs about. The ones I know of are too far of a walk, especially without a cloak." She rubbed her arms and stood before stepping toward the woman's feet. She tugged on one of the shoes. It finally popped free, but Miss Wycliffe lost her balance and fell backward. Her skirts flew up in the air, and she was in a barrel roll.

Stunned, John stared for a moment before he gained his wits. *Damnation.* He rushed over and offered his hand, although he struggled to find her hands amongst the abundance of skirts, cloak, and underclothes. "Miss, I . . ." he stammered like a schoolboy.

Flounces of material shifted and shuffled. From the bundle emerged Miss Wycliffe's face, flushed with color. John's stomach dropped through the ground. *She is a beauty.* And so unassuming. Did he know a lady who would not have wept in embarrassment?

"Such maneuverings I have never seen before," he offered.

She grasped his gloved hand, and he helped her up.

"At least I didn't lose the shoe." She lifted the woman's slipper in the air.

"I'm glad I didn't lose you in that tumble and toss."

"No worries there, sir. I'm clumsy, but not weak. It shall take something stronger than gravity to claim me from this earth." She brushed a wave of loose hair from her face.

He stared. His heart stilled at the certainty and clarity of her voice. A small thread of relief uncoiled in his body. Perhaps the loss of her parents had not broken her after all. "No doubt, Miss Wycliffe."

"She couldn't have been planning to be out of doors long with only these thin slippers." She pressed her lips together and awkwardly released his hand, returning to the body. "The mud and dirt soaked her stockings." She rolled the thin material down from above the woman's knees and studied her bare feet. "Even her toes are soiled. And there are splashes of mud upon the hem and back of her dress."

"She ran from her attacker," John added. "Perhaps he overcame her here." He stopped himself from further details.

"Why would she stop here?" She studied the material on the front of the yellow dress. "And if he had tackled her, there would be mud or grass stains, but there are neither."

"Perhaps she knew him."

"Or her."

John balked. "A female attacker?"

"Why not? Women can kill as well."

A female attacker? He paused and blinked.

"I'm not saying it *is* a female, only that it could be. Although by the twist of her body, I believe her neck was broken, and that would have required the brute strength of a man." She ran a hand along the woman's cheek. "At least such a death is quick. There is some peace in knowing she didn't linger in pain."

Shame flushed John's body, and his pulse quickened. Lucy's parents had not had a quick death. When John had found them, his brother Sean was standing over their bludgeoned bodies with a shovel. The voice of Miss Wycliffe's mother echoed in John's ears.

Please . . . please don't hurt my daughters.

And he silently promised her again that he never would.

Chapter 3
The Boar and Sable

"Thank you for joining me to notify Miss Cunningham's parents this afternoon. I know it must have been trying, but you being there gave them much comfort." Mr. Brodie stepped aside and opened the door for Lucy as she walked under the faded Boar and Sable sign. The warmth and noise from the men, already deep in their cups at Clun's largest pub, proved an unexpected comfort. She longed to be around the chaos of life.

Far too much death surrounded her this day.

Weaving through the crowd, they found an empty table. Mr. Brodie pulled out a chair for her, and Lucy sank into it. Her limbs screamed in exhaustion. Removing his hat, he settled into the chair across from her.

The Rudds' eldest daughter greeted them, her plump figure and ready smile gifts from her mother. "What can I get you, sir? Miss Wycliffe?"

"Two ales and two of tonight's special."

"Be back shortly with two ales and two stews." She disappeared into a cluster of young men just arriving.

Lucy mustered a smile. "I am most appreciative of your offer to buy me dinner, Mr. Brodie. Despite the horrors of the day, I find myself famished."

"My apologies. That is my fault. We seemed to have worked all the day without pause. I'm afraid I can lose myself in my work." He ran a hand through his mussed hair.

"I understand. I can be prepping a body for hours and not realize it. The work can consume me."

Ales and bowls of steaming stew with hearty slices of bread arrived. Lucy adored Mrs. Rudd's stew. It was one of the foods she could still savor despite her lack of smell because of its many spices.

"What brought you to such work, Miss Wycliffe?" Mr. Brodie asked between bites. "'Tis unusual for a woman to be in such employ."

He wiped the corner of his mouth with the customary brown cloth napkin provided at the pub. His motions were deft and deliberate, moving from the left corner to the right. When he folded it exactly twice and placed it back in his lap, she hid a smile. Such precision was a reminder of her grandfather, who'd been an officer in the army.

What a turn this day had taken. Finding Miriam, being offered unexpected work, and feasting on a delicious meal. Lucy savored a bite of her beef stew and then smiled. "I imagine my past has merely shaped my life as it has yours, sir. Your military service reflects off you like the candlelight."

The corner of his mouth quirked up in amusement. "Ah." He sniffed and rested his palms on the table. "So easy to read, am I?" He drummed his index finger on the battered grain between them.

A chuckle escaped her, as much to her surprise as perhaps his. "It is part of my nature to note details. I could not dull it if I tried. Were you in the army?"

"Royal Navy until I was wounded." He tapped his leg and leaned back into his chair. "Now I have decided to stay on land for the rest of my years. Lost my taste for the water." His irises, the shade of bluebird wings, darkened and he glanced away. Whatever else hid behind those words would remain there, for now.

"And you? I noticed you skillfully avoiding an answer." He laced his hands before him.

"I suppose I don't quite know how to answer. It couldn't be fate, but tragedy that thrust me into work as a layer-out.

Yet I find I'm quite skilled at it, so I cannot begrudge the blessing or gift I have in my work."

The intensity of his gaze unsettled her. Had she shocked him? She knew she was no lady in the usual sense of the word. Did she speak too plainly? Had she said too much? Father always claimed she was far too direct. Worry skittered up her spine.

He cleared his throat. "Tragedy, Miss Wycliffe? May I ask what occurred?" His fingertip traced the indents along the scarred table.

Mr. Rudd set another pint of bitter on the table for Mr. Brodie. Liquid sloshed gently over the side and slid down the glass, scurrying toward the crevices of the wood. "Anything else I can do you for, sir?" He addressed Mr. Brodie as if she were invisible, which wasn't unusual. The man held no regard for women in general, and as a layer-out she was seen as even lower than most.

Mr. Brodie's gaze rested on her. "Anything else you desire this evening, Miss Wycliffe?"

Mr. Rudd glanced in her direction. The barkeeper's cheeks remained in a constant flush as the man was known to sample a nip from every barrel of ale. Tonight seemed no different. Lucy held her reply a few moments longer, until the poor man began to fidget and shift on his feet.

"No, sir. Thank you kindly for the meal. It was a heavenly treat." She turned toward Mr. Rudd. "Give my regards to Mrs. Rudd. She makes a delicious beef stew."

He grunted an answer before he walked away. No doubt he wouldn't be giving his poor wife any credit. Nor would he ever exchange more than a grunt with Lucy. He'd made it clear, long ago, he thought her unnatural. Glancing at her lap, she brushed a breadcrumb from the napkin still splayed out over her dress.

No matter.

She was able to support herself, her sister, and niece. Mr. Rudd could be damned. Lifting her chin, she took a deep breath. When her eyes met Mr. Brodie's, the concern in them surprised her. She worked to maintain her smile.

"Mr. Rudd doesn't seem to hold you in the same esteem as I do, Miss Wycliffe. His loss, to be sure."

"I'm afraid he is not the only one to think me odd for what I do. That, and with what happened to my parents, some think my sister and me to be touched by evil." She fidgeted with the edges of her napkin. "Nonsense, of course."

"Is that the tragedy you speak of? The one that thrust you into such a life?" His eyes seemed to implore her, his focus so intense against the candlelight on their table, she hesitated to answer. But he was the new constable. He would know soon enough, wouldn't he? And he'd trusted her thus far, even offered her employment. There seemed no harm in telling him.

"Yes," she whispered. "They were killed by an intruder almost ten years ago. My sister and I weren't home. I found them when I returned from my walk. My only hope is they didn't suffer overly much. And that they forgive my absence."

Once the words were out, a rush of relief coursed through her body, only to be quickly replaced by dread. Why had she told him? They'd only just met.

Silence stretched out between them. The manly shouts and laughter gathered along the bar filled the air. She watched these rough customers, so carefree and drunk, a life she couldn't imagine for herself. Not even in her wildest of fancies.

"Surely you do not blame yourself for what befell them? You were but a child. What could you have done?"

She met his searching gaze. His hands rested on the table, fingers woven together like the wings of a closed butterfly. He didn't understand, but then, how could he? "I should have been home." She adjusted the shawl she'd draped across the grass stains on her shirt from her earlier tumble. "I was cross because they'd left the door open and let my pet starling escape. I was a silly girl. I ran out in search of him. The last words I spoke to them were hateful and angry. When I'd returned, still without my bird, they were dead."

"Where was your sister?" Deep lines creased along his brow. A muscle worked in his jaw.

"She was with her friend. They were playing with her new dolly. It was a miracle she didn't arrive home before me. If she had . . ."

At the time, Lucy had still been in her teens. The shock of it had almost undone her. Heaven only knew what would have become of her sister, had she found their parents first. Poor Cil might not have recovered.

"I am sorry. And for the burden you carry from it." Empathy rested in the soft tones of his words.

"I can see you have an understanding of life's burdens, Mr. Brodie."

He nodded. "I do. But one mustn't let that sort of weight become greater than ourselves."

"One of the reasons I have chosen this work. Or perhaps it has chosen me. The action, the doing, helps shift some of the weight of their loss around. And there are days I break free of it." She smiled. "Such as today."

She flushed. *What a ridiculous thing to say.* "I'm sorry. I know it sounds dreadful on account of finding Miriam." She repositioned herself and fidgeted with loose strands of her hair. "I do not mean to discount the horror of her loss."

"Of course not. I wouldn't think that."

Her heart raged in her chest. She had to try to explain so he didn't think her a monster. "To be needed for my services. To be useful in some way in solving a murder. To help figure out what happened to her, instead of just finding ways to hide her trauma, has lightened my spirit."

A brilliant smile greeted her. "Another reason we shall get on so well, Miss Wycliffe. It is the complexities of crime-solving that fuels my being. Knowing I may help in granting a family peace and also put a murderer to his death at the end of a rope. Together we may be able to close this case yet." He lifted his glass to her.

"To Miss Cunningham," he added.

Lucy lifted her own half-empty glass. "To my sweet, dear friend, Miriam. May you rest in peace and know your soul will be set free on the wings of birds."

As she took a draw of her ale, she hoped her words were true and her parents' spirits flew alongside Miriam's. That their deaths had borne them wings. That they did not blame her. That they had not suffered as she imagined. Her throat thickened with emotion. Time healed so many things, but it had never healed this. It had never healed her.

"Ah, Miss Wycliffe. Fancy seeing you here."

Lucy's throat constricted. *Mr. Fiske.* Her gaze rested on his overly-large dilated pupils and rather ample double chin. She'd forgotten he often frequented here since he was still a bachelor. *Even if he is a bachelor well past his prime.*

A droplet of stew clung desperately to the corner of his mouth.

Past his prime for so many reasons.

She smothered a cringe.

Resting her glass on the table, she forced a smile. "Good evening, sir. May I introduce you to Constable Brodie?"

Fiske nodded to Mr. Brodie and introduced himself. Lucy wrung her hands in her lap. She could only hope he would leave without further torment. When he turned his body toward her, she stilled. It seemed her hope would not be realized, not today.

"I'm pleased to see your finances much improved, since you are out this eve." He tucked his hands in his pockets and leaned closer to her, which made his chin transform into swinging jowls. "I shall expect to see the amount paid in full by the end of the month," he said in a whisper.

Commanding herself not to flinch, she held his horrid gaze. "Of course, sir."

He stalled, his eyes lingering along her décolletage— what little there was of it in her shapeless frock—but finally left.

Shame and anger crept along her skin. All she wanted to do was flee before another man from Clun showcased his power over her. At least Mr. Brodie hadn't. He'd been a gentleman on all accounts, and she was grateful for it.

"Shall we go, sir? I fear I have left Becca too long. Her funeral is soon, and I promised I would do all I could to make her as she once was."

"Of course. Let me settle up, and I'll see a hansom takes you home."

A hansom for such a short walk home?

She hesitated. "I am grateful for the employ and delicious meal, but I can make my own way. I don't require a drive home. The walk will no doubt serve me well. I fear I have overdone it with such a dinner."

"Then you will allow me to see you home on foot. I cannot allow you to walk home alone. With all that's happened . . ." Mr. Brodie paused and lowered his voice. "I don't think it's safe for you to be unaccompanied, Miss Wycliffe."

She fidgeted with the ribbons along her bonnet. Although she despised the notion of being coddled, perhaps he was right. She'd have to learn to be more cautious until they determined what linked the two murders. A flash of her friends' faces and memories of their sweet laughter assailed her. Such laughter would be no longer.

The ribbons fell from Lucy's hands. She didn't desire a similar fate.

Mr. Brodie retrieved her bonnet and handed it to her. He ran a finger over the brim of his black topper, awaiting her answer.

"Thank you, sir. I appreciate your offer to accompany me home."

His shoulders relaxed as if relief had sunk through his bones like water. He truly seemed a kind, attractive man. He walked over to the bar and left some coin on the counter for Mr. Rudd, who smiled widely.

"Do come back now, Constable," he called after him.

Mr. Rudd didn't bother to repeat the polite farewell to Lucy. He knew she couldn't afford to frequent his place regularly, if at all. She and her sister were barely making it by as it was. Lucy would soon be forced to relinquish their childhood home if she didn't have the full payment to make to Mr. Fiske in three weeks' time.

When she'd originally agreed to pay her parents' loan in full on a ten-year note, it had seemed so far away. Now the ten-year anniversary hovered but weeks away, and she couldn't imagine having even enough hours in the day to earn what she needed. She prayed Mr. Fiske would reconsider her request for a year's extension on the repayment, once he realized she hadn't purchased her own meal.

But the man pinched and stored his coin tighter than a squirrel collecting nuts with but one cheek.

With a soft smile, she shrugged into her cloak and tied the bonnet ribbons under her chin. She hadn't counted on finding Constable John Brodie at her door this morn, either.

Chapter 4
The Walk Home

A cool evening breeze rippled along John's face. Dusk settled into the edges of Clun, and the lamplighter brought a glow to each of the oil lamps dotting the lanes of the small village. It wasn't proper to walk Miss Lucy Wycliffe home alone without a chaperone, but he couldn't bear to leave her unescorted after seeing the horrible end that had come to her friends. He also knew she had no chaperone.

As a woman of seven and twenty, she seemed to have cast aside any worries regarding her reputation. Or perhaps that was the way of the country? He'd been here too short a time to know. Nor did he truly care. Reputation and the rules of society had brought him little except heartache.

A dull throb in his leg began. The pulse of it sang in rhythm with each step. He stifled a groan. Two fingers of whiskey were definitely in order this evening, after the day he'd had.

A couple passed by and the flash of the woman's yellow dress from beneath her dark cloak reminded him of Miss Cunningham. His mind shivered at the memory of her resting on the silent shore of the lake. Still. Lifeless. *Dead*. Silently, he cursed himself. He was alive, was he not? It was more than he could say for Miss Cunningham or the other woman resting on Miss Wycliffe's preparations table. More than he could say for the Wycliffe parents who lay well beneath the dirt of the earth. He had to remember to be grateful for what life he had and for the blessing he'd been granted this day in finding Miss Wycliffe. Perhaps helping her and her sister would bring him peace.

A peace he longed for like a thirsty man in the desert.

"So, how do you find our village?" Miss Wycliffe's voice hummed along the air.

"To be truthful, I have seen little except for the station house since my arrival." And it was the truth. The state of disrepair of his new lodgings and workhouse had claimed more time than expected.

Miss Wycliffe chuckled. "Then are the rumors about Old Man Codger true?"

"Rumors?"

Shadows danced across her face as the lamplighter breathed life into the lamppost beside them. His body ached at the simple beauty of her. He wished he could stop noticing it, but he couldn't.

Miss Wycliffe leaned closer to his ear, and his body heated. "Word had it he was quite a collector. Of everything."

John nodded as they began their journey over Clun Bridge, one of the few landmarks he knew. "I can confirm that to be true. I've never seen so many boxes in such a confined space. He seems to have kept every file, scrap of paper, and piece of correspondence ever to grace the doors of the station house. What I cannot figure is how the constable after him could stand the disorder. It's as if the man never used the space."

"Ah, you are very perceptive. He didn't. It was Codger's son who assumed duties after the old man's death ten years back. He took the loss of his father hard and never used the station house for his work. He lived with his mother, and since there is generally little crime and dispute here in the village, he had no need of it."

"Did he relocate to another jurisdiction before I came? Magistrate Kieran provided few details about my predecessor. And what seems to be his rather hasty departure."

Miss Wycliffe paused. "It may be due to the fact the man just disappeared."

John came to a sudden stop in the middle of the bridge. He met her gaze. "Disappeared? And no one searched for him? He's not been found?" Questions assailed him.

She dropped her gaze and readjusted her bonnet, looping the pale shimmery ribbons together into a new bow. "Well, people *did* search for him for a time. When nothing was found, his mother chalked it up to him running away from his duties. Seems she found a note explaining his leaving. Said he went to Scotland to stay with a second cousin. I always thought it odd, but the Codgers were different. They always have been."

"How so?"

He battled unease as he rested his palms on the cool gray stone of the old bridge walls. Staring into the dark waters of the river below, he wrestled with the bizarre new facts. A constable, abandoning his post? He'd never heard of the like. Especially with an elderly mother most likely dependent on the man's earnings.

Miss Wycliffe worried her gloved hands. "I shouldn't have said that. It's gossip, and I know the sting when you are on the receiving end of it."

Surprise gripped him. A woman who was uncomfortable with gossip? Things were different here in the country. Or perhaps it was Miss Wycliffe's especial quirks. He tried to ease her concern. "Think of it not as gossip but as assistance to help me better understand my new post, new town, and its inhabitants. And what happened to the man before me."

She sighed. "I appreciate your attempt to ease my guilt, but I'm still being a horrible gossip. I'll tell you only because you are the town Constable."

The wind whipped up, sending a few loose tendrils of her hair into the air. The weather would turn soon.

"Shall we?" He stepped forward. "I can almost smell the snow in the air. It won't be long now, and I don't wish to get you caught up in it."

"No doubt you must also feel it in the ache in your leg. I must introduce you to Miss Clara. She can make a tonic to ease any ache. She is gifted in herbs and plant remedies. Her mother was a healer."

John smiled at her pleased by her keen observation. "I'll remember that. Now, on to the Codgers. Tell me more."

"The Codgers are an old established family in Clun. They used to tell everyone their ancestors helped gather and lay the very stone used to build Clun Castle." She gestured to a hill to their left. He could see the outline of grey ruins catching the moonlight but little else. "There were also stories about one branch of their family suffering from instabilities of the mind. Odd interests. Internal voices that would not allow them rest, which made some folks deem them insane. I am unsure if either, neither, or both of those stories are true, and I have lived here all my life. Perhaps you will get to the truth of it."

"And how does this relate to the son's disappearance?"

"Some of the villagers believe his mother wrote the letter herself to hide that the son may have given in to self-slaughter."

"And others? What do they think?"

She shrugged and chewed her bottom lip. Her voice dropped into a whisper. "Others think he may be living in the stretch of woods between here and the water mill."

"A man living in the woods? Alone? How long ago did he disappear?"

She looked skyward and seemed to be counting. "Since last March, so almost a year's time now."

"I doubt a man could survive on his own in the woods alone for so long. Especially without shelter and food."

"That is what I believe as well, though time has also taught me not to discount any possibilities. And there are people who say their things have gone missing. Pies cooling on a window's ledge. Coats and hats left out of doors to air."

John shook his head. "Remarkable. Another mystery in Clun in need of solving."

"You jest, but you know as well as I people are capable of so many things one doesn't often expect. Good and bad. And the human body and mind are more resilient than most people give them credit for. A fact I'm sure you would agree with in your line of work and past service in the Royal Navy."

"Ah. I suppose you make a point. The human spirit can drive a man to do far beyond what seems possible."

They continued on in silence along the single road leading away from the village. Miss Wycliffe's cottage loomed off in the distance. The sight of it sent a ripple of dread down his chilled limbs. Other than the larger shrubs and trees surrounding it now, the cottage remained unchanged from the night he'd stumbled upon it in search of his brother. The whitewash paint was still chipped. The dark wooden shutters surrounding the windows still watched his approach, the judgment in them a folly of his imagination which he batted away.

Rocks crunched under their boots as they walked the remaining distance to the front door. On the curved pathway, a lean orange tabby rushed toward them. It meowed at Miss Wycliffe's feet and rubbed against her legs. She stooped and petted the little beast.

"A friend?" he asked with a smile.

"She appears when it's cold. Otherwise, she roams about the village. This is Apricot."

A few snowflakes drifted down from the sky, sprinkling on Miss Wycliffe's cloak like powdered sugar on a cake. John's breath caught. The sight of it tugged at him. How could he feel so strong a connection and attraction to her after mere hours together? This sort of response was unlike him in every way. He was practical and resolute. Was it guilt? Was it a romantic fancy?

He sighed. Perhaps he did hold a bit of a romantic nature of the world, but he was desperately trying to right a wrong for her. And for Miss Cunningham. And himself if he were indeed honest. He didn't want to muck up the lady's life further by adding in attraction.

But could he stop it? Should he? He nested his hands in his pockets and forced himself back into the present.

"Why Apricot? 'Tis an unusual name for a cat."

"When I was a child, my father went into town and they had apricots. He spent far too much on them and brought back one for each of us to try. The taste of it was heavenly. I can still remember how sweet it was and the juice exploding into my cheeks. Naming her Apricot reminds me of that memory. 'Tis one I would like to remember always."

A woman, wooed over an apricot? John could not steal his gaze away from her. Nor did he want to.

"Thank you for dinner and the escort home, sir." She fiddled with the buttons on her cloak.

Her nervous gesture thrust him back into awareness. He was making her uncomfortable, the last thing he wished to do.

"You are most welcome. I am grateful for your help." He cleared his throat. "Especially with accompanying me to notify the Cunninghams. Having you there made a trying situation easier." And he meant it. Her kindness, the way she'd held the mother's hand as he interviewed them, had eased the woman's burden. Truth be told, there was something about Miss Wycliffe's warm, gentle presence that eased his own.

Until he remembered the horrid secret he kept from her, festering like rot under his skin. How would this woman ever understand, once he mustered the courage to tell her how his brother had changed her world forever? That he had hidden the truth and his brother away, never allowing her the peace of knowing what had happened to her parents and why?

I'm a bastard, plain and simple.

"I was glad I could be there for them and you, sir. I only wish I could have prevented it somehow. I shall miss Miriam dearly. As will all of us in Clun."

His pulse increased as he realized she might think this the end of their working partnership. He had to extend his time with her. Offer a more fixed relationship, of sorts. He had to make things right, especially with the financial strain he knew rested on her shoulders.

"Would you be interested in extending our brief working arrangement into a more permanent venture, Miss Wycliffe? I'm new here and from the city. A combination that may make many of the locals hesitant to my inquiries." He held his breath.

"I am flattered by your request."

"I would pay you for your assistance, of course. And pardon my bluntness, but from what you alluded to today, perhaps a bit of extra coin would ease some of your burden?"

As well as my own.

She tugged at her gloved fingertips. No doubt a flush crept along her neck into her cheeks, even though he couldn't see it in the moonlight.

"You are quite perceptive," she said.

"I could not help overhear Mr. Fiske at supper. And Mrs. Cunningham's inquiry about the note for your cottage coming due."

He'd also seen the older woman press a shilling in Miss Wycliffe's hand. A kind, unexpected act for a woman entombed in her own grief. It rang of devotion. He knew he played upon Miss Wycliffe's situation in the worst of ways, but he couldn't let her slip away from him. Not yet. There was too much for which he needed to make amends.

She sighed. "My financial difficulties are no secret, I suppose. When my parents died, I extended their note on the cottage. At the time ten years sounded like more than enough to repay the sum." She shook her head. "Now, it seems an impossible task. It comes due in a few weeks. I have asked for an extension on repayment of the note. However, Mr. Fiske is quite a stubborn man."

"Is that a yes to continuing our arrangement?" John sent an encouraging smile. If he could help her, perhaps he could heal part of himself.

Seconds spiraled out in a slow breath like the snowflakes swirling down around her. One landed on her nose, another on her eyelash. For a moment he wondered how it would feel to be a bit of frozen snow, close enough to her beauty to touch her.

His musing evaporated as the flakes melted into her skin. Her hesitation seemed a death knell to his plan and his hope to salvage some part of the past into goodness.

"I would be a fool not to accept your kindness, but do not offer out of charity or pity, sir."

"It is I who would be a fool not to take advantage of your skill. Not only can you help me garner more information from your neighbors here in Clun, but you can help me further examine the bodies for clues. I would very much like to officially determine if Miss Cunningham's demise is related to the death of the poor woman now resting upon your table, as we suspect it to be. You will earn your pay, I assure you."

"Then I accept, and I must take your leave as I am chilled to the bone." She rubbed her arms. The cold had settled in quickly along with the rate of the snowfall. John suppressed the urge to drape his coat around her.

"May I call upon you in the morning?" His words rushed out as he moved forward to open the door for her. "I would like to have a further look at the woman you are tending before she is returned to her parents for burial. See if she has any markings in common with Miss Cunningham."

"Of course. I rise early, so any time after eight shall be fine."

There were so many other things he wished to say, but he pressed them down into the silence and left with a nod and tip of his hat.

Chapter 5
The Cottage

Staring down at Becca's pale face, Lucy frowned. Concentration eluded her, and it showed in her work. The uneven powder placement lacked precision. She stepped away from her prepping table, climbed the cellar stairs, and walked over to the window. A thin veil of darkness clung to the edges of the sky as the light struggled to burst through. Perhaps the sun didn't wish to shine this morning either, nor could Lucy blame it. She loathed this time of year.

Whenever she neared the anniversary of her parents' death, her nightmares of that night emerged, hungry from hibernation. After waking in a cold sweat for the third time in the night, she'd risen and lit the candelabrum on her bedside table, heading downstairs to work, but her efforts were lackluster.

Becca deserved her best.

Two hours had passed since Lucy had awoken, and her stomach growled. Despite the fact she *should* be hungry, every time she eyed her stove and thought of even the most meager meal of cooked oats, her stomach churned. Her body and mind were on edge. And she'd learned over the years to let it pass on its own. No amount of fresh air, work, or food would quell the worry and unease. Being busy helped to push it back for a while, so she'd continue on.

For now.

In the cellar, shivering at the shift in temperature, she snuggled further into her wool wrap. Batting a wisp of hair from her brow, she gazed down at Becca. Lucy's time with her this morning had helped, despite the uneven layering of powder. Gone were the bluish-black marks along her neck, but much work needed to be done before the girl could be dressed into her final resting clothes and accompanying flowers. Noting adequate light from the early dawn finally edging in from the ground-level windows, Lucy blew out one of the candles from the candelabrum near Becca's pale form. The spirals of smoke served as a reminder of how poor Becca's life had been extinguished and taken far too early from this world.

So had Miriam.

"Becca, did you have such a similar end? I cannot stand the thought of it." Lucy selected a few more powders and ointments from the cabinet near the table.

She always talked to the people she worked on, a quirk her sister Cil thought morbid. But how could Lucy make anyone understand? Speaking to them, even when they could not hear her, leant some kindness to the intimacy of what she did. Sewing them, washing them, and trying to cover what marks she could with the oils, ointments, and powders she'd created with Miss Clara's help had become Lucy's life. And she knew what she did was important for those who loved them, no matter what townsfolk like Mr. Rudd thought. She dabbed powder along the brow of Becca's forehead with her finger, then bent closer. Instead of a smooth even texture, a series of tiny red bumps dotted and pocked Becca's brow. Lucy pursed her lips. Why did they seem so familiar?

She closed her eyes. *Think. Think.*

"Of course!"

She'd seen a similar rash on Becca's arm earlier last fall. Lucy had even teased her about it because the girl had been scratching at it like a cat with fleas. A reaction to hogweed her mother had asked her to plant in their front flower box.

All of it had later been removed due to Becca's reaction. At least that was what Becca had told her.

So where had *this* rash come from? Lucy would have to see Miss Clara. She would know if anything else could have created such a reaction on Becca's skin. And it might get them closer to figuring out who had killed her . . . and Miriam, if indeed the two were related.

Continuing to add powder along the edge of Becca's cheek, Lucy smiled. She had not one, but two jobs now. Perhaps somehow she might have enough money to give Mr. Fiske to convince him to extend her note repayment for another year.

The sharp rap at the door startled her, and the container of powder fell from her hands to the dirt floor of the cellar.

"Thistles!"

"Miss Wycliffe?"

Blast. "One moment, sir," she answered.

The crisp commanding tones of Mr. Brodie's voice were unmistakable even after knowing him such a short time. Bending down, she carefully swept the powder she could salvage from the floor back into its container. She hated to waste such an expensive mixture, but how did one extract powder from packed dirt?

Frowning down at the powder remaining, she sighed. Nothing could be done. She secured the small jar's lid and placed it back on the shelf next to the jar of rouge. At least no more of it would be lost. Dusting off her skirts, she climbed the stairs to the main level and trooped to the door. Swinging it open, she couldn't help smiling.

Mr. Brodie stood holding a basket of colorful fruit. As if on cue, Lucy's stomach growled. *Loudly.* She cringed.

"Good morning, Miss Wycliffe." He lifted the basket toward her. "To thank you for being my assistant." He smiled. "It sounds as if I may have arrived just in time."

"Thank you. You didn't need to. However, I am grateful. Fruit is a luxury I can't often afford." Her mouth watered at the sight of the collection of apples and pears, and her stomach regained its desire to eat.

"I am only sorry I couldn't locate an apricot for you." He tapped his boots against the stoop to shake off the packed snow and plucked his hat from his head before he stepped inside. Apricot wove in and around his boots. To Lucy's surprise, he bent down and rubbed behind the cat's ears. Not many men agreed with the keeping of pets indoors. At least not here in Clun. Perhaps men in the city didn't mind such frivolities?

Or perhaps only Mr. Brodie didn't mind.

"Please do come in, sir." Lucy gestured to one of the two embroidered chairs in front of the hearth, her only seating other than the kitchen table.

She washed her hands in the basin in the kitchen and dried them. As he settled into a chair by the fire, she selected an apple and rubbed it along her blouse sleeve until it shone, then took a big bite from it.

He chuckled and a smile greeted her. "I find you quite refreshing, Miss Wycliffe."

Lucy savored the apple and swallowed. "How so? And the apple is delicious, thank you."

"You've a way of ease about you. There are no pretenses." His gaze danced along her face.

"Should there be?" She gnawed on the edge of her lip.

"Never." He paused a moment. "How is your work coming along?"

"I have found nothing of interest except for a rash along Becca's brow and forehead," she began. "I think it's from hogweed as she was allergic, but I must see Miss Clara to be sure. I think I'll know more once I have time to properly tend to Miriam."

"May I see her?" He gestured to the open trapdoor leading to the cellar.

Lucy set aside her apple. "Of course."

Mr. Brodie rested his hat on a nearby chair and followed her below. He approached Becca and, bending over, studied her brow. Lucy appreciated his concentration and care for her friend. Old Man Codger wouldn't have dared to edge so close. The man despised the dead. An irony for a constable, one that everyone overlooked.

Mr. Brodie rubbed his chin with his index finger, a habit of deep thought she'd noted yesterday while he studied the scene at the lake. "I can see the bumps, but I didn't notice any like them on Miss Cunningham. Though the neck marks on this poor girl are similar." He narrowed his eyes and bent closer. "I can scarce tell where Miss Lusk's were. What kind of ointment did you use to cover the bruising?" Scrunching his nose, he moved back. "'Tis remarkable even though it smells like the devil."

"I can make no claim to it," Lucy admitted. "'Tis Miss Clara's creation. And, I'm sorry if it has an odor. Perhaps you could give me a clue as to its smell? Between the two of us we may be able to unearth her secret."

"Ah, that explains it. It has a very peculiar odor. An unpleasant one. It smells of chalk and rotten eggs."

"Then I will think it a blessing I cannot smell, sir, for I spilled some of it on the floor. I fear it may reek forever as it is now in the soil."

"I'd take a bucket to it later. Poor Apricot will thank you." He glanced around the small cellar. "'Tis unusual to have a root cellar below one's cottage, is it not?"

"It is. The farmer who owned it prior built it with the root cellar below the cottage rather than outside as his wife was of a delicate nature and sickly. It allowed her to lift the trapdoor and travel below stairs for her goods rather than venture out of doors during the cold winter. Evidently, when my mother saw it, she was entranced by the idea of not having to do the same, so here we are."

"You have made a quite remarkable transformation of it to a preparations room." He ran his fingertips over the top of several of her jars and tins of ointments, lotions, and herbs.

"It also adds a nice sense of safety for those I prepare. The layer-out before me had more than one body stolen from her own root cellar that was detached from her cottage."

"Unfortunately, such body-snatching still happens in London as well. I am glad she is safe under your care here. Once she is ready, my men will bring Miss Cunningham to you as her parents have requested."

Lucy inhaled sharply. How would she prepare yet another dear friend for the grave?

Mr. Brodie gestured to Becca. "When is she due to be returned to her family?"

Lucy pulled at her fingertips. "Tomorrow afternoon."

A crease knitted between his brows. "Are you concerned you will not have her ready?"

"I will, but I don't wish her to leave me. Becca is . . ." she faltered. "She *was* my oldest friend. Other than my sister, not a soul knew me better, and the thought of her leaving here and being placed in the darkness of the earth alone unsettles me." Lucy's eyes stung as her emotions betrayed her. "'Tis not rational or reasonable even, but it is how I feel." She met his gaze.

The concern she found there anchored her. Did she dare move under the weight of his stare? Did she even wish to? For seconds, their gazes held in a quiet grace that settled between her ribs and down into her stomach. If any man understood loss, it was this man, Mr. Shiny Boots.

John Brodie. His eyes, his soul told her so without a word falling from his lips.

"Loss is never rational, nor reasonable, Miss Wycliffe. There is no need for you to be."

Her throat dried. If he didn't stop being so kind, so understanding, so bloody perfect, she might unravel like bound yarn on the floor. "Is there anything else you wish to examine of her before I finish up?" Lucy forced a tight smile.

"A dirt sample from the sole of her boot, and I will be on." However, he didn't move. "Is there anything you need? Anything I can do for you?"

Wiping her damp eyes, she tried to chuckle. "You are my employer, Mr. Brodie. It is I who should be asking you."

"Well, all I have need of is your presence at the office after your work here is done this morn. If you feel up to it."

"Work is a blessed distraction and a great comfort for me in times of distress. I shall be there as soon as I can."

Mr. Brodie scraped a slice of dirt from Becca's shoe into his handkerchief and tucked it in his trouser pocket. He climbed the stairs before donning his hat and coat, then crossed to the door. "Wear your warmest cloak, hat, and gloves. We will be out of doors."

"Oh?"

"Yes, and good walking boots as well."

"Anything else?" she asked, as he opened the door.

He turned and flashed a wicked smile. "Just you, Miss Wycliffe. That shall be enough."

The door closed and Lucy blinked after him. Was he flirting with her? Did such a serious, handsome man as he even need to? No doubt women would swoon and gather at his feet like bees to a honeycomb. Perhaps her overwrought emotion caused her imagination to run wild and free in hopes of such a thing.

Apricot meowed at her.

"You're right. The man would no sooner be interested in me than the king's regent. I am a layer-out of the dead. And a spinster." She rested her hand on the top of her head and cringed as her eyes fluttered closed. "And I forgot to brush my hair. *Again.* What the man must think of me, I can scarce imagine."

~ ~ ~

Lucy Wycliffe commanded his thoughts, her cinnamon hair and fine ivory skin, luminescent like a pearl. The clock chimed on the wall, and John rubbed his palm down his face.

Fool.

She would never consider him a match, yet he sat in his office, mooning over her, worse than a schoolboy.

A schoolboy.

Despite having little to nothing to offer her. And what he understood of women could be held in a bloody thimble, so even if he dared give in to his feelings, the results would be disaster.

Pure disaster.

His few dabbles into courtship had been foibles at best. He wasn't even amusing. Many women had told him so. Boring, they'd said. A waste of a handsome face, they'd said. Such successes with women had been one of the many reasons the sea and the Royal Navy had appealed to him.

And the sea had ravaged him further still. He ran a hand down his thigh and felt the familiar marbled flesh beneath his trousers. No woman would scarce want him at all now, even if they could stand to look at his wound. He could offer them only his name and what he could hold in his hands, which amounted to nothing. Since his father had disowned him, he had no future prospects for inheritance. What he would have in this world he would earn, and a constable's earnings were not impressive.

Now he could no longer run from his shortcomings. Or his growing attraction to the very woman whose life and circumstances his family had ruined so many years ago.

I'm a bastard.

Surely she would arrive soon. The clock chimed half past two, and the sun shone brilliant against the buildings and windows of the town square. Vendors called out their goods as folk bustled by his window. A few peered in and waved a greeting while others studied him without a word.

Being an outsider and from the city served as a double-edged blade to his progress. He'd have his work cut out for him. Time might win them over to trust him and solving these two murders would be a good start. If only he knew where to begin.

He studied the soil he'd taken from Miss Lusk's shoe. Moving it about in the round glass dish he had unearthed from a battered box earlier, he examined it with the magnifier. *Dirt*. He sniffed it. It smelled like the mixture that had been on the soles of Miss Cunningham's boots. The commonality was helpful, but such a discovery would not lead them far. Not in a countryside full of it. He had to do what he always did.

Go back to the body.

Then, he'd return to the site of first discovery.

He dribbled a bit of water from a nearby glass on the mud, and as the soil moistened and loosened, tiny bumps emerged. With tweezers, he tugged the mud apart into smaller segments. He squinted. *Seeds?* So small, one could scarcely identify them in the dark, thick mud. But there they were.

His heart soared. Finally, a clue.

Frowning, he sighed. He knew as much about botany as he did women.

John stood and scanned the crowded, cluttered room. His gaze drifted from box to box, and he scrubbed a hand through his hair. He had seen a book on botany, an old, dusty and rather smelly leather backed version. It even had plates of plants and seeds in it for easy identification. How many boxes ago had he spied it? Yesterday, or perhaps the day before? Time spent in this stuffy space ran together. He closed his eyes, trying to remember.

A knock on the window startled him, and his eyes flicked open. He turned to see Miss Wycliffe, a vision before the mottled glass of his windows, though she appeared murky on the other side of them. The panes were in dire need of washing, yet another task to add to his list. Heaven knew he couldn't afford to hire anyone. Not with his meager salary and him taking on Miss Wycliffe as an assistant.

The bell above the door jingled in approval as she entered. Tugging the cloak down from her head to rest in a neat fold at her neck, she smiled at him. "You have made great progress in your office, I see."

"You jest."

"No, quite the contrary." She shook her head and removed her bonnet. "You have made great improvements. I can see the floor and some of the walls. I cannot remember a time prior to being a child that it was so orderly in here."

John couldn't help but be amused. Most women would fuss at the disrepair of the room. She somehow noted the improvements. Yet another reason he needed to be wary around her. Her innate goodness and optimism had become a beacon of hope to his tired, weary soul.

He stepped away from her to gain some distance. "Yet, I cannot for the very life of me find the book I desire despite seeing it before."

"Oh? And which book is it you desire?"

When he faced her, the eager smile she set upon him undercut his thoughts, and he paused. "A book on botany. I have found some seeds in the mud I took from Miss Lusk's shoe this morn. And I know little of plants."

"Yet another reason to seek out Miss Clara if it cannot be found. Where have you searched? I am good at finding lost things. My sister Cil always tells me so."

"Why does that not surprise me in the least?" He shrugged off his suit coat and laced it around the back of his chair. "I believe it is on the left side. I'll pull down some boxes, and we'll set to digging. If we can't locate it in a quarter hour, we'll claim defeat and set off on the other task I have for us today."

Miss Wycliffe hung her cloak and bonnet on the lopsided hooks next to the door. "Oh? And what task is that?"

"We'll retrace the area where the bodies were found."

She stilled and visibly swallowed. "Do you think something was missed?"

"Well, many times one doesn't know what to even look for at first. Now that we believe they are linked by a similar means of death and the soil on their shoes, we can look for other commonalities to make it official." He set a few boxes before her and pulled back the lids. "Here are two for you to peruse."

She set to the task in silence with a creased brow. Had he said or done something he shouldn't have? John dug into his own boxes, and they continued in silence except for the soft shuffle of books and boots on the wooden floor.

"Does it become easier?" she asked.

"Does what become easier?" He stood to see her brushing off the leather cover of the botany book he sought. The dust particles twirled and danced in a shaft of sunlight seeping through the window. Her lithe fingers moved in a gentle ripple along the dark edges.

"Seeing them as parts of puzzles to be solved rather than real people." She met his gaze, and the sadness in her eyes nearly pulled him under.

He swallowed hard. He wished he had another answer, but he'd tell her the truth. "No. Not for me. Every case feels like the first one."

Chapter 6
Investigating at Summerland

The wind whipped through the warmest cloak Lucy owned. The day and its damp temperament chilled her to the bone. She hurried just ahead of Mr. Brodie in a quest for the sun awaiting them on the other side of a copse of evergreen trees. Lake Summerland glistened in the afternoon rays and for the briefest of moments it blinked back, tranquil and beautiful as it always had been.

When her gaze cast in the direction where they'd found Miriam, Lucy shuddered.

"Miss Wycliffe?" Mr. Brodie called, yanking her from her thoughts.

Lucy spied him circling the very spot where Miriam had taken her last breath. Covered in a thin blanket of snow, the spot seemed serene against the dark green of the treetops and blue of the sky. Picturesque, charming, and perfect, yet now it would always be related to death. *Miriam's death.* And the loss shook Lucy more deeply than she expected.

She caught the way Mr. Brodie studied her. No doubt he could sense her hesitation. His military service and time as a detective would allow him to decipher what every hitch in her step and line in her brow meant. Mustering her courage to earn her pay and impress her new employer, Lucy set her jaw and walked over to him.

Each soft step into the snow proved a reminder Miriam would no longer do the same. With each footfall, Lucy's grief began to shift to anger. With her focus and skill, she'd find who'd taken her friend from this world. She just had to muster it from beneath her grief, as she had done before when she'd lost her parents.

"Perhaps it's too soon to have come, Miss Wycliffe. I can see the distress on your face. If you'd like for me to take you back, I can." A deep notch formed between his brows and his lips settled into a frown.

Lucy scanned the landscape before daring to meet his gaze. "It is difficult. As I approached you some of my sadness shifted into anger, and I wish to use it to help you find who has done this. Miriam deserves full justice."

He nodded. "I will assist you in that endeavor. I'm moved by your resolve. Miss Cunningham was lucky to have you as a friend."

"As I was to have her as mine," she replied. "Tell me what we hope to find under this new blanket of snow. Won't all of our evidence have been lost?"

"Preserved, actually. Frozen into the earth where it cannot dare disappear."

Brilliant.

Why had she not realized it? The cold would preserve evidence similar to how it preserved a body. "You're right. I wouldn't have thought of it. If there are any clues remaining, they will be packed beneath the snow cover."

"And since it is only a thumb's depth of new groundcover, it will not be overly difficult to see what may have been out of place."

"Out of place?"

"Since you know the area so well, I had hoped you could scan here first and then look about more closely at the spot where she was discovered. I wish to try to discern why the killer left her here of all the places he could have in Clun. Seems an odd choice for a winter night, does it not?" He stared out in the distance, scouting the edges of the forest and nearby fields surrounding the lake.

"Yes. It is an odd place for her." She pressed a hand to her forehead. "I don't know why I didn't think of it earlier. Miriam feared the lake. She couldn't swim well, so she never dared too close."

He edged nearer.

"Do you know exactly where they found Becca in relation to Miriam?"

"Abe discovered her closer to the woods, near the line of evergreens to the left."

"Abe?"

"Miss Clara's nephew. He lives with her and is a gardener and caretaker of sorts. There isn't much he can't grow or fix." Lucy smiled at the thought of her childhood friend.

"Do you know what he was doing about these parts?"

"He traverses this path to get to the mill. He works there when he can. Seems he found her on his way home from an early shift that day." Would she ever forget when he came to give her the news of finding Becca? Lucy doubted it. One didn't forget the worst days in the blink of an eye. They lingered about like fog.

"Could you point me in the vicinity of their homes, so I have an idea of what direction they would have traveled from to reach here? I assume they wouldn't have bothered with the road. Do you believe they would have dared travel this path at night?"

She took a deep breath and spied the path Becca most likely would have used, then pointed it out to him. "She would have chosen this one since it runs between her parents' property and the Codgers'."

Mr. Brodie gathered two wet branches and rested one before her feet, another slightly behind her. "Does this fashion a line to where she was found behind us?"

Lucy shook her head. "No. The line should run closer to the road." She shifted the branches so they made a more direct cut in the snow between the path Becca would have taken and where Lucy remembered Abe describing it. She frowned. "However, this was relayed secondhand from Abe. I never saw Becca here or the exact spot where she died. Her father and Abe brought her to my cottage."

Mr. Brodie stopped sketching in his small black ledger and glanced up. Emotion flashed brightly in his eyes, and he paused. "I will ask him the precise location, but your estimate is helpful. Please continue. You knew them, perhaps even walked this same stretch together. Trust yourself." He offered a smile of encouragement, and her worry fluttered away like a butterfly.

Lucy lifted her chin. "Miriam preferred to walk farther from the lake's edge. She would have taken a route away from the waterline."

Mr. Brodie finished his sketch and gathered two more branches before approaching once more. "And Miss Cunningham? Where is her home in relation?"

Lucy took the branches and placed them in the direction of Miriam's home, located far off on the other side diagonally across the water. "There is nothing on this side of the lake I can imagine her trying to get to. This leads to a patch of woods, a stretch of farmland, and finally town. It is much more direct to travel along the road."

"Show me," Mr. Brodie encouraged and handed her two branches.

Lucy placed one before her and the other behind, between Miriam's home and where she was found. Mr. Brodie added to his sketch while she studied the direction of Becca's line and Miriam's to see if they might intersect somewhere, somehow, but they didn't. She frowned and propped her hands on her hips. "This makes little sense."

Mr. Brodie continued to sketch in his small ledger, focusing his attention on what he was creating. "It rarely does in the beginning. We are just gathering the pieces."

"That's what puzzles me." She chewed her lip. "Her home is on the other side entirely. She would have had to traverse the full length of this lake to get here when she could have run into the woods or back onto the road for help. She would only have been—" Her breath hitched. Tears burned hot at the back of her eyes as her throat closed.

Mr. Brodie stopped sketching and approached her. "Miss Wycliffe? What is it?"

Dread coiled tightly in Lucy's chest, too similar to the night she'd found her parents dead. "Miriam would only have run here to this spot—so close to the water's edge—*to* someone she felt safe with." She met Mr. Brodie's gaze and blinked back tears. "Someone she knew. Most likely someone *I* know."

~ ~ ~

The wind whipped Miss Wycliffe's skirts and cloak about her body. Rogue tendrils danced wildly like flames of fire about her face.

John's throat tightened.

Despite how he tried, he could not quell his attraction to her nor his intense desire and need to protect her from the world as he knew it. The look of her standing before him in distress, with such beauty nestled all about her, stole his words, his breath, his logic. A woman he wished to make amends to.

A woman now under his employ.

Miss Wycliffe. *Lucy*. How he longed to say her name aloud and hear it twirl and twine out in the cold empty air, and the knowledge of it startled him. He had to focus on the present and investigating this murder. Two murders, and yet his thoughts spun out to her, not them. He had to regain his focus.

And fast.

He dropped his gaze and counted divots in the snow. Five, ten, fifteen, twenty; then he steeled himself, clamped off his emotions, as he had done so many times before. Before battle, before a widow's tears at a notification, before Miss Wycliffe now as she realized for the first time that a person she knew could have ended the lives of two others she loved and cared for. He knew what that sort of shock lent the body and mind as well as the ravages it took upon a soul, but he said none of this. He pressed his lips together, took a breath, and nodded. "I agree."

"You agree?" Her brows knit together and her breath came out in a puff before it disappeared into the air.

He shrugged. "I've thought from the start it had to be a local."

"Why? How could you possibly know, this early on?" She wiped her eyes. Crossing her arms about her chest, she watched him, awaiting an answer.

"Do you truly wish to know such unpleasantness?"

"Does it matter whether I wish to know it? This is part of my position now, is it not?" Her skin had flushed, and her eyes brightened to a hyacinth once more.

"Shootings or stabbings are often distant impulsive acts done by strangers. It's careless and leaves clues and material evidence. Done for thievery, panic, or rage, it's reckless." He approached her until the toes of his boots almost touched her own. "Strangling is a more intimate act. A personal death, if you will. The killer must look their victim in the eyes, squeeze and hold until the last breath escapes their lips and the last stream of life flickers away."

They stood in silence, their gazes locked, with ribbons of cold air extending and disappearing about them. She stared at him so long, he wondered if she had been struck dumb or ill or if she might faint straight away. Part of him knew she would do none of these things. She was a layer-out of the dead, and her spine of steel would not crumble under such truth. Would anything? Perhaps if he faced her now and uttered the truth of what his brother had done and what he, John, had failed to do, she would shrug it away.

"And what of beatings, sir? What kind of killings are those?"

"Why do you ask?" The lie caught in his throat, and he shifted on his feet. He knew exactly why. They had been holding the same dreadful memory between them at the same moment. A shared moment of loss only they would understand. An ugly past history binding them together as only pain could.

She looked away first, severing the thread holding them close, and stepped away. Carving the snow with the toe of her boot, she created a semicircle. "My parents were beaten to death. And when you spoke of the intimacy and distance of crimes, I wondered what a beating would be." Once she completed the circle in the snow, she met his gaze. "I have never understood what happened to them. Or why it had to happen at all."

Why did it happen?

Another question he wished he had an answer for. Only his brother and her parents knew, and all of them were long dead, by his dear brother's own hands. "I wish I had an answer as to how or why."

"Can you tell me what it reveals about the killer?"

Did he dare reveal anything? Would he unravel the whole truth by tugging along this one frail thread? He didn't know, yet he could not stop his tongue from uttering the truth.

"Beatings are acts of rage, anger, and desperation," he began. "Such acts are often precipitated by interruption."

"So, it is also an intimate act. To be so violent with one's bare hands."

"Yes, but not as much as a strangling."

"I see," she whispered, tugging at the cuffs of her gloves. Her words trickled through the air like raindrops. "Miriam was so close to reaching the woods. Do you believe she hoped to escape her killer?"

He eyed the forest and glanced back at the lake behind them. "While I fear she looked into the eyes of her killer, I'd prefer to believe she stared past him at a midnight blue sky. And I pray she beheld a moment of peace and beauty at the last."

She smiled at him and nodded. "That is a prayer I shall wish too."

Why would I utter such nonsense around her?

Perhaps they were his thoughts, but to voice them aloud to her, in a moment of investigation, was weak and unseemly. They had a killer to find. One who used skill to entice, trap, and kill its prey. A mountain lion of a predator who, once detected, only signaled its presence too late, for its prey was already in its reach.

John cleared his throat and settled on the task at hand. "I'll trace a path along where you believe she most likely journeyed. Will you look about the wider scope of the scene to see what, if anything, might be amiss or out of place? Even the smallest of details is of great import." He pulled a few red strips of cloth from his pocket. "And if you find anything, don't retrieve it. Merely mark it in the snow with one of these until I return."

"Yes, sir," she answered, accepting the cloth strips. A slight tremble traveled from her hand to his.

"And if you have need of me, call out. I will not be far." He gifted her a smile in an attempt to reassure her. Her lips pressed together in a thin line, indicating his failure to do so. She turned away to begin her search.

The afternoon chill shifted into a more menacing cold, and the sharp sweet smell of coming snow sang in the air. They'd have another hour before they'd need to return. Mother Nature waited for no one. This John knew, more than other men, his years at sea a lesson in respecting Her wishes and listening to Her warnings.

With every step, his leg throbbed, and the pain shot into his thigh. Another step leant a hard, unusual feel beneath the sole of his boot.

Crack.

He paused and carefully lifted his foot. Leaning down, he brushed a layer of snow away with his glove. A shattered glass watch dial glittered back at him in the stark white snow. Lifting it carefully, he removed the silver watch and its long chain from the snow surrounding it. The timepiece had no closure and little remained of its glass facing. He turned it in his palm. No engraving, either. Only the intricate detailing upon the metal sang of finery, wealth, and privilege. He glanced around him. It seemed as out of place here as he did.

Frowning, he placed it in a handkerchief and tucked it in his coat pocket. He nested a red strip of cloth in the snow where he'd found it and marked its location in the crude sketch he'd been outlining, a portion at a time, after they'd arrived about the lake. It lay along the imaginary path Miss Cunningham might have followed as she entered this area after leaving her home.

He froze. Dread crawled along his skin. Or perhaps from the path her killer had taken as he began his trek before killing her.

Or after.

Chapter 7
The Clues and the Stars

"Find anything of note?" Mr. Brodie asked as he approached.

Lucy frowned. "I'm not at all sure what I *should* be finding. I've marked two spots ahead, closer to the tree line." She pointed toward the dusty shadows a few yards behind her. The two red fabric strips rippled in the breeze, side by side. The odd and chaotic crimson screamed against its serene white surroundings, much as she felt being here, doing this. As if she didn't belong at all. Any moment, she might be called out as a pretender.

"Show me what you've found." He gestured for her to continue on ahead of him.

Encouraged, she lifted her skirts to ease her steps and mustered her fortitude as she neared her markings. If they were nothing, she would feel a fool. "The pitch in the ground is lower here. Perhaps something heavy had rested on these two spots before the snowfall. Do you see how the snowpack is lower only in these two small ovals?" She pointed. Her pulse picked up speed as she awaited his response.

Mr. Brodie studied the ground and then walked behind the two markers. He stared back out at the lake. The area where Miriam had taken her final breath. Lucy shuddered. He grimaced and stooped to analyze the indentions in the snow once more. Pain etched along the pull of his mouth.

She fought the urge to assist him and instead pondered his movements. If only she knew the twirling of his mind and the stream of his thoughts.

After scanning out in the distance, he glanced up at her. "Well done, Miss Wycliffe. I believe you have found his perch."

"Perch? The way a bird perches on a branch?" She walked closer.

"I shall regret this later, but this is the best way to show you what I mean." He knelt before her, emitting a small groan as his knees fell directly into the two rounded marks in the ground tagged with crimson ribbons. "He sat here, in this position, for some time. Waiting. Waiting for her."

Dread coiled through Lucy's chest as the cold breath stilled in her lungs. "An animal, hunting its prey?" Her words seemed to fall from her lips in fragile puffs of snowy air.

"Yes." His gaze softened as it met her own.

"I see." She could imagine it all too well. He had waited for dear Miriam.

"It is a horror," he added, "but what you've found will make a case much easier against whomever did this. We have evidence to show it was a planned attack. An intentional killing." Rising, he brushed the snow from his trousers, and then added markings to his bound ledger.

"If these two deaths are related, do you believe the killer waited for poor Becca, too?"

He continued to sketch. "Killers are creatures of habit, same as the rest of us. No doubt if they are related, which I do believe they are at this point, he most likely did. He may have gained confidence if he'd been lying in wait once and succeeded. It could have propelled him to try it once more."

"And he was successful." She rubbed her arms to ward away the chill deep in her bones. "Do you believe he will try again?"

Mr. Brodie met her gaze and paused, pressing his lips together before answering. "Truthfully?"

"Yes."

He frowned. "I do."

Discomfort silenced her, and he continued on with his notes.

"Did you find anything?" she asked as he tucked his ledger back into the interior pocket of his coat. Secretly, she prayed he would say no.

Yet he nodded. "A watch, of all things." He pulled a handkerchief from his pocket and folded back the linen material. "Mind the glass. I stepped upon it."

Lucy studied the timepiece. "Something about it is familiar. I cannot place why exactly. I can tell you it was not Miriam's. Nor Becca's. It is far too fine a piece for them to have owned. Or their families, either." Peering closer at it, she frowned. "I have seen it before, though. 'Tis the chain I recognize and the stenciling around the face of the dial."

"When you remember, do tell me." He tucked it away and glanced at the sky. "I'm afraid we have little time left before another round of snow makes its way upon us. Perhaps take one more look in the area along the edge of the lake, and I'll follow closer to the tree line where you left off."

"I fear I may be missing things. I don't know exactly what I'm looking for." She wrung her hands. What if she passed over something of import, and Miriam and Becca's killer was never found?

"Do not doubt yourself," he replied. "You've a fine eye for detail. Whatever seems unusual is what we want. And even if anything seems missing or out of place, it would also serve our purpose." He walked away from her toward the evergreens.

Why does he believe in me so?

Mr. Brodie's confidence in her confused her. Of course, she knew how to prepare bodies and accomplish some minor medical procedures. But finding clues and solving a murder—two in this case—exceeded her capabilities.

Didn't it?

Lucy swallowed her hesitation and tugged her cloak closer as she headed back to the lake where Miriam had been found. Fat gray clouds nested above her. No time remained to doubt herself. The storm would soon be upon them. Daring to venture to the very edge, she scanned the snow and mud around the lake's borders, where it sloped to what she knew to be the water line. A thin, frozen cover made the lake a glassy mirror beneath the fine layer of powdery snow. It reminded her of a day, long ago, before Miriam began to fear the water's edge.

~ ~ ~

"Wait, Lucy!" Miriam called, giggling as she clumped through the snow in her brother's old boots.

"Mir!" Lucy laughed, watching her friend wobble from side to side with each struggling step in the knee-deep snow. "You look like a tot taking its first steps. Those boots are far too large for you."

"My others were soaked through, and I didn't want to miss the stars."

"How did you talk me into this? It'll be pitch black soon. And we'll be turned to icicles. We shouldn't even be out here."

"You can't see the stars in the day," Miriam panted. "And they will be beautiful. They always are after the first snow." Coils of air puffed out of her mouth. Then, she smiled and fell back into the fresh snowfall.

A dusting of flakes flew up like flour around her, and Lucy fell back in the snow as well and laughed until she lost her breath.

"Look," Miriam whispered. They stared up into the sky, rushing on to darkness, no doubt from Miriam's bidding.

Lucy blinked up at the emerging stars. So perfect and glorious. She should have been cold and chilled to the bone, but the beauty of the stars, amidst the tiny stray flakes of falling snow kissing her cheeks, filled every facet of her soul.

"It's perfect," she murmured.

Miriam turned to her and grabbed her hand, squeezing it. "Beyond perfection, I think. It's heaven."

~ ~ ~

"Miss Wycliffe?" The sound of Mr. Brodie's voice and the crunching of snow underfoot grabbed Lucy from her woolgathering. Concern knitted along his furrowed brow. "Shall we return? You seem unwell." His gaze swept her face.

Lucy blinked the memory away. Tracks of tears cooled her cheeks, and she swiped at them with her gloves. Heat flushed her body. How long had she been lost in thought? How long had he been calling her name?

She took an uneasy breath. "Merely memories."

He said nothing as he studied her.

Staring out into the distance, she knew what she had to do. *For Miriam.* "I've remembered something. I hope it might be of help. Will you hold these a moment?" She reached out to him with the strips of remaining fabric in her gloved hands.

He took them from her without a word.

The snow was far too sparse to flop onto it as she had that night, more than ten years ago. Carefully, Lucy lay down upon the thin snow. Spreading her arms to recreate her memories, she gazed up at the gray sky and then around at the other landmarks.

Oh, Miriam.

Lucy squeezed her eyes shut and hoped the stars were the last thing her dear friend had seen before her death.

Opening her eyes, Lucy took a breath to quell the rapidly uneven thunder of her heart, and clutched Mr. Brodie's steady hand as he offered to help her back up.

"What is it?" he asked. "Another clue?"

Despite her efforts to keep it at bay, another tear spilled down her cheek before she batted it away. "I think she came here to see the stars. She loved to see them after the first snowfall. She would lie back and watch the first flakes fall."

He sucked in a breath. "Alone?"

"I doubt it. When we were younger, I went with her. I imagine she invited someone to join her. Most likely they were holding hands, staring up to the heavens." She couldn't complete the rest. Emotion filled her throat.

"And she would dare to step so close to the water's edge? I believe you said she feared the lake."

She nodded. "Not until a few years ago after her foot got caught between rocks on the lake bottom while swimming, and she almost drowned. Her older brother rescued her. However, she'd had quite a fright. She claimed the lake—" Her words faltered as the rest of what Miriam had said came rushing back to her.

"Go on," Mr. Brodie murmured encouragingly.

Lucy's pulse picked up speed. "She said the lake had spoken to her and wanted to claim her as its own." She wrung her hands. Discomfort roared along her skin as she recounted the story. "We'd laughed it off at the time, but now, it seems so vulgar to speak of."

"Well, you and I both know the lake did not claim her. She died by the hands of a man, not Mother Nature."

Lucy shook off her fear and settled back into the reassurance Mr. Brodie gifted her. Calm slowly coated her insides like honey. "You're right. Thank you."

"But such a story of the love of the stars would explain the body's positioning. I do believe the night she died was a new moon. The sky would have been near perfect for star gazing." He frowned as he began to sketch and write in his ledger, the one she now loathed. Could a person's death be reduced to a few words and sketches on a page bound in leather? Was that all Becca and Miriam were now? Notes, scribbles, and sketches?

I hope not.

She stared beyond him and listened to the rhythmic sound of graphite on parchment.

"Well done today, Miss Wycliffe." He offered his arm to her, and she hesitated before allowing him to walk her to the road.

"It does not feel well done. It feels horrid. Horrid to realize she knew and very well may have invited the killer to join her on a night when she expected only peace, beauty, and a sea of stars." Lucy plodded along in the snow.

Steps Miriam and Becca would never take again.

A copper-colored fox darted out in front of them and chased after an unsuspecting brown hare. To the fox's dismay, the rabbit scurried into a hole too narrow for him to continue through. Soon it gave up chase and trotted off.

"That is often when death comes," Mr. Brodie replied. "Uninvited, unwelcome, and with no conscience for timing."

Chapter 8
Meeting Miss Clara

A crunch of snow startled Lucy, and she turned to see Mr. Brodie approaching around the tree line on the road. She smiled in relief. After yesterday's trip to the lake, she had been unsettled, her sleep a fragmented and fitful attempt at rest.

She'd left her cottage early this morn, eager to do something to busy herself. Her restlessness even prevented her attending to Becca, who waited patiently back in the cellar on Lucy's prepping table for a few final touches before being retrieved by her family. Even though the cold weather didn't require her to complete the full process of embalming to preserve her friend for burial, Lucy did need to add a layer of lavender, chamomile, and rosemary oil solution to Becca's skin before returning her to her parents.

"Good morn, sir." She hoped he did not hear the tremor in her voice as she called out.

He smiled and nodded in greeting. "Thank you for the precise directions on how to get here, Miss Wycliffe. Otherwise, I might still be about the woods, attempting to find it."

He offered his arm to escort her the remaining distance to her friend's cottage. "Miss Clara values her privacy and would never live along the main road. Too much noise, she claims. I am impressed you found it upon your first try." She studied his face. Shadows rested beneath his eyes. His sleep had been as fitful as hers.

"Well, I must admit, this isn't where I settled on my first endeavor. I took a wrong turn a ways back. This I found by accident and by the forked tree you noted." He pointed to Miss Clara's 'favorite sitting tree,' as she called it, a lovely oak towering high above many of the other trees in Clun.

"I am glad you made it. I cannot wait for you to meet her. She is a treasure and will be of great help in figuring out the heritage of the soil as well as the nature of the seeds you've brought."

Lucy pulled the bell outside of the tidy cottage. Despite the sun shining overhead, a winter chill challenged the air. An ample garden, often filled with blossoming herbs in the spring and summer, lay dormant under another fresh blanket of snow. The soft shuffle of Miss Clara's shoes sounded on the wooden planks inside. One final creak let them know the woman was close.

Lucy tapped the heel of each of her worn boots against the stacked rocks on the stoop to release the snow caked on the bottoms of her soles. Miss Clara would know if Lucy tracked in one new snowflake.

The door squeaked open.

A smile bloomed on the old woman's face. "Lucy! What a surprise this morn. I didn't expect you 'til tomorrow, girl." Before Lucy could answer, Miss Clara sniffed the air. Her smile evaporated. "Who's the man with you? He's no' from around here, is he?" She sniffed the air again with a twist to her lips. "Smells fussy. Is he from the city?" She clutched the door, and her voice dropped. "And you know I don't like strangers."

Lucy bit her lip and smiled. Leaning forward, she whispered, "I know, Miss Clara. He's the new constable." She bent closer to the old woman's ear. "And he seems nice even if he is from the city."

The old woman pulled her dark gray shawl up to cover her shoulders and straightened to her full height, a mere head above the doorknob. Tucking a loose lock of her silver hair behind her petite ear, she stepped to the side. "Come in. Best we get acquainted then."

Lucy glanced back at a frozen Constable Brodie. She touched his arm. "Mesmerizing, isn't she?"

He nodded and took a step forward. "She has a way about her." He stooped and murmured low, "Is she blind?"

Before Lucy could answer, Miss Clara chimed in. "Yes, son, I'm blind, but no' deaf. Come in or no' but close the door. I can't have the cold killing my plants."

Lucy entered the warm, cozy cottage as Mr. Brodie knocked the snow from his shoes and followed her inside. She stilled, allowing her eyes to adjust. *Heavenly.* Every shelf held flourishing plants and herbs, and a tidy group of flowering plants sat in an oval ring beneath Miss Clara's only window.

"Is the smell as glorious as I've always imagined?" Lucy asked.

He nodded, removing his hat. "The most luxurious of perfumes, I would think. It's the lavender I find most curious. How can she possibly get it to grow in winter?"

Miss Clara poked along ahead of them and sat in her rocking chair in front of the fire. She felt for her yarn and needles in her basket on the floor. Lucy's gaze followed the growing mound of gray woven wool cascading down. A new shawl, no doubt. As Miss Clara's fingers began their busy wavelike motions, she added in the slow smooth cadence of her rocker. Lucy walked toward her and sat in the chair opposite the old woman, then gestured for Mr. Brodie to stand near the hearth between them. Miss Clara had only two chairs in her small home.

The woman's rocking halted, as did her hands. "You're quite large for a man, aren't you?"

He cleared his throat. "I suppose so. How could you possibly tell my size from there?"

She pursed her lips. "You're blocking my heat. Move to the right. I'm an old woman. It doesn't take but a chill to put me underground, and I've no mind to go anytime soon."

Lucy laughed. "Miss Clara, I do adore you."

"Oh, go on. Why've you come?" Miss Clara resumed her rocking and needlework as a smile curved her lips, clearly pleased with their unexpected visit.

"Well, since Mr. Brodie is the new constable, he's investigating the deaths of Becca . . ." Lucy paused, willing herself to be stronger than she felt. "And Miriam."

"They related?"

Lucy glanced at Mr. Brodie and nodded. This wasn't her investigation to explain.

"We believe they are, Miss Clara," Mr. Brodie began. "And Miss Wycliffe tells me your keen sense of smell may be able to help us with some of the items we found with the bodies."

"I'm no' too keen on smelling the dead, sir. No' even for a man of the law such as yerself. No' even for those two sweet girls."

He sputtered. "No, no, I would never ask you to do such. Perhaps you could smell some of the evidence? Soil and some seeds, to be precise."

"Dirt? You wish me to smell yer dirt?"

Lucy jumped in. "Yes, Miss Clara. If you could tell us what decay and scents you recognize, it may help us in figuring out where they had been before they were killed."

"Before they were killed? You think them murdered, sir?" Miss Clara had frozen. Her chair had ceased its movements, and her hands rested along the arms of wood.

"Sadly, I do."

"Two murders? Here? In Clun?" She frowned. "No' possible. I've lived here all my life. Such things don't happen here. No' ever."

"I'm afraid they have, and my deepest desire is to prevent another from happening. We must catch whomever has done such to these girls."

Silence settled in and around them with only the faint crackling of wood burning in the hearth. Lucy held her breath. Miss Clara's hesitation surprised her. If her friend didn't agree to help, Lucy would have to try to unearth the soil type by her wits and Mr. Brodie's nose, which would take far too long. She nibbled her lower lip until the creases in Miss Clara's brow relaxed.

"You a soldier, sir?" Miss Clara asked and sniffed the air.

"Yes, ma'am. Out of the Royal Navy a few years past now."

"Because of the leg?" Her rocking chair started its usual rhythm.

Mr. Brodie smiled and slid a glance to Lucy. "Yes. How can you tell?"

"I can hear the uneven cadence in yer gait." She scrunched her nose. "And I can smell that foul liniment oil. No good for a leg injury. I'll mix you something right and proper for it if you'd prefer. Can you tell me what kind of wound it is?" She folded her hands in her lap.

Lucy smiled. Miss Clara would only help if Mr. Brodie showed he trusted her by sharing something. Something personal and private. Lucy recognized the tactic. Miss Clara had used it on her many years ago as well.

And it had worked.

Mr. Brodie searched Lucy's face and shifted his stance. When Lucy nodded in encouragement, he rubbed the back of his neck. Was sharing unnatural to him?

His jaw muscle flexed, and he dropped his gaze. "Bullet wound. It ravaged the muscles along with the burn from a fire. It plagues me, especially from exertion in the cold."

The rocking chair continued its even cadence and Miss

Clara resumed her knitting. "I've an ointment for you. I'll have it ready for you tomorrow."

"Thank you."

"Well?" she prompted. When neither of them replied, she frowned. "Bring me the dirt you wish me to smell. I haven't got all day. I'm old, you know."

Mr. Brodie chuckled. "Of course." He stepped to her side and extracted the samples from his trouser pocket, pressing them into her hands.

After opening each pouch and sniffing them several times, she set them down. "Peat. Some of it can be found out near the farmland between the Cunninghams' and the forest. A ways off from the lake, though. Quite a walk on a cold night."

"May I ask how you know it could have only come from there?"

"Only place no' overused by farming. Peat is dense, rich with nutrients. The farmland nearby has a thinner base to it. The nutrients are stripped from the crops or consumed by the grazing herds. Dig some yerself if you don't believe me." She shook her head and grumbled something so low, even Lucy couldn't decipher it.

"Thank you," he added as he jotted down her words in his ledger. "I may do just that. As evidence of course. And in hopes of finding the killer's exact path."

"Path?"

Lucy jumped in. "Constable Brodie believes the man may have habits in his killings. Methods to help us discover his identity and prevent any further attacks."

"Habits, you say?"

Lucy shrugged and eyed Mr. Brodie. He nested his ledger back in his pocket and cleared his throat.

"From my experience," he began, "killers have habits and ways they cannot shake. Patterns. Rituals, if you prefer an actual term. I think this man enjoys the hunt, waiting for his victims to come to him."

Lucy shivered. *Hunted?* Poor Miriam and Becca, hunted as if they were prey? The thought of it sickened her, causing her stomach to sour and lurch. If she hadn't been so schooled in managing such feelings during her work, she might have become ill right then and there.

She channeled the image she always used when the world seemed to shift and twirl into madness, and imagined the smooth, tranquil lakes and evergreen fields of Grasmere. A family holiday she could remember in grand detail from when she was very young. The yellow daffodils, swaying in the breeze, danced to a rhythm only they could hear. The wind, rippling against her face, cooled her cheeks after running. And the smell of flowers . . . she could almost taste their sweetness on her tongue.

Finally, her stomach settled and her mind calmed. The threat of sickness passed, and she unclenched her fists at her side. She could do this. She wanted to learn everything she could from Mr. Brodie. Other than her father, no man had ever taken an interest in her intellect and abilities. She feared disappointing him.

Or her sister and niece who counted on her.

"There are also seeds in the dirt. Could you feel them and have Miss Wycliffe describe them to you, Miss Clara?" Mr. Brodie brought out the bags of seeds and passed them to Lucy. The brush of their gloves against one another sparked a tiny tingle of awareness, a lovely, gentle reminder of the admiration she felt for him and needed to keep to herself. She was his employee, nothing else.

Lucy stepped nearer to Miss Clara and sprinkled a few of the tiny seeds onto her glove.

"Lucy, tell me what you see, girl. I've no interest in getting my hands dirty while I'm knitting." Miss Clara shook her head.

Lucy brought the seeds closer to the fire to get a better view from the added light. "I'm not sure how they look different from any seeds, other than they are tiny. The size of the head of the smallest needle."

Miss Clara rocked back and forth in silence. "I've no guess upon it yet." She tilted her head to the side. "Come back in two days' time, and I'll have an idea. Leave the seeds on the table. Be on with you, I've knitting to tend to. And then my plants."

Miss Clara was never shy about ending their visits. Lucy left the seeds on the table and kissed the old woman's soft cheek.

"A pleasure to meet you, Miss Clara," Mr. Brodie offered as he donned his hat. "And your assistance in this is greatly appreciated."

"You best find who's done this. If another one of our young girls gets hurt, you'll hear from me, Mr. Brodie." Her rocking chair came to an abrupt stop.

"Yes, ma'am."

"We'll see you tomorrow then, Miss Clara," Lucy added.

"I'll be seeing only Mr. Brodie, Lucy. Too dangerous for young girls like you to be out and about 'til this monster is caught."

Lucy frowned. Miss Clara had never banned her from coming to see her. "Miss Clara, I can—"

"I'll have no more of it. Now go on."

Lucy knew better than to attempt to dissuade Miss Clara from anything. Once she decided upon something, nothing changed her mind. She walked ahead of Mr. Brodie as they left the cottage in silence. Emerging into the cold air, Lucy snuggled into her cloak, wrapping it tightly around herself.

Mr. Brodie offered his arm, and Lucy took it without question. As she neared him, his warmth tugged her body as close to him as she dared. He radiated heat like a hearth on two legs. Such an image made her smile.

"I see why you adore her," he said, walking along the snow, their steps punching through the now hardened top layer. "To live here in the woods alone, blind, yet able to keep her house of plants alive and in such order. Remarkable." He stared off ahead of them.

"Well, she has a great many friends and people who look in upon her. Sadly, there will be two less to care for her with Becca and Miriam gone. They joined me to see her when they could."

"Does she have no family?"

"Other than Abe, she had a son. He died quite young. I never knew him. She's been a widow as long as I've lived here."

"Do you know what happened to him?"

"No. She rarely speaks of him, and I've never seen a sketch or keepsake from him. I don't even know how long he lived. Perhaps she set aside the memory, so she could move forward."

Lucy could understand such a decision. That sort of loss cut clean and quick to the bone when you least expected it. If you kept it buried and locked away, it could harm no one, could it?

"Is that what you have done with yours?" He turned to face her. His gaze heated her body the way whiskey had, the one time she dared drink it. It had warmed her to the core before the spasms of coughing had set in.

Lucy held his stare. "I suppose. Most days it's easier to bury it along with days past. The burden of regret weighs far too much to carry along with me every day." She tried for a smile but the lies she told nearly choked her. She never left her load behind. Never. It was her burden to carry, and hers alone. "And you, sir?"

"Evidently, I drown mine in liniment that smells far too foul for Miss Clara."

Lucy smiled. It pained him to share, which she understood. She would push no further. Not today.

"You've been doing a fine job, Miss Wycliffe. I daresay you may have made quite an officer of the law."

"If I had but been born a man."

"Well, yes. However, you could still train to be a nurse. If you ever decided this work didn't suit you of course."

"At one time, I had thought of doing just that." She stared into the sky. "However, those classes take coin I don't have. And there are no places to train around here, plus leaving Cil was never an option. I have responsibilities."

His lips quirked into a smile. "Your sister is quite lucky to have you."

"As I'm sure your siblings are to have you, sir."

"Not quite. We never had the affection for one another as you and your sister seem to share. My remaining brother has no interest in me, nor I him."

What did one say to such a statement? "I'm sorry," she murmured.

"It's for the best for both of us. It took me a long time, but after being at sea and then wounded I realized some people are meant to live in my heart rather than in my life."

Lucy ached for him. She could never say similar words about her sister, her family, and her friends. What kind of man was this brother of his? And what had happened to his other siblings? Questions fluttered about her amidst the silence. For a moment, she wondered if he could hear them battling around, seeking freedom and release from her mind.

"Do you prefer the solitude?" she asked.

"Perhaps. I find I am rarely lonely when I am alone. It is with others I feel like an island."

"You speak in riddles to me today, Mr. Brodie."

"I don't mean to. Perhaps Miss Clara's visit loosened all of this within me. Her resolve to be who she is and be happy is quite inspiring. Even to a man such as myself."

Lucy nodded. "She has a similar effect on me as well. She is strong and truthful and as settled into herself, her life, as I one day hope to be."

"Ah, and what would such a picture resemble?" he asked, tugging her closer. So close, her forearm brushed his side, a firm muscled plane. Her body tingled. She wished she had not felt it, for she longed to feel it again and again.

But he was Mr. Brodie, her boss, her superior. A gentleman as well.

She sighed. Could it hurt to tell him of her dreams? To release them to the wind to fly and flutter away and melt into nothingness?

Lucy crinkled her brow. *Yes, it could.*

She could lose her job.

He brought her to the walkway to her cottage. "Perhaps one day you will tell me what the contented and happy Miss Wycliffe would look like. What your dreams are, beyond your responsibilities. For now, I know we both have work to attend to. Me to a mound of others' belongings, you to prepare a friend for final rest."

"Yes. Perhaps I will stop in the day after next in the afternoon to see if you have need of me at your office."

"Only if you feel up to it. I will think of you all tomorrow morn."

The funeral.

Her throat clogged. She'd not wanted to think of Becca's funeral, fast approaching. "Thank you. It will be a tough day for all of us."

Especially if the killer was gathered among them, a mourner of a different kind altogether.

Chapter 9
What Wasn't There

Pain yanked John from sleep. The exertion of the last two days had settled deep into his strained, taut muscles. He blinked in the darkness as he lay on his mattress and forced deep breaths of air into his lungs to slow his heartbeat and thus, the throbbing in his leg. He'd felt worse. And with all pain, it was about willing oneself past it or through it. Otherwise it would devour you whole.

As it had the night his brother had killed the Wycliffes.

John struggled to sit on the edge of the bed. The moon glowed brightly outside his window. *Bollocks*. Usually he could gather a few more hours of sleep before the pain woke him. Tonight, he would manage on little rest. Unless he took another thimble of whiskey, of course, which might well be in order.

Pressing his feet flat on the cool wooden floorboards, he wrestled with the decision. He needed to be fresh and able when he met with Miss Clara in the morn, not dulled by drink.

He sighed. No drink it was, then. Which meant no more sleep for him this eve.

A loud pounding on the door below in the office startled him. He grabbed for the bedpost to hoist himself upright. His thigh muscles seized and clenched at the sudden movement, and he gritted his teeth. *What a time for a muscle spasm.*

Hitting his thigh with his free hand, he groaned at the slashes of pain echoing his movements. Soon, the muscle released, and he took one step and then another. He grabbed the oil lantern on the bedside table where he'd left it and turned the subtle winking flame to full strength. At the top of the stairs, he sighed and began the slow tedious descent.

Silence replaced the pounding. Whomever had wished to see him had abandoned their efforts.

John reached the office door and yanked it open.

Nothing. No one.

Darkness greeted him. Cold blew against his thin linen nightshirt. Sparse snowflakes swirled in the wind.

Shifting the lantern slowly, he searched for proof he hadn't been imagining the noise, and spied footprints. Were they merely his own from earlier in the day? The evidence he found near the old iron rod anchored in the ground, serving as a boot scraper, startled him to his core.

A threepence winked back at him in the snow, as familiar-looking as the set of five-jacks that flanked it. Toys he and his brothers used to play with every summer here in Clun. Such things had importance to him, but why would they be important to anyone else?

How would anyone know what these items meant to him? His parents were long dead. And other than his brothers . . .

John's throat closed.

He sucked in a greedy breath and scanned the empty town square for movement. Shadows crept behind the gleam of snow illuminated by the moon and flickering light of his lantern.

Nothing.

An owl hooted in the distance.

Fear threatened to overtake his logic. He needed time to think, not react.

Gathering all the items, John closed the door and latched it behind him. His heart hammered in his chest as he brought the contents to the table and spread them out. As he studied them, his pulse slowed to its normal pace. This was a warning shot, nothing more. A blow across his bow, as he'd seen in wartime. The criminal was baiting him, but why?

Was the man feeling threatened by John's investigation? Or was the past somehow relevant to these present crimes?

Did someone know about his younger brother Sean, what he had done so many years ago? *How?* John rubbed his chin. Great pains, great *care* had been taken to seal away any evidence of his family's presence here in Clun so long ago.

Sean had been confined until the very night of his death. Not in a jail, but a fancy prison of its own where the rich hid away their unwell relations. The ones they didn't wish to interfere with their lives or social standing. His father and eldest brother, dear Cameron, had commanded such a confinement. Soon after, his father had disowned John for entering the Royal Navy against his wishes, which gave Cameron all the reason he needed to sever ties with John completely.

However, not even the open seas could quiet the unrest in John after Sean's untimely and unnatural death. While the sea never silenced his rage over Sean's self-slaughter and the part John felt he played in it, it served as a welcome distraction.

Separation from the world had been a blessing to John at first, no matter how strange it seemed to anyone else, especially Cameron. For what brother could sentence his youngest sibling to such a death? Sean was unwell, as he always had been. Their parents' refusal to acknowledge his behaviors and sickness were a direct cause of the murders. Repeated rescues and denial of Sean's "misadventures" only amplified his behaviors, and the lack of treatment for his melancholy had ultimately led to his death.

John could never forgive himself for not being brave enough to challenge his father and older brother until it had been too late, far too late, for everyone. Nor would he ever forgive himself for allowing Sean to take Miss Wycliffe's parents from her. And for never giving her and her sister the peace of knowing who had killed them.

Guilt became one of the reasons he'd left London. Being such an imposter, pretending to uphold a law he hadn't always followed, sickened him. After he helped Miss Wycliffe secure her cottage for good and captured this killer, he would remove himself as constable and pursue some other employ. One where he wasn't the hypocrite he was now.

John collapsed on the bench seat and fingered each of the items. Emotion thickened his throat. He and Sean had wasted hours, days over such a game of five-jacks. He smiled at the cool feel of the coin in his fingers. The winner got to keep the shiny threepence until the next game.

Gifted to them by their grandfather, the coin was a treasure they had passed between them like gold after his early death; the smooth, worn feel of it between his fingers, a reminder of all John had lost since then.

Of all he could yet lose.

This series of clues was a warning. Of what? Blackmail? A threat? Did the killer mean to harm him? Or was it merely a threat made to cease his inquiry?

He stilled. Perhaps they were heading in the right direction and making someone uneasy. Such uneasiness would please him. *Deeply*. Jailing this killer would be John's last official act as an investigator. He needed it to count for something.

Studying the items once more, he smiled. No doubt Miss Wycliffe would have many ideas and suppositions if he showed them to her, but he could not ask her about them. He feared he would give himself away. The woman missed nothing. Hopefully she would miss his budding attraction to her, for he struggled to squelch it. And he needed all of his wits about him if the murderer felt threatened or wished to scare them off.

John stood and lit the stove. He shook the kettle; some water remained. He set it upon the meager wood stove. Perhaps tea would right his thinking. It sure as hell couldn't hurt. The chill hit his bare legs. Nor could a pair of trousers, if only the damned things weren't all the way up the stairs. He needed them, so he'd begin the slow tasking ascent. Perhaps by the time he returned, the kettle would whistle.

~ ~ ~

Hours later, John had made progress in the investigation, and his resolve to attend Becca Lusk's funeral had settled into stone. His visit to Miss Clara for ointment would have to wait. The best way to see the town was to attend church and funerals. He opted for the funeral.

Pushing open the heavy wooden doors of St. George's Church, John couldn't help but note the black crepe tied with white ribbon hanging off the handles in honor of Miss Lusk. Although most funerals in small towns such as this would have been in the family home, the Lusks had asked the pastor for special permission to gather here, so all who loved her could be in attendance. And by the look of the large crowd, they were.

Entering, John tipped his hat in greeting to the women standing inside the door, removed his topper, and settled into an available seat in a pew on the last row. A sea of townsfolk wearing black sat in the rows ahead of him. If the show of people in attendance reflected devotion, Miss Lusk had been loved by these people and this town.

Save for the killer.

John scanned the forms and profiles. General restlessness abounded in the room. If the bastard roamed among them, he pressed down his excitement amidst everyone's grief. The thought soured John's stomach, as did the strongly scented candles burning about the altar, ones reserved to cover the smell of the dead.

The church bells tolled and quiet descended on the crowd. The pastor, an older man named Hume, readjusted his cloak and began. Each word rang dull and void in John's ears. He'd seen far too much of the darkness of humanity to have much faith or hope in anything.

His eyes settled on Miss Wycliffe.

Lucy.

A knot settled under his ribs. He would allow himself to think of her as *Lucy* in these moments of quiet and peace when she didn't know he saw her. The sweet nub of her nose, the coy strands of wavy hair escaping the knot she had attempted at the nape of her neck, quieted the loudest parts of him. Longing budded in his gut. He believed in her resilience, her kindness, her intelligence. She could save a man far better than any faith he had ever known.

And if he allowed her, and if she somehow wanted the shell of a man he was, she could set a new course for his life.

Tightness filled his chest. What fool would believe a woman of Lucy's caliber would risk anything for him? He had nothing to offer her beyond what he owned, which fit in a trunk, and what he could earn, limited by his injury.

Suddenly she stilled, frozen in time like a deer snagged alone in the woods. No doubt she had sensed him. Perhaps his attraction to her burned too brightly. A slight turn and she caught his eye.

Did a smile lift the corner of her lips? He wanted to think so, longed to hope for her response, despite his purpose here this day. He turned his attentions back to Hume and picked out a few words—

. . . taken too soon . . . a heaven of bright light and hope.

John shifted and tapped a tune along his leg. He'd heard such empty words during a Sunday sermon a decade before when his family had visited and sat in this very church. John had been too eager to return to London to take notice of much of the town or the people who lived there. He'd noted little then, but he noted everything now.

Scanning the room, he noted the Cunninghams sat close to one of the many stained-glass windows. Mrs. Cunningham stared out one of them. The woman and her husband had come to offer the Lusks comfort despite their own loss. John's throat dried. Even Miss Clara sat next to a younger man with a tattered black coat. Perhaps the nephew and helper Miss Wycliffe had described? *Abe*. A man John needed to speak with. The boy might have seen something in his travels from the mill to Miss Clara's. John filed it away as he continued his study of the room.

An odd mix of old and young, somewhat well-off tradesmen and shopkeepers, next to lean farmers in their Sunday finery, mingled about him. Yet, they all loved Miss Lusk as they seemed to all love Clun. The town had won their hearts long before it had won his, and with love came protection. Loyalty. Secrets. But would loyalty burn their sweet town to embers?

The last amen echoed from the crowd as the coffin holding Miss Lusk was lifted by the pallbearers. The young woman shone in purity, covered with purple, white, and blue chains of flowers, and a look of peace upon her face. Quaint scenes of children playing beneath towering trees covered the simple wooden coffin. The handmade carvings edged along the sides offered a subtle, beautiful detail to an otherwise forgettable creation of wood.

And as the scene of children passed by, it struck him. The clues he'd found outside his door were incomplete. One couldn't play five-jacks without the wooden ball, could they? What the hell did it mean? Had the bastard lost it or did its absence reveal a clue to the killer himself? John rubbed the back of his neck.

Blast.

Why hadn't he noticed it earlier? Was it fatigue? Pain? Did it matter? Watching the pallbearers go and Miss Lusk along with them, John's resolve settled in his gut. He would find whoever had killed her—and Miss Cunningham—before anyone else died. Meeting Miss Wycliffe's even gaze across the aisle, he clenched his fists at his sides.

He wouldn't lose Lucy to such a fate either, even if he had to turn fate on its own bloody head.

Chapter 10
The Gathering

Lucy didn't know if she suffered more from the strains of the day or if Mr. Brodie did. Watching him across the small room at the gathering back at the Lusks' cottage after the funeral, she swallowed a twinge of compassion for him. The tightness of his jawline and the pull of his shoulders in his jacket illustrated the pressure the case placed on him. Or perhaps it wasn't the case but merely the vulnerability of being so close to two families who each lost their child. Either way, she wished to bring him some reprieve from it.

"Mr. Brodie." She nodded a greeting to him as she reached his side. "I am surprised to see you here. It was thoughtful of you to come."

When he turned completely to face her, his shoulders relaxed, and the lines in his brow evened out. His response flushed her with warmth.

"The least I could do. I was unsure if it was appropriate, however, I wanted to show what support I could." He studied her before his eyes flitted away, back to the crowd of mourners greeting the Lusks at their door. "How are they?"

"Poor, I'm afraid. Becca was their only child."

Glancing away, he tugged on his coat sleeves. "I didn't know. I should have."

What?

"How would you know? You've been here less than a week's time. One cannot take in the whole of a town in a mere few days." She edged closer to him and gently touched his elbow. "Whatever you chide yourself for this day," she whispered, "you shouldn't. There has been enough loss and despair. Let us give our sympathies and seek some air. You look as if you could use it."

"Even in the face of this, you are sunshine itself. One of the many things I do not wholly understand about you, but I will embrace it."

After issuing a goodbye and granting the Lusks the warmest of hugs, Lucy left. She couldn't bear to look upon the covered mirrors, black wreaths, or facedown charcoal sketches any longer. Their home had always been a beacon of life for her, but now it was merely a sober reminder of loss.

Cold winter air shocked her body to awareness as she accepted Mr. Brodie's arm, a movement she had grown accustomed to. The regular, firm warmth, she now missed when she walked alone. Having him here by her side on this harrowing day was a blessing she didn't take for granted. And should *not* become used to.

He would most likely move on to another post after a few months. City dwellers never stayed here for long. It seemed there wasn't enough to occupy their attention. Perhaps Mr. Brodie would be different.

"I'm sorry for the loss of your friend," Mr. Brodie offered. "I can see the sadness in your eyes although you set out the bravest of faces, Miss Wycliffe."

That he would know this warmed every part of her. After a handful of days, he knew some of her many expressions and understood them. Just as she could comprehend some of his. Was this the truth of intimacy with a man? Him knowing every part of a woman, of who she was without asking? What heaven that would be.

"Much like the brave face you have set upon me now. I can tell your leg plagues you, sir. It seems we are both full of masks." She smiled at him, and he chuckled before gifting her one in return.

"I am in agony today, but it is not only the pain. This case is so very different from the crimes of London. There, murders are dark, dastardly things of impulse and hate and greed. Here, other than impulse . . . or rashness, I cannot imagine the motivation for the crimes. You are a kind cluster of people. Who would wish to end the lives of these two women? And in such a brutal way."

Lucy pondered his words. Other than their steps on the snow, the occasional call of a bird, or drop of a dead branch, there was only silence.

"Perhaps. You forget we are an old town with some black marks upon our history," she added.

"Not a surprise for a town meshed between the worlds of the Welsh and Scottish."

"I suppose. Yet, it is not history set on killing now. It is someone far more alive and among us." She narrowed her gaze and lowered her voice. "Is that the true reason you came to the funeral today, or are you trying to find a possible suspect?"

"Yes." He leaned closer to her. "And I am pleased at your deduction. You are a fine assistant. Hiring you is the best decision I have made yet since my arrival here."

His praise bloomed tight and full in her chest. To be valued and appreciated was a new and refreshing feeling. One could get used to such kindness. She fidgeted with her bonnet ribbons.

One could also lose it.

The edge of her cottage came into view and disappointment greeted her. Not only would her time with Mr. Brodie end, but Miriam waited on the other side of the door. A sigh escaped Lucy's lips. For once, she wished she had yet another profession.

"I'm sorry you've had such a difficult day," he said quietly, guiding her to the front stoop. Softness entered his dark, searching eyes. "If there is anything I can do . . ."

Stay.

She brushed the rogue thought away. There were so many things she wished he would do, and yet so few she would ever utter aloud, at least not yet. She let go of his arm and immediately loss consumed her.

"Time will heal as it always does," she began. "It's Miriam I wish not to see this day, but she must be prepped for the next life as well." She rubbed her hands together, trying to warm them despite her thin gloves. Clouds had gathered and blocked out the warmth of the sun, and she dreaded what awaited her.

Another friend to prep for another burial.

He opened his mouth to answer as the cottage door flew open. Stepping in front of her, he blocked her with his body.

An impulse of a military man, or perhaps simply of a man who cares for her?

At the sight of Cil, Lucy relaxed. Mr. Brodie remained uneasy and stiff, yet he stepped aside as Cil threw herself into Lucy's arms for a fierce embrace.

"I have missed you, sister," Lucy murmured into Cil's mass of blonde curls cascading along her neck and back.

"And, I you." She pulled back and attempted to straighten her day dress. "I heard of what happened to Becca. And Miriam. Sick with worry, I rushed here to find the cottage empty. My mind swarmed with fear, and when I saw you round the bend in the road . . ." Cil's sweet caramel eyes filled with tears. "I was flooded with relief."

Lucy squeezed her sister's hands in her own. "I know, sis. But I am well. At least as well as one can be."

Cil's eyes slid past Lucy's shoulder.

Thistles.

"My apologies. Constable Brodie, this is my younger sister, Mrs. Priscilla Newberry."

They exchanged pleasantries, and Mr. Brodie lifted his topper in greeting.

How else to continue? "He is our new constable. He's been investigating the deaths of Becca and Miriam."

"And Miss Wycliffe has been a most helpful and able assistant."

Did affection coat his words? She wished so, longed so, but alas did that make it so?

"Thank you, sir," she finally replied. "I have learned much in a mere few days."

"Well, I don't wish to keep you from one another." Mr. Brodie smiled. "Much work awaits me. A pleasure to meet you, Mrs. Newberry." Another tip of his hat, and he was gone.

Lucy stared after him, wishing she'd said something, anything to keep him here.

"Sister," Cil whispered, and tugged her back inside. "I leave you for less than a fortnight, and I find a man, a handsome man no less, on your stoop? You must tell me everything."

Lucy closed the door behind them and removed her cloak and bonnet before resting them on the wall hook. "Only if you will help me with Miriam. She must be ready by the morrow, and I have been putting it off."

"Blast." Cil's shoulders sagged. "I feared you might ask, but I cannot refuse you." She rolled her sleeves. "I'm most glad I left Norah Jane with her grandparents in Obley. We had a glorious visit, and she wished to stay longer. I obliged."

"Perhaps you could stay here with me while she is away?" Hope bloomed in Lucy's chest. To have them together as sisters beneath the same roof once more would be bliss.

Cil nibbled her lip, brow furrowed. "Yes, I will. I wished to speak to you about the cottage."

Her uneasy, wavering glance set Lucy on edge. She held her breath, pushed her sleeves to her elbows, and pulled open the root cellar door. She began down the stairs and Cil followed.

"I will be packing up. Leaving. I decided to move to Obley and stay with Ethan's parents. For good."

The knot of her hair Lucy had been tying back fell from her hands, and her heart plunged. "What?" she asked, as they reached the cellar.

Cil rushed to her and grabbed her hand. "'Tis not a decision I made lightly. I think, *I know*, this is best for Norah Jane. And for me. With Ethan gone and his parents aging, it will be a help to us all. Norah Jane will have more time with them, and I can help them with the upkeep of the house and farm. And I will not have Fiske looming and threatening me with the note I owe. I will sell my cottage and gift you the proceeds. What is left of them after the note is repaid, you can put toward this cottage, your home."

Lucy's eyes heated with tears. The loss of Becca and Miriam, and now this? Her tight throat choked off her words.

"And, you, dear sister, who has cared for me and for us, can have your own life. You are so beautiful, intelligent, and capable. You could leave here and pursue training for a profession outside of this. Or, you may find a man who deserves you, with whom to begin your own family and life. I will not be bogging down your dreams any longer. You will be free to choose your own path. Even if you decide to stay here and continue on in this role as layer-out."

"You cannot leave me, sister." Lucy didn't recognize the weak, trembling voice as her own. Her foundation had been shaken the last few days.

"I can and I must. For the both of us. I want you to be happy." Cil's lips curved into a devilish smile. "And perhaps this timing of Constable John Brodie's arrival is perfection. I noted how he moved in front of you in a gesture of protection. It was quite dashing." She sighed and pressed a hand to her chest.

Leave it to Cil to make her laugh. Lucy batted at her sister's shoulder. "He is former Royal Navy and a detective from London. No doubt such a response is from years of duty, nothing more."

The explanation sounded ridiculous even to her own ears.

"Oh? And does that also explain the dreamy look on your face as he turned to leave?"

Blast.

No, it didn't. Only her growing affection for him could explain it.

A knock on the door startled Lucy from her thoughts and saved her from having to answer her sister's question. Pivoting to the ground-level window, she peered up and groaned.

Mr. Fiske.

Ugh.

She couldn't *not* answer as he held the note of her home, but oh, how she wished to. Mouthing who it was to her sister, Cil soon echoed her moan.

"He always smells of cooked onions," Cil complained in a whisper. "Must you answer?"

"If I wish to continue to own a home then yes, I must answer." Lucy tromped back up the stairs, dragging herself to the door, and forced a smile. As Cil crowded in behind, Lucy swung the heavy wood open.

"Good day, Mr. Fiske. What brings you by this afternoon?"

Mr. Fiske lifted his chin and sniffed. "I see you're back in Clun, Mrs. Newberry." He ran his hands around his ample waistline before his hands rested in his coat pockets. "How do your in-laws fare these days?"

"Well, thank you for asking. I came back early to check on my sister when I heard the news."

"As am I. Thought I would check in upon you, Miss Wycliffe, after Miss Lusk's funeral. A single young lady such as yourself living alone in the woods . . ." He shook his head. "Can't be too careful."

His eyes roved over Lucy's form. *All* of her form. She shuddered and clung desperately to the strained smile on her lips. He was a wretched man. *The* wretched man holding her bank note coming due all too soon.

"I am well enough, Mr. Fiske. Thank you for your concern. My sister and I were about to continue final preparations for Miss Cunningham before her burial later this week." Stepping aside, she motioned him downstairs where he'd be afforded a full view of Miriam, prone upon the table in the root cellar. Knowing well of his weak countenance, he'd not last much longer, should he deign to actually descend into the depths of her prepping room.

Putting his hand to his mouth, the craven Mr. Fiske stepped back. He coughed and recovered with a bow. "I will leave you to your work, ladies. 'Til our next meeting." He scuttled out.

The *next* meeting. There would always be a next meeting with him. She closed the door and leaned hard against it.

"He is such a weasel of a man, sis. How can you stand his visits? He makes my skin crawl. And feel blessed you cannot smell him."

Lucy laughed. "I shall count it as a blessing." Pushing off the door, she rested in one of the set of chairs in front of the hearth. Fear crept along her skin, and she lifted her hands toward the fire. "Thank you for lighting the hearth. I am chilled to the bone."

"Now we may finish our talk," Cil said. Excitement laced the ends of her lilting words, and she settled into the chair by Lucy.

She rolled her eyes. "What is there to further discuss? You know I do not wish you to leave."

Cil grabbed one of Lucy's hands and held it in her own.

"Of course. This is what is best for all of us. You deserve to live your life and be happy."

"But you and Norah Jane *are* my life. And I have my work. I need nothing more." She pinched the bridge of her nose. The thought of losing them, even if only by distance, pained her. What would she do without them a mere walk away?

Cil smirked at her. "Really?"

Lucy squirmed in her seat. Perhaps she'd *prefer* more, but she didn't require it. She had enough. Why long for more and be disappointed?

"So, the flush upon your cheeks is also my imagination? He is a fine-looking man. A gentleman, it seemed, by the cut of his jacket and his movements." Cil lifted her eyebrows and held Lucy's gaze.

Did she dare deny her attraction further? Her sister was no fool. Lucy's shoulders slumped. "I do find myself attracted to him, caring for him. Far more than is reasonable. I have known him less than a week's time, *and* he is my employer. He is paying me to assist him in these murders."

"Well, I believe the attraction mutual. I could not mistake his disappointment at my interruption as anything other than loss. And although I am quite sure he admires your intellect, affection rested in his gaze, beyond hiring you as his assistant."

Leave it to Cil to put hope and ideas of romance in Lucy's head. Her sister had fallen for her now-deceased husband in less than a fortnight and been married within the month. Their love had been fierce and deep for the few years their union had lasted before he died in battle.

"What I feel is of little consequence." Even as the words echoed in the air, Lucy could hear the dull tones of deceit.

"Nonsense." Cil pulled Lucy to her feet. "What you feel *is* the only thing that matters. You must let go of all of your fears and embrace what bubbles in your chest and consumes your dreams." She smiled and sighed. "I envy that sort of love, you know. I have had it. I know what a gift it is."

Sadness resonated in Cil's eyes and the tilt of her head. She squeezed Lucy's hand. "I have hoped for a love match for you. I should have known the man would be extraordinary in all ways, to catch your eye."

Lucy shook her head. "What do you mean?"

"He is an attractive, intelligent military man with an openness of mind and spirit to employ a woman, a female layer-out of the dead no less, to assist in his cases as the new constable. I know of no other man who would dare to think it, much less do it."

Hmm. Cil did have a point. Most constables never took an assistant, never mind a female one with Lucy's unusual experience.

"So why do you think he did?"

"Did you never ask?"

Lucy approached the window and stared out. Snow had begun to fall once more, and the light of the afternoon sun receded low along the treetops, their bare arms reaching toward the heavens. "I did, I suppose. He said he needed a person to look upon a body, and they recommended he see me at The Boar and Sable."

"Oh?" Cil arched her eyebrows and leaned against the window frame.

Lucy flushed at the memory of their first meeting. He'd stood so fresh and proper in her tiny cottage, all crisp lines and full of tidiness. And she with hair messier than a bird's nest, with corpse flesh smeared upon her cheek. "Yes. I made a horrid first impression. I know not why he's continued to seek me out for help."

"You are the most brilliant woman I know, that's why."

Apricot meowed and rubbed against Lucy's legs. She stooped and scratched behind her ears. "Did you sneak in with Auntie Cil?"

"She did. As soon as I turned the key in the door, she came bounding up the walk and got inside scarce before I did. Little sneak."

"Which is why I adore her." Lucy watched as Apricot pranced back along the floor and swished her tail in the air. She batted something between her paws.

"What have you there, sweet girl? Best not be any of my supplies." She bent down and chuckled. "She must have carried it in with her."

Cil shook her head. "No, it was on the floor when I first walked in. I thought you'd purchased a toy for Apricot to bat about." She picked it up and smiled. "Reminds me of the wooden ball you use for five-jacks."

"No matter. It looks like Apricot will be staying, as you will. The snow's begun."

"Then aren't I lucky? Trapped with you in your cottage to assist you in preparations. What dreams are made of." Cil rolled her eyes.

"It's for Miriam."

Cil sighed. "I know. I only wish things were different."

"As do I," Lucy murmured, tying back her hair. She stared down into the cellar at Miriam's pale, translucent skin. "As do I."

Chapter 11
The Find

John finished off the last drop of his first pint of ale and rested the tankard on the table. The noise in The Boar and Sable served as a strange comfort to the eerie silence of his office. He chided himself. That was a lie. The loneliness of the space *and* his lack of any real progress in the case ate away at him this eve.

As the snow fell in thick downy sheets outside, he mulled over what few clues and new information he'd gathered during the day at the funeral and at the Lusks. These people of Clun were tightlipped around him. As a stranger, a constable, and from the city, he had three resounding strikes against him.

Mr. Rudd approached his table with a grin and the stench of ale. "Another for you, sir?"

What did it matter?

John nodded and tapped the tankard on the table. "And a bowl of stew, sir."

"Right away." Mr. Rudd shouted the order back to the kitchen.

Might as well eat something to dull the effect of the drink.

His stomach rumbled. He was hungry. Hungry for food, for comfort, for meaning, for companionship. For a life.

Miss Wycliffe's face swam before him. He had no right to want anything further from her, but he could not stop the longing he felt each time he touched her or the sense of loss when she stepped away. Or the fear edging into his reason when he thought of something happening to her.

Or of her finding out the truth about him and his brother.

He reached inside his coat pocket and rubbed his fingers along the threepence he'd found outside his door. Did a stranger somehow know John's biggest secret? Or was the stranger not certain and merely trying to flush him out and the truth along with it?

Rudd slid a fresh tankard of ale onto the table and nodded. "Food be out shortly."

"Thank you." John drank from the tankard and studied the patrons frequenting the bar and those tucked away in the booths around him. He'd seen many of them at Miss Lusk's funeral earlier in the day. A pair of voices in the booth behind him amplified in volume and tone. John leaned back into his booth to listen. After all, who knew what information he might glean? Drink often loosened one's lips.

"You've no right to tell me nothin'. Never done a bit of good for anyone here. What you do is unnatural. Unnatural, I tell you. Should have told 'em about you and your doin's long ago."

"You're wrong." The other voice seethed with anger. "What I do is holy and needed for the sake of the village. Without my work, our harvest would yield nothing. People would starve."

Laughter boomed. "Is that what you think? Crazier than I remember you bein'. I'm done with you. The devil can have you for all I care. I'll not be protectin' you any longer."

A tankard slammed hard on a table and the scuffling of shoes on the wooden floor muffled the rest of the exchange. John drank more and listened, only to hear more cursing. A young man he'd never seen before stalked off, heading past him with speed as he shrugged on his coat and readjusted his meager cap and scarf.

"Good to see you, Bobby," Rudd called after the young man.

The man turned to him and nodded. "Good food as always, sir."

The other man, the "unnatural" as this Bobby fellow had called him, must still be sitting in the booth. John itched to discover who Bobby had argued with and called a name, but he couldn't risk such a blatant move.

John rested his head against the high back of the tall wooden booth, straining to listen, hoping to hear something, some other fragment about what the men had discussed. To his disappointment, he heard merely mutterings from behind. To his further disappointment, the Magistrate of Clun, Wynn Kieran, entered and headed right toward him with hat in hand, preventing any further inquiry about the strange man.

Bollocks.

No doubt the day was about to get even worse.

Kieran had not replied to any of John's updates on the case or his request for greater assistance. However, funerals often spurred even the most inept and lazy of men into action. Most likely the sorrow of the Lusks had propelled the sloth into motion.

Finally.

John straightened and nodded as Kieran settled into the seat across from him. The magistrate was not the type of man to ask for admittance, for he'd never been denied anywhere. *Not yet, anyway.* Miss Wycliffe would rattle the bastard to his core. The mere thought of it made John almost smile.

Almost.

Kieran rested his hat on the table and sat rigidly upright with his hands in his lap. No doubt this was not a place he frequented. And not a place he'd remain for long.

Rudd approached to greet him. Kieran raised his hand in dismissal without a word. Rudd flushed and returned to the bar. Being a gentleman often made one an ass to the rest of the world. A lesson John had learned from his older brother and one he preferred to never repeat. And another reason he didn't mind being disowned.

"I say," Kieran began. His overly waxed, salt-and-pepper mustache twitched on his pinched face, making him look even more like the weasel John had already discovered him to be. "This business with the dead girls needs to be concluded. Word is spreading through Shropshire that we've some sort of a—" He paused and bent forward. "Lunatic," he continued in a lower voice, "running about like some wild child in the woods. We cannot let such ridiculous notions continue. When will you solve the case, Brodie?"

John took a deep breath and let it settle in his belly. He'd met other men like Kieran. Raving at them made no difference. Nor could he use reason or make the man grow a heart and have empathy. "I am making progress, sir. Bringing closure to these families is of greatest importance to me. We will return peace and safety back to Clun, however I can give you no exact date as to the *conclusion* of the cases."

Kieran sniffed. "Not good enough, Brodie. Not at all. I've a ball to host for my eldest daughter in less than a fortnight. These cases will be concluded by then. I will not have her celebration tainted by the deaths of some local farm girls."

John counted the striations in the paneling on the far wall in the distance. He reached thirty before he dared glance back at Kieran. "These young women deserve justice even if they are merely *farm girls*, sir."

Kieran narrowed his beady gaze at John and twitched his mustache again before speaking. He leaned forward in his chair, careful not to touch the table. "And, I'll remind you of some truths. *You* were not my first choice as constable. Your superiors earned you this position. Why they have such faith in you, I don't know. Your mistake in engaging the unnatural layer-out woman, Miss Wycliffe, as an assistant has already earned you one strike, Brodie. A poor decision on your part. What worthy constable needs to hire an assistant? Especially a woman of such unusual breeding and strange tendencies."

He sighed and gathered his hat. "If you fail to close this case before my daughter's ball, consider yourself dismissed."

John met the man's dark eyes and thin, hollowed face. It would take one well-placed strike at the base of the neck to silence him, but John pressed his palms to the table instead. The man mattered little to him now, and he could take insults from someone he didn't respect. They bounded off him like sleet. But to insult a lady, especially Miss Wycliffe, ignited white hot anger in him.

He wanted to respond in kind for the magistrate's disrespect but wouldn't spur the man's displeasure in her direction. As the most powerful man in Clun, Kieran could make her life miserable if he chose to. John nodded and said the only words he trusted himself to utter. "Yes, sir."

"I'm glad we have an understanding." Kieran stood and turned in a flourish. His dark coat swished behind him like a serpent's tail.

Rudd brought a bowl of fragrant stew and a spoon to the table. The aroma of chicken and vegetables made John's mouth water. The steam rising from the bowl created a blessed distraction to the anger and frustration coiled tight in his chest.

He forced himself back to task. "Nice young man you were talking to, earlier." John stirred the stew and glanced back to Rudd.

The man's brow furrowed.

John needed to offer a reason for such an inquiry. Rudd didn't trust him yet, despite how often John frequented his pub. "Looking to hire a man to fix up the office. Do you know if he needs the work?"

Rudd shook his head and gave a toothy smile. "That's Bobby. Lives in the next town. Came in to see his family and attend the funeral. He'd have done good work for you, but he's got a job at the mill. Good folk. Took Miss Lusk's death hard. Used to be sweet on her when they were younger."

"I can imagine the young woman had many admirers."

Rudd nodded. "Aye. She and Miss Cunningham both did. And they were the best of friends since they wore braids in their hair. Nasty business, all this killing."

For all his bruskness, perhaps kindness lurked in the depths of Mr. Rudd. Not like Kieran, whose heart seemed as dark as the sky on a new moon.

Rudd paused. "If you need some work done, I know Miss Clara's nephew, Abe, would be interested. He only has a few shifts a week at the mill. He'd appreciate some extra coin. He struggles as it is. Nice boy, though."

"Thank you," John replied. "I'll speak with him tomorrow. I appreciate the suggestion."

Rudd nodded and started to walk away from the table. He came back and lowered his voice. "Keep an eye on him while he works for you though. A light finger from what other folk say, and his need for coin doesn't help matters. If you take my meaning."

"I do."

John took a hearty spoonful of stew, savoring it as he did the night he'd first come here. *A bit of a light finger, eh?* An unexpected twist in the investigation. Gaining some traction, John dared another question.

"What about the other young man sitting behind me? Is he in need of work as well?"

Rudd glanced into the booth behind him and frowned. "Don't know who sat here with Bobby. Didn't see him. Wasn't here long enough, I guess. Done and gone now."

Unease settled along John's bones. How had the man come and gone without detection? Perhaps he practiced being invisible and moving about the place unseen. A definite plus if one was a killer, but it was John's job to shed a light on the bastard.

A hot, bright, white light.

That is exactly what I'll do.

Chapter 12
Uninvited

Lucy worked by the dull glow of light from her candelabrum. Shadows shifted along the wall as the flames flickered every so often, a brief reminder time passed regardless of the tightness of Lucy's limbs and the deep ache in her chest. Cil retired long ago. Lucy wouldn't sleep for hours.

Even if she would have liked to rest, too much work awaited her. Miriam's funeral was tomorrow, only a handful of hours away. Yet another friend to say a final goodbye to.

Snow drifted down at a steady rate outside the ground level window above her as she continued to weave Miriam's golden hair into fine petite braids, creating a crown atop her head as Mrs. Cunningham had requested. Cil's soft snores echoed from the bedroom above, and Lucy smiled. She adored having her sister here. While Lucy often had guests waiting for preparations, they were a far cry from having a living, breathing person with her.

Apricot curled around Lucy's legs. "And of course there's you, my sweet," she whispered, smiling at the shining topaz eyes blinking back at her.

A scratching sound came from the back of the cottage. A branch of a tree against the roof, perhaps? She finished her braid and began another. The scratching sound amplified and increased, almost as if something longed to come in from the cold. Her brow knitted in a frown. What if some poor animal like Apricot wandered about in this?

Outside, the snow swirled as the wind whipped up.

She shivered. What if something altogether more sinister lurked about? Mr. Fiske and Mr. Brodie's warnings echoed in her mind. Although she wasn't exactly alone, she and Cil couldn't overpower a large brute of a man. Especially one bent on death. A killer. *A murderer*. A man now confident in his killings.

Lucy refused to be the next victim. She felt in the pocket of her dressing gown for the putty knife she usually stashed when she worked on flesh, reassured at its outline there.

Bolstering her courage, she stayed put, determined not to go outside unless she was certain of what or who it was.

Tying off her friend's final braid, Lucy sighed.

"Miriam," she whispered. "I will find you some of those beautiful crocus flowers you adore. Perhaps white or purple or both. You will be beautiful, I tell you."

Lucy studied what she had accomplished. All of the bruises were covered and invisible to the eye. Miriam had a sweet rose pink to her lips and a slight blush to her cheeks, the way Lucy had always remembered. She hoped the Cunninghams would be pleased. If only she could soften some of their pain.

A meow sounded outside the cottage. Lucy ascended to the main floor and peered out the front window. A tiny tricolored kitten meowed and scratched along the door, its orange, black, and white fur wet from the snow. Lucy hurried to the door and cracked it open, so the cold didn't rush in.

"Belle, what are you doing out?" In all the horrors of the day, the Cunninghams must have failed to leave their barn door open for her. Why else would she have wandered all this way to find warmth?

Lucy scooped the kitten into her arms, hugging her to her chest. "Or did you know Miriam rested here? I know you miss her, sweet girl. As do I."

The poor creature dug its claws into the front of Lucy's nightclothes. Its tiny, shaking form clung to her. Once inside,

Lucy set her down. It was then she noted the smudges on her gown and the dark paw prints the cat left with every step across the floor.

"Belle, what have you gotten into?" Lucy stooped to look closer. "Is that blood?" Pressing a finger to one of the smudgy prints and lifting it to the dim light, her pulse increased.

Mud.

She released a shaky breath and chided herself for her paranoia.

Get hold of yourself. It's just mud.

The kitten had tracked in mud, as creatures often do. Lucy dabbed at herself, finding more stains.

Blast, now she'd have to wash it.

She went to the door to drop the latch. As she reached the door, a strong force pushed against it, sending her sprawling. She scrambled back, staring at the large form covered in head to toe black, filling her entire doorway. Even his mouth and nose were covered with a dark scarf. Other than his eyes, she could see nothing of him.

The sheer size of him revealed his gender, though. It was definitely a man.

She froze. His dark, beady eyes bore through her. His gigantic boots were caked with mud, his dark trousers stained with fresh splotches as if he'd been running in a wet field. Lucy trembled.

Or kneeling somewhere in wait. In a new perch as yet undiscovered.

Waiting for her.

Was this the man? The killer? The one who had taken her friends from this world? Did he wish to claim her now?

Lucy's mouth opened, but she couldn't scream. No air escaped her lungs. Paralysis seized her. She could not shout or warn. She just stared back. Like a daft crazed woman, she stared.

The wind whipped the door fully open, causing it to slam against the wall, spurring her body and mind into action. "Lucy?" her sister slurred from the bedroom, still in a slumber.

"Cil!" Lucy shouted, clambering against the floorboards and grabbing the only weapon within reach—her fireplace bellows. Wielding it like a sword, she lunged at the stranger looming above her. He wasn't as tall as Mr. Brodie, but he was formidable. She darted to the left, narrowly escaping his grasp. The cats scattered and huddled together in a far corner of the cottage.

"What do you want?" Lucy yelled.

He said nothing.

Cil stirred from bed and padded out of the room. "Sister, what—" Seeing the intruder, she released a loud scream. A high, bloodcurdling scream Lucy envied. Why hadn't she been able to muster such a scream?

"Stay behind me," Lucy commanded, poking the bellows toward the stranger. Nothing would happen to Cil. Norah Jane had already lost a father. She would not lose her mother.

And Lucy would not lose her sister, her only real tether to the past and the family she'd once had.

The intruder lunged for her and Lucy took the opportunity to land a solid blow to his ribs. A crack sounded, followed by a curse. Before she could pull back, he grabbed her and twisted her wrist. A lightning bolt of pain seared up her arm. The bellows clattered to the floor. He yanked her toward him, and shivers scurried along her spine. Paralysis seized her once more.

Fight back, fight back.

Fear swallowed her whole, as it had the night long ago when she'd found her parents dead.

He shoved her aside roughly. She stumbled and tried to catch herself but landed with a hard knock to her head.

Skidding across the floor, she scraped her legs and thighs as her dressing gown slid up and twisted around her body.

"Lucy!" Cil cried out.

Lucy could hear them struggling. Everything came in and out of focus violently as her stomach churned. Items crashed amid muffled groans, until a final thud sounded.

Boots echoed away from her.

An eerie silence swallowed the room. Had he left?

Panic seized her as her heart thundered in her ears. What had he done to Cil? Why did she not scream or cry out? Lucy fumbled about, attempting to untangle herself and rise from the now spinning floor. She got to her knees first and grasped the table leg for support. Blinking, she willed the room to stop whirling. It only slowed. She scanned the area for her sister.

Her heart faltered to see Cil sprawled between the kitchen and bedroom, motionless.

The dark stranger turned to her and readjusted his gloves.

"What do you want?" Lucy demanded. "I've nothing."

He stalked past her, heading to the open cellar . . .

To Miriam.

"Her," he growled.

Gooseflesh rose along Lucy's skin.

"Leave her alone," she pleaded. "She has suffered enough." She crawled toward the trapdoor to block his advance, pitching forward as the room continued its ugly twist and turn.

Jamming her hand into her pocket, she gripped her putty knife and eased it out, waiting for him to come nearer. If he got close enough, she could stab him, wound him, slow him down. And if she perished, at least she would have done something to protect Miriam and Cil.

"I'll not leave without her." He loomed even closer.

"Why do you need her? She is gone from this world.

You've killed her." Lucy's heart raced in her chest. Why would he want Miriam, already dead?

"Move aside," he ordered.

There was something familiar in the timbre of his voice and the memory it stirred.

Do I know him?

"Move."

She could hear the desperation in his voice now. Hints his patience and control were withering away. One more step, and he would be within reach.

Lucy clutched the knife tightly. Tensing, she mustered all the strength she could.

"I'll not let you take her. Not without a fight," Lucy hissed, rising from her knees.

He grabbed for the front of her dressing gown, lifting her off the floor. She reached out and snatched the edge of the scarf around his mouth. It sagged, revealing a cleft chin and a dimple she remembered from long ago.

She gasped. The knife she held in her hand clattered to the floor.

I know him.

Chapter 13
Rage

When the newly installed sleigh bells clanged on the office door, John halted from his paperwork at his desk with a start. Perhaps leaving the single bell in place would have been better, however he wanted to ensure he could hear someone enter even from upstairs in his bedroom. After the gifts left to him the other morning outside his office door, he needed to be more careful.

And more prepared. He frowned at the wall clock.

Who would be by at half past seven in the morning?

A young boy rushed in, skidded across the wooden floor with boots covered in wet snow, and tugged his hat from his head. Squeezing it between his hands, he panted out, "Excuse me, sir."

Alarm sang through John's body at the visible fear in the boy's wide bright eyes. He'd met the child once before. John searched his memory until the boy's face clicked into place.

"You're one of Augustus Travers' boys. What can I do for you?" John removed his glasses and rose from his desk.

"Yes, sir." The boy gave a brief nod. "Will Travers, sir." His breath shuffled in and out in uneven spurts, and he twisted his hat in his hands. "There's need of you at the Wycliffes. I was helping out Miss Clara this morn, and when Miss Wycliffe failed to stop in as she'd promised to, yesterday after the funeral, Miss Clara sent me over. And . . ." He paused and tears blurred his eyes. "I tried, sir. I couldn't wake them. I ran here first, and I . . ."

John's heart raged in his chest. Every fiber of his body tautened with fear. Why had he not put someone on watch at her door? He was a fool. A bloody fool. And if they were dead . . .

He clamped down on the thought. "Find the doctor and send him on to the cottage. On your way, tell your father to meet me in the square. I have need of him."

The boy nodded as he donned his hat and disappeared through the same door he'd stumbled in. John grabbed his hat and outer garments. Unlocking the top drawer of his desk, he found his revolver and loaded it, shoving the weapon in the back waistband of his trousers.

Snatching up his ledger and pencil, he slammed the door shut behind him.

Mr. Travers locked his general goods store across the street. The tightness of his gait, as he hurried to John's side, signaled he knew exactly why he'd been beckoned.

"Travers." John nodded as they headed through the town square toward the road to the Wycliffes. The speedy pace pulled and strained every muscle in his thigh, but he ignored it. He had to get there and quickly.

"Will tells me something's happened at the Wycliffes." Travers met John's pace, and his gaze narrowed off into the distance. Travers scanned the horizon from side to side as he strode, a remnant of the man's past military training.

"Remember when you said you'd help out if ever this case became too big for one man?"

Travers spat on the ground and readjusted his hat. "Yep."

"Well, consider such a time now. If anything happens to me before this killer is caught, you're in charge of this town."

"You've my word."

"That's all I need."

~ ~ ~

John used the cold, fast clip to the cottage as a way to burn off the rage, anxiety, and fear coursing along his body. If he'd been a stronger man, he would have run. If he tried, his muscles would seize and cripple him, and then what use would he be to anyone? And he couldn't wait for a hackney. Too much needed to be done. Too many things were unknown. Uncertain. He clenched his teeth.

And he refused to acknowledge they might be too late.

The Wycliffe cottage came into view, serenely peaceful with the fresh snow banking the stone walls and windows. From the outside, nothing seemed amiss. Except for the quiet. The bloody eerie quiet. Even the animals and birds did not stir.

Wide footfalls from men's boots pocked the fresh snow, and John's stomach clenched. Someone had been here. Someone uninvited. Unable to wait further, John started a slow jog across the final walkway and nudged the door to the cottage open.

Bloody hell.

Cold consumed the room as if they were still out of doors. The hearth fire had died out long ago. Lucy Wycliffe's form lay sprawled on the floor, motionless, clothed in a thin dressing gown and woolen stockings. John froze.

Is she dead?

Her pale skin, closed eyes, and slightly parted mouth stopped his heart in his chest. A flash of the past seized him and he could almost see Mrs. Wycliffe, superimposed over Lucy's body as she lay upon the floor. Shaking off the horror, he rushed to her, kneeling by her side, ignoring the slice of pain sailing along his leg.

Travers hurried to the sister, lying in a heap toward the bedroom.

"Miss Wycliffe?" John urged, cupping her face. Cold greeted him, thankfully not the rigid feel of death, and his heart soared. "She is alive," he said aloud, relieved. His hands shook as he stroked the hair back from her temples.

"So is her sister," Travers answered.

John shrugged off his coat and covered Lucy. "See if you can warm her, Travers. It's frigid in here." He removed his gloves and rubbed Lucy's icy hands in his own, blowing his warm breath on them. "You must wake, Miss Wycliffe. The doctor is coming. You are safe now."

And I think I love you.

He couldn't keep the words from rushing into his head. *Love her?* Perhaps he was merely overcome by the moment. He barely knew her, and yet some part of him could place every freckle across the bridge of her nose, could understand what made her tilt her head in confusion. And the thought of losing her, now or ever, struck him dumb with fear.

And anger.

"She wakes!" Travers called. "Don't try to move, miss. The doctor is coming."

The woman moaned. "Lucy? My sister?"

"She is here. Alive. Mr. Brodie is trying to wake her now."

And try he did. John rubbed her arms. Even through the heavy wool of his coat, he could feel the cold within her limbs, deep within her bones. "Lucy," he murmured, a hint above a whisper. "You must wake. You must. I cannot abide anything else than your waking. Please, wake."

He focused his hope, his attention upon her, awaiting even the slightest change in her breath or the color of her cheeks. Anything to show she heard or felt something. He turned her head gently to the side and studied the egg sized knot growing there. *Bloody hell.* She'd been knocked about hard. She needed a doctor, now. He removed his scarf and placed it beneath her nape to cradle her head and prevent further movement or trauma.

Whenever he found the bastard who'd done this, he would snap his bloody neck.

Her eyelids fluttered. The tiny, ginger colored lashes twitched, and she opened her eyes. He smiled down at her. *Thank God.* He brushed his fingers across her forehead.

She started and her eyes flickered. "What's happened? Cil?" Her words rang high and thready, but she squeezed his hand.

"Quiet yourself. Mr. Travers and I are here. Your sister is awake. The doctor is coming."

Apricot came over and nested herself against Lucy's neck. Another kitten John had never seen before meowed plaintively and ran its tiny matted frame along his leg. "And I have not met this one before. Seems you are gathering woodland creatures." He tried to add some levity to distract her. Her pulse throbbed weakly at her wrist. Too much excitement could overwhelm her.

"Bella. Miriam's kitten," Lucy croaked, struggling to talk.

"Relax. You need not speak."

"She is how he came in. He fooled me." Tears sprang to her eyes. She gripped his hand harder, and her breathing increased.

He needed to soothe her. "Look at me. You are safe. Calm yourself. He is gone. We are here."

Her eyes darted wildly. "You do not understand," she sputtered, wilder, more desperate as her breathing became rapid and uneven. "I *know* him."

"You know him?" John settled closer to her, stroking her hair to comfort her. And he hadn't killed her? Why would he leave her here, alive, after attacking her? It made no sense, but little in this case did.

She coughed and relaxed her head against his palm. Her eyes fluttered and opened once more. "Yes. His scarf slipped, and I could see his face. He has a cleft chin. A dimple, and . . ." She moaned. "I am so dizzy, sir. Please stop moving me."

He stilled. He wasn't moving her.

"We can speak of this later—"

"There is no time. He has her. I tried to stop him, but he's taken her."

He couldn't decipher her riddles. She and her sister *were* here. "He's taken your niece?"

"No." Lucy's eyes fluttered closed. "She is safe." Her head lolled to the side.

John patted her cheek in an attempt to rouse her. *Bollocks*. He leaned over her until he could feel her breath on his cheek, then relaxed. She'd merely lost consciousness again.

"Lucy? Miss Wycliffe?" If he could wake her a moment longer, he might know who had attacked her and what she meant by *he'd taken her*.

Doctor Sykes, an old man a few years past his prime, yet good and decent from what Travers had said, hurried in.

"Constable." Dr. Sykes nodded to him and came to Lucy's side.

John rose to give room for the doctor to attend to her. Immediately, loss consumed him. He'd tried to protect her, and he'd failed. He rubbed his forehead.

"Any details you can tell me about what's happened?" Sykes asked as he felt for her pulse.

"She gained awareness and spoke for a few minutes before she fainted once more. I noted a sizable wound to her head. Near the temple. She and her sister were attacked, sir." John shoved his hands in his trousers and watched as the doctor carefully examined her head and neck.

"If you will grant me a few moments, Constable, I can complete my examination." Sykes looked up at him.

"Of course, my apologies." John shook his head and

stepped away. He'd lost all his senses this morn. He crossed to Travers who had knelt beside Mrs. Newberry.

The poor woman shook and her cheeks were stained with tears. Augustus Travers continued to murmur to her and speak softly as he held her hand. Kindness emanated from the man, and John knew he had been right to trust his gut about him after their chance meeting at the tavern not long after his arrival in Clun. Travers was also a good, decent man, and if anything did happen to John before this case was solved, the man would see justice despite what Magistrate Kieran might do.

"Lucy?" she called in a faint tremble of air. Her eyes searched John's face, fear etched along her brow.

"Dr. Sykes is examining her, as he will you shortly."

"She is alive?" A tear spilled down her cheek.

"Yes. She is alive. She is strong, much the same as you."

A wavering smile formed on her lips, and she half sobbed.

"Easy there," Travers whispered to her. "Take care. Slow, even breaths. 'Tis what your sister would want. And your daughter. Close your eyes and think of her face. Slow breaths."

She obeyed and slowed her breathing. John nodded to him. Travers had her well in order. "I'll make a fire to try to warm the room."

And to keep busy. Stillness didn't become him. The longer the doctor examined Lucy, the more restless John became. If the man who had attacked her had touched her, done anything untoward . . . He snapped some twigs and branches in half and settled them on the grate before adding a seasoned log atop it. Using flint by the fire, he lit it and the tinder grew into a hot flame.

He would kill the man with his bare hands if he'd interfered with her. He would. It didn't matter if John was the law itself. The man would be dead.

"Constable?" Sykes asked.

John stood and grimaced as his leg muscles pulled. He walked over to the doctor, who led him outside. "Yes, Doctor."

"Miss Wycliffe has had a nasty blow to the head. With care and rest over the next few days, she should be fine."

"Was she . . ." John cleared his throat and glanced out into the distance. He began again. "Harmed or interfered with in any other way?"

"A few scratches and bruises from quite a scuffle, I'd guess. No additional injuries, I'm happy to report. Found some blood and skin under her nails. She gave her attacker a fight. Most likely left a mark or two on him if you take my meaning."

John pressed his lips together and willed his heartrate to slow. *Thank God.* She had fought him off and saved herself and her sister. Emotion thickened his throat. "Thank you for the update. Is she safe to be moved to her bed to rest?"

"Yes. Please see to it while I check upon Mrs. Newberry."

Back inside, Sykes went in search for his next patient, while relief and a rush of fatigue washed over John. Lucy seemed fast asleep. A hint of color had returned to her cheeks, which gave him hope. Perhaps warmth and rest would aid her recovery the most. She would be all right, and he would be there for her the next time.

"Miss Wycliffe? Dr. Sykes says you are well enough to be put to bed to rest."

She didn't move or stir.

"I'm going to carry you. Don't be alarmed." John lifted her and gently cradled her against him. Her weight and frame seemed as fragile as a bird, but he knew better. She was strong, formidable, and would recover. The feel of her against him soothed his spirit. His body longed for her so deeply, a tremble traveled through him. As he carried her to her bed, she stirred and snuggled against the side of his neck as she increased her hold on him.

"Please do not leave me, John," she murmured.

Never.

Laying her upon the bed, he removed the coat he'd draped around her as she shivered. The sweetness of her there in her thin dressing gown almost undid him. So beautiful and delicate and female. And vulnerable.

And lucky to be alive.

He tucked her into bed and she sighed, shifting beneath the covers. As he turned to leave, she took his hand. "Thank you," she whispered, as her eyes fluttered closed. Her hand relaxed, dropping from his as she fell asleep.

Lord above.

John released a ragged breath. His emotions fought his logic, needing to analyze what he could while he could. He exited the room to find Mrs. Newberry settled in a chair pulled close to the fire, looking past him into the bedroom.

"She is resting." John answered her unspoken question. "She will be fine, in time. How are you feeling?"

Blankets and quilts entombed her as her eyes darted about. Palpable fear consumed her, and Travers studied her carefully with a furrowed brow.

He approached John. "Doctor went out to get some draughts for them to ease their sleep later. He'll return shortly." He sniffed and dropped his voice to a hum. "He says she'll be fine. Only scrapes and bruises. There's something she's not saying. Or perhaps not wanting to ask."

"And you know this how?"

"My gut."

Travers crossed his arms over his chest as they approached Mrs. Newberry.

"Can you tell us what happened?" John asked.

The woman lifted her eyes to him and then dropped her gaze to her lap where she rubbed her hands together. "I—"

She faltered and took a breath. "I don't know exactly. I woke to a crash. I came in the doorway, confused with sleep." She met John's gaze. Fear burned bright in hers. "This man all in black was standing there. Lucy tried to warn me. I couldn't move fast enough. And when he struck me, I remember hitting the floor and nothing after." She lifted her gaze to Travers. Warmth emanated from her face, and she blushed. "Until you were here, Mr. Travers." She studied her hands.

"Does anything seem to be missing? Did he want something?"

She stilled and stood, the quilts cascading from her. She stared toward the open trapdoor, but almost toppled over.

Travers caught her and held her arm. "Miss, I don't think you should be troubling yourself—"

"Did they already take her for burial?" Mrs. Newberry scanned the room.

"Who?" John asked.

Her voice faltered, and she clung to Travers's arm. "Miriam," she whispered. The final *m* of the name ended on a tremble.

Dread screeched along John's skin, and hairs stood on the back of his neck. Lucy's words echoed back to him now and it all clicked into place.

"There is no time. He has her. I tried to stop him, but he's taken her."

"Not that I know of." John strode across the room to peer down into the dim cellar.

The table where Lucy prepared the dead stood empty, the stained sheet she placed underneath the bodies missing. The scratched wood of the barren table blinked back at him. His stomach dropped.

"He's taken Miriam," Mrs. Newberry whispered. "She is gone."

Chapter 14
Taken

"Gone?" John faltered in disbelief. Air whooshed out of his lungs.

Mrs. Newberry nodded and sobbed, covering her mouth with her hand. Her hair fell in a curtain, obscuring part of her face.

"Miriam," she muttered. "He has taken her. Poor Miriam." Her body began to fold beneath the horror of it, and Travers guided her back to her chair by the fire, supporting her as they walked, his words indecipherable and low.

John turned away from the hearth and moved toward the front of the cottage to stare out the window. What man of this earth, what crazed person would break into a cottage to steal a body? A grave robber? Some unnatural man who studied the dead to better understand the living? A ritualist with tendencies John couldn't comprehend?

His head throbbed, and he rubbed the back of his neck. His mind raced with theories. His heart thundered. His leg ached. And his relief over Lucy and her sister being alive faded into a new, unsuspecting rage regarding the cruelty of the situation. A woman who had already been defamed and murdered had now been denied her final rest on this earth.

John clenched his fists at his sides. Not while he breathed. She would have her eternal rest. Her family would have theirs. He glanced into the bedroom where Lucy now slept.

And Lucy would have peace. He would protect her from whatever man, whatever creature roamed this town threatening its people.

"Bloody hell," he grumbled and rubbed his eyes.

"I couldn't agree more." Travers stood beside John and stared out the window. Tucking his hands in his trouser pockets, the shopkeeper shook his head. "When you asked for help this morn, I had no idea what the day would bring."

"Nor did I." John glanced back to see Mrs. Newberry rocking slowly in the chair with her eyes closed. No doubt she was worn out and would soon be asleep. At least he prayed she would. He turned back to Travers.

"Sure you're prepared for what may come, Augustus? I fear this may get worse before all is said and done. And you've family and a business to care for."

Travers met his gaze. A certain steady resolve reflected in his eyes. "Yes, sir. Most alive and of use I've felt since my Violet left this earth." He sniffed and glanced away.

John nodded. The man had been a widower a handful of years now, the love for his late wife evident in his eyes and in the words he'd spoken of her when they'd first met at the tavern. Raising his three boys and daughter on his own with his mother-in-law had to be a challenge. One John could scarce imagine.

What a mess this day, this case had become. Had he made a mistake in coming here? He had hoped to help the Wycliffes, the town, himself. Yet, here he stood, not even a full week at his new post, and the carnage of this case was strewn about him like rubbish. Two murders, a threat to himself and Lucy, a break-in, and now a missing body.

"What next?" Travers asked, scrubbing a hand down his face.

A great question.

"We'll need to have someone here to watch over the ladies in case they need further care."

"Doc should be back shortly with the draughts, so they can rest. Asked him to bring my mother-in-law with him. I know she'd be happy to sit with the women a spell. She's got a house of boys most days, me included." Travers shook his head. "Time with them might do her a world of good."

John smiled. "A solid plan, indeed. It will give us time to examine the cottage for clues, analyze what we find, and begin the search for whomever dared break in and seize Miss Cunningham."

"Did Miss Wycliffe say much when she came to earlier?"

"Quite a bit. I wish she could have stayed awake long enough to tell me the rest of it." He dropped his voice to a hint above a whisper.

"Oh?" Travers lifted his eyebrows.

"She recognized her attacker."

Travers blew out a low whistle. "Lord above."

"I know. She recognized him, and the bastard no doubt knows her."

"Why did he leave her alive?"

John shrugged. "At the moment, I have no idea." He stared into the bedroom where Lucy dozed. "Perhaps she does."

~ ~ ~

"The ladies should sleep for a few hours, then see if you can rouse them to have some warm broth, Mrs. Dobbs." Dr. Syke's instructions drifted to John's ears through the open cellar trapdoor. "Send word if they take a turn before I check in on them tomorrow."

"Will do. Thank you, sir." The rocker creaked in time with the kind lady's response.

As the cottage door rattled upstairs, John continued searching for evidence, stooping to examine the dirt floor beneath the empty preparations table.

"Poor creatures." Mrs. Dobbs' Scottish brogue lilted from the bedroom, interrupting his search.

Rising, John climbed to the main level, closing the cellar trapdoor behind him and crossing to the bedroom to glance in. The gray-haired woman, ample in size and heart, rocked back and forth in the chair they'd carried from beside the hearth to where the sisters now slept. Her movements kept time with the knitting she worked on in her lap. He'd liked Travers' mother-in-law the instant he had met her.

"Thank you for caring for them. I'm grateful beyond words." John gifted her a smile.

"As we are grateful ye took on such a post, Mr. Brodie. Not having a constable so long has made Kieran a bloody pain in my arse. Can't abide the foul creature. Raising taxes, squeezing us dry, I tell ye."

John couldn't smother his smile. A chuckle broke free in the air. "I do appreciate your candor, ma'am."

"Lord above, Ena," Travers added. He shot John a glare. "Do *not* be encouraging her."

"I'm afraid I might have to. Tell me what else you know about these parts, Mrs. Dobbs," he called to her. "How long have you lived in Clun?" John smiled at Travers and joined his friend's search under the kitchen table.

"Finally, a man who values the thoughts of a lady such as meself." Her voice carried easily in the quiet cottage.

Travers grumbled and sighed. A long-suffering sigh.

"Lived here since the fall of 1820," Mrs. Dobbs continued. "A right fine place to settle in and raise a family for a long while. Since Codger Senior passed on, bless his soul, there hasn't been any real law or order about here. Codger Junior tried for a while, but he had no stomach for it. He also had no backbone. Couldn't stand up to the youngest Kieran once his older brother passed on."

John spied an object far beneath the table out of arm's reach. *Blast.* He grabbed the fireplace bellows and poked it through to the other side. As he tried to stand, his thigh muscle seized. He gritted his teeth as a moan escaped him.

Travers made to approach, and John waved him off. "Just my leg. It'll pass."

He distracted himself by questioning Mrs. Dobbs further. "Do you believe Junior lives in the woods?"

Her laugh tinkled from the bedroom. "I'd wager not. Not as tough as his father and he resented this place."

John frowned. "Why? Seems a quaint town."

"As bad as Kieran is, his father was worse. Drove poor Codger Senior hard. Many say he pushed him to an early grave."

"Is that why there hasn't been a rush to fill the position?" John shook his head. It explained a great deal. Too much, perhaps. Now he understood why Kieran disliked him, and why the town cowered to him. They feared what his family and name could do to them. John probably should be leery as well, but he had nothing to lose.

Except Lucy.

His muscle spasm passed, and he slowly stood.

"That be the truth of it," the lady answered.

John circled the table. The sight of the object he'd dislodged shook him to the core.

"What'd you find?" Travers stared at him.

"A wooden ball. For a five-jacks set."

One of the last things John had hoped to *never* see again.

Chapter 15
Abe

"A what?" Travers approached to look.

"A ball for five-jacks." John turned it over in his fingers. The smooth, worn shape rang of memories, of times when he'd played for hours with his brother on the shore while they visited in Clun. Before they'd gotten older and known death and tragedy. While not their exact set, it could have been its twin.

John clenched his fist around it. The bastard had *been* here. In this cottage. He'd left this other part of the clue in her house. To taunt him.

I've been a fool.

When the killer had left the threepence and jacks, the bastard had warned him of the impending danger, yet John had ignored it. And Lucy had paid the price for it. So had Mrs. Newberry.

And Miriam.

Lord above.

His arrogance and his secrecy had cost them dearly.

"I take it this means more to you than it does to me."

"Yes." John nested it in his trouser pockets. How much did he tell him? How much could he afford not to? If anything happened to him, John needed the reassurance someone else knew the truth and could protect Lucy and the other young women of Clun.

But what if Travers were somehow involved? A ridiculous thought altogether. John stamped down his fear and returned to logic. He had to trust someone. He clenched his jaw. "The killer contacted me already. He warned me. I didn't listen. I didn't know it would happen so soon after."

Travers frowned and eased closer to John. His eyes were dark. "You *knew* he might attack them, and you did nothing?"

"I hadn't put it all together yet. It's a mistake I will regret for the rest of my days. I couldn't imagine he would do something such as this."

Travers nodded as his expression lightened. "Can't blame yourself for not being able to read the mind of a coldblooded killer."

But couldn't I?

Wasn't he still lying to Augustus even now? John had protected a killer once before, and now, was he doing it again to hide his own shame of his past? His gut clenched.

Shame and fear drove his reasoning rather than facts and logic. *It* had to stop. *He* had to stop.

"Let's finish here, collect anything of significance, and get back to town. We have to find Miss Cunningham." John ran a hand down his face. "But first, we need to tell the Cunninghams Miriam is missing. Of what happened here at the cottage."

"Best not put it off. Funeral's set for today."

John nodded. As if he could forget. As if any of them could.

"Abe," a familiar female voice croaked from behind them.

John's stomach dropped. *Lucy.* He fought the urge to run to her side.

Mrs. Dobbs ceased her rocking. "She's awake! Come quickly."

The men hurried to the bedroom with John entering first.

Lucy's eyes fluttered, then opened and focused on his face. Her breathing uneven, she reached for him. He hesitated. As a gentleman and as her employer, it wasn't appropriate, yet he longed to comfort her. When she reached for him once more, he smiled and settled his hand within her own, casting propriety aside.

For once he followed his heart, and the cold, fragile feel of her petite hand in his undid any remaining resolve to keep his distance. She meant too much to him even after mere days. There was so much he hadn't told her, so much he needed to tell her, but he clamped his teeth down on the truth. It had to wait. For now, he needed to listen.

Clutching his fingers, she searched his face. "It was Abe."

John's heartbeat picked up speed, and his throat dried. "The man who attacked you?"

As she nodded, a tear slid along her cheek. "Ready to stab him with my putty knife, I tugged down his scarf in our struggle. Once I recognized him, I knew he wouldn't kill me, nor I, him." She struggled for breath.

John sat on the edge of the bed, and it creaked under his weight. Mrs. Newberry didn't even stir, deeply in slumber from the draught Sykes had given her. "Take your time, Miss Wycliffe."

She faltered, swallowed, and began again. "He said he'd suffered too much and so had Miriam. And he would take her to where she would have peace from this world."

Mrs. Dobbs murmured under her breath, crossing herself.

"Abe, as in Miss Clara's nephew?" Travers' tone wavered in disbelief.

"Yes. If I had not seen his face, I wouldn't have believed it either. We've been friends for as long as I can remember. All of us." Lucy gestured weakly. "I don't understand why he would do it."

"Nor I." John studied her face.

He understood her confusion. When he'd discovered his brother standing over her parents with a weapon in his hands and blood upon the floor, John had fought to accept the truth of it, the horror of it for quite some time. Now he understood disorders of the mind, the confusion it caused, and the carnage it could leave in its wake. He rubbed the back of her hand with his thumb.

But he could tell her none of this. Not now. Would he ever?

"You will find her," she pleaded. "I cannot abide the idea of him having her after what he's done."

"You believe he killed Miss Cunningham and Miss Lusk?" Travers asked.

She nodded as tears fell anew upon her cheek. "If I had not seen his eyes, heard what he said, I wouldn't have thought so. Yet how he seemed last night . . . Darkness haunted him. I believe him capable of anything."

Travers rubbed his jaw. "Wouldn't believe it if you hadn't spoken the words, miss. A real shame."

Lucy hiccupped. "There was a time we were the best of friends. The eight of us. Now, it seems we are a fractured lot. Three of us lost to the world already."

"Three?" John asked.

Lucy shifted and glanced away from him to the wall. "Jeremy. He died a few months after he became a soldier." When she faced him again, her features were tight and strained. Fatigue crowded her, and he needed to let her rest.

"Best you sleep," John said. "Close your eyes. Travers and I will find him. Rest now."

Lucy nodded and closed her sweet violet eyes. One last tear fell upon her cheek. John's chest tightened anew, as he released her hand. He nodded to Mrs. Dobbs and followed Travers from the room.

"Tell me everything about this group of eight. I need to know who else may be in danger." John grabbed his hat and gloves and shrugged on his coat and scarf. They needed to notify the Cunninghams and begin their search before this fellow Abe had time to strike once more.

Travers followed suit, donning his outer clothes before following John out the door. When they reached the main road, Travers stated, "There were eight of them close in age who schooled together. Did everything together far as I can recall. Miss Wycliffe, Mrs. Newberry, Miss Cunningham, and Miss Lusk were the girls of their group. Jeremy Foss, who passed away years ago, Abe Jenkins, Bobby Dunn, and of course Old Man Codger's boy, Sherman."

"Sherman? Odd name for a boy."

Travers shook his head. "Some family name. As a junior, most called him such. He hated the name Sherman. I don't blame him."

Recognition dawned. *Bobby*. From that night at The Boar and Sable.

"And this Bobby Dunn. Do you remember if he was here for Miss Lusk's funeral?" John asked.

"He was. Came in just for the day. He lives with his family a town over but works at the mill. Nice boy."

"That's it then. It had to have been him and Abe that I overheard at the pub after the funeral."

"You *saw* Abe there?" Travers tensed.

"No. I heard two men arguing behind me. When I asked Rudd about them, he said he'd only seen Bobby, but it had to have been Abe with him."

"Why?" Travers asked, turning his head from a gust of wind.

"Bobby called him unnatural, crazy even. Said he wouldn't be covering for him anymore. We've a need to find and interview this Bobby Dunn."

Travers blew out a breath. "Won't be able to. At least not for two weeks. Overheard him telling the Lusks he was traveling north to see his sister and his newest niece."

"Of course." John sighed, kicking a downed branch off

the path. "That would have been far too easy."

On their walk to the Cunninghams, the sun finally broke free of its clouds, warming John's face. The air provided a refreshing balm to his skin. "Such an odd crime to happen in such a beautiful place."

"Seems you brought the odd happenings of the city with you, Constable." Travers glanced off into the woods in a continuous scan as they traveled.

John shook his head. "I hope not. Whatever luck I have tends to be bad."

They walked in silence until the Cunningham's cottage came into view. It stood resolute as an enlarged version of Lucy's home with a sleeping garden plot off to the side and a well in the front. John's gut churned. He dreaded this conversation, yet there was no way to prevent it. At least Travers stood by his side, the way Lucy had a few days prior when he'd first met the Cunninghams for the notification of Miriam's death.

Now he had to tell them she'd been taken from them.
Again.

"Any idea what you'll say?" Travers asked as he kicked the snow from his boots on the stoop.

John lifted his hand and knocked. "The only thing I can. The truth."

~ ~ ~

"Well, it went better than I expected." Travers pulled the collar of his coat high along the back of his neck. A cold evening wind whirled about them, the temperature having fallen since they'd left Lucy's place earlier in the day.

"Oh? Here I thought it would be far too soon if I ever had to have such a conversation again." John tugged his hat down and frowned. Mrs. Cunningham's weeping still echoed in his ears.

Travers shrugged. "Just trying to lighten a dreary day."

"I appreciate the effort. I'm grateful you came along today. You've your own business and family to tend to, so why don't we stop by the Wycliffes, and I'll take up post while you escort Mrs. Dobbs home with you?"

"You keeping watch all night?"

"Don't see any other option. I can't leave them on their own. Nor can I ask your mother-in-law to stay the night with them, unprotected. Who knows where Abe is and what the next part of his plan might be? He's been one step ahead of me thus far. I'd rather him not make any additional progress on whatever his scheme is."

"And what about tomorrow and the day after?" Travers shook his head. "You're only one man. You need help. You can't protect them *and* hunt a killer. Especially one such as him."

Travers was right. John couldn't do both, but he didn't have a police station with other men to help and support him. Only this morning, he'd wrangled in help by asking Travers for support.

There was always the magistrate. John could plead for another man to help resolve the case, but would Kieran even listen? The man didn't approve of John being here. How would he possibly approve another man interfering in his control over this town?

He wouldn't.

"You and I both know Kieran will be reluctant to add any additional support to solve our case," John began. "The man despises me as it is. Gave me a two-week end date on this case already. If I don't have it solved by his daughter's ball, I'm fired and released from my post." His head started throbbing and he rubbed his left temple.

"Bastard," Travers grumbled, kicking a loose stone in the snow.

"My thoughts exactly."

The edge of the Wycliffe cottage came into view. John's

pulse increased. He wanted to see her. Protect her. Sleep, he could do without.

But Lucy, he couldn't.

"Then we form a detail to make sure they're both covered as best we can," Travers suggested. "I can ask my eldest boys to mind the store, and Ena and I will take turns guarding the women. I'll even assist you with the case when I can."

"Why? You've so much already to tend to. I can't in good conscience accept your offer. I can't pay you, and this will interfere with your very livelihood. You'll also be placing your life at risk." John stopped and Travers did the same.

Did the man even realize what he was saying?

Travers lifted his chin. "This is my home. The home of my family. I won't in good conscience, as you say, sit by and do less than everything I can to help you catch this killer. If anything happens to either of those women . . ." He paused. "I would never forgive myself. Miss Cunningham has a right to eternal rest and her family, a bit of peace. Losing some sleep and income is worth it to do those things." He set his jaw and held John's stare. "Don't deny me what little I can do for them."

John smiled and nodded. "You're a persuasive man. I imagine the men in your care would have followed you anywhere onto the battlefield."

"Well, war wasn't much to my liking. The enemy was fuzzy and unclear, but with this we know who we're looking for and why. We need to find a way to get him before he hurts anyone else."

"Then that's just what we'll do." John reached out his hand to Travers and shook it hard.

Now all John had to do was catch a man he'd never met or seen—

Who traveled about town and the woods like a ghost, then faded into the ether.

Chapter 16
The Question

Lucy woke in a sea of warmth surrounded by daylight and the sweet calming murmurings of a woman humming a tune she didn't quite recognize. Blinking her eyes open, she noted the familiar surroundings of her bedroom, her sister asleep beside her. The faint creaking of a rocking chair beckoned her to turn.

Mrs. Dobbs, a lovely old Scottish woman who'd lived in Clun ever since Lucy could remember, sat in the chair knitting. Whenever she and Cil had gone into Mr. Dobbs' General Store, now Mr. Travers' store, the woman had snuck them boiled sweets. They'd shoved them joyfully in their pockets, savoring the lemony treat for as long as it would last.

Lucy sighed aloud at the pleasing memory, and Mrs. Dobbs turned to her. She ceased her rocking and smiled. "Well, there ye are, sweet girl. Awake at the sight of the afternoon sun. Took quite a tumble according to the doc. How are ye feeling?" Settling her knitting on the nightstand, Mrs. Dobbs rose and approached the bed.

Lucy croaked an answer. "Better." Her skull didn't pound and threaten to crack open as before. "What time is it?"

"Ye and yer sister have been asleep almost a full day. I've been home and back. Best to get some broth in ye. Some's been warming over the fire."

"Thank you, Mrs. Dobbs." Lucy struggled to sit up and winced. The aches of her fight with Abe lingered. It hardly seemed to have happened, yet her limbs screamed otherwise.

Flashes of her struggle with him, his dark angry eyes, and the force of his hands on her flooded her mind. Her pulse quickened. She tried to will the memories away by squeezing her eyes shut, yet they rushed forth once more.

Resting against the pillows, she pressed the heels of her hands to her eyes to keep the horrid memories at bay. The sounds of her own pleas and Cil screaming . . . The dull thud of her sister hitting the floor . . . The images and memories wouldn't stop whirling about her.

Lucy panted as her body and mind remembered what the sleep had repressed.

"Dearest?"

Lucy's breath caught as the woman helped her sit up and wrapped a warm, comforting arm about her waist as her mother always had.

"Ye are safe now. So is yer sister."

"And Miriam?" Lucy asked in a whisper behind her hands.

"No, luv. They haven't found her yet. They will. Mr. Brodie and my Augustus are on the case. For now, uncover yer eyes and see all that *is* right with the world."

Slowly, Lucy lowered her hands and opened her eyes.

Mrs. Dobbs smiled at her. "Ye and yer sister are alive. Let us celebrate this current miracle and let God focus on the rest, hmmm?"

Choking back her doubts about such a celebration, Lucy propped herself against the pillows once more. The real question remained. Where had Miriam been taken and how could they catch Abe before he killed again? What news about the case had she missed while she'd been asleep?

Something Mrs. Dobbs said hit her like a stone.

"I've been asleep a full day?"

"Aye. The draught Dr. Sykes made might have been a wee bit too strong. Missed a few visitors, ye did. Constable

Brodie and Augustus have taken turns keeping watch on both of ye at night."

How had Lucy not known any of this? She rubbed her eyes in an attempt to untangle the cobwebs in her mind.

"The Lusks and Cunninghams even dropped by." Mrs. Dobbs brought a bowl of steaming broth to her.

"Oh?" Lucy glanced away. Her throat dried.

Did they blame her for losing Miriam?

She folded the quilt at her lap. Staring at her hands, she chided herself. Why had she not fought harder? Or tried to reason with him? They were friends, were they not? She *knew* Abe. She had known him most of her life. So why would he have killed Miriam and Becca?

And left her and Cil alive.

Her heart thundered in her chest. Perhaps she'd been wrong. Could Abe be only a thief and not a killer? Why would he have wanted to take the body if not as some horrid prize?

Mrs. Dobbs draped a cloth over Lucy's lap and patted her shoulder. "Shouldn't be worrying yerself. Mr. Brodie and my Augustus will find the girl. And him."

"Mr. Travers has agreed to help?" Lucy accepted the bowl of broth. The warmth on her hands and steam against her face seemed a gift.

"Aye. Bless the man. He's been all but lost without Violet. First signs of life I've seen out of him for years. And I'm so grateful for it despite the cause."

Lucy swallowed a warm spoonful of broth. Perhaps some nourishment would soothe some tiny part of her and help her think more clearly.

"Oh, and yer horrid sniveling banker man came by." Mrs. Dobbs grimaced. "Fiske seemed more concerned about when ye'd be paying yer note off rather than yer wellbeing. If the Constable hadn't already been here, I would have driven the man out by the whip of my apron tail."

"I wish I could one day see such." Lucy giggled.

Fiske had more money than one man ever should and all he did was worry about when more was coming in. Her money. Money she didn't have. She glanced around her familiar cozy cottage, a place she might not have for much longer.

"Please eat, my dear."

Lucy smiled and took another spoonful although her mind whirled. Fiske had been here. Constable Brodie had been here. John knew of her dilemma, but to learn he and Mrs. Dobbs had been reminded of her meager circumstances stung what inkling of pride Lucy still had.

With the attack, her services for the constable would most likely be suspended. Another cut to her earnings. Her cottage would soon be lost to Fiske. A reality she'd kept at bay long enough, and one she'd soon have to face. She'd best enjoy what time she had left here. Suddenly, the broth tasted sour on her tongue.

Could she leave this place without ever knowing what happened to her parents so long ago? Without putting to rest their memories? She'd not considered she would ever be forced out on her own without her work. Yet, the future stared back at her; unflinching, unyielding for the first time since her parents' death. Since the first day she'd become a layer-out. A day long ago when she and Cil had taken care of Old Man Codger, their first job, and prepared him for the grave.

Cil stirred beside her, yet she didn't wake. What would become of her life without Cil so close by? She and Norah Jane would be a mere town away, a day's trip in fact. Not far, but not close. And Lucy would be alone.

Truly alone for the first time in her life.

"Dear, ye best have more while it's warm. Or shall I reheat it?"

Lucy eyed her half-eaten broth. She needed to have more, yet her stomach lurched. Fear of the future and worry over the past churned what contents remained there into a boil.

Her life was crumbling around her feet despite every effort she'd made to keep it upright.

"I'm sorry, I cannot eat more. My stomach turns."

Mrs. Dobbs took the bowl from her. "We'll try again later, dear. Best ye lay back and rest. Perhaps it was too soon."

Or too late for so many things. A flash of Abe's face hovered as weariness pressed upon her, and despite how she fought it, her eyes closed. Worry and fear crept in with her fatigue. Would Abe come back? Did he watch her even now?

Was that the door opening and closing? Her heart raced in her chest and she wished to scream but dizziness and confusion consumed her. She commanded her eyes to open, yet they wouldn't obey. Was she awake or asleep?

Muffled voices sounded, but she couldn't distinguish them. Panic set in, and Lucy tried to garner the strength to stop the racing images of fear bounding about her mind. Her eyes opened a sliver. Fuzzy shapes approached her.

Abe?

She wouldn't let him take her. Lucy batted the air until her arms collided with something hard. Hands encircled her wrists. Strong, masculine hands, and a man spoke to her in docent, soothing tones. Was it a trick? She couldn't give in or give up.

Not yet, not yet.

She couldn't let anything happen to Cil or Mrs. Dobbs. The old woman couldn't protect herself.

Can I?

"Miss Wycliffe? Please. Stop." Hands held her down on the bed. She fought and kicked. A hard thud landed on an arm or perhaps a leg, followed by a groan. After a pause, the words continued. "You are safe," a smooth baritone soothed. "No one will hurt you. Not again. I'm here. You're safe. Stop fighting me. Please, Lucy."

When she heard her given name, the subtle sweetness of it calmed her to the bone. She recognized the voice at last. Her name didn't sound as beautiful from any other man's lips. *John.*

He *was* here. She *was* safe. She stilled and settled against the bed, concentrating on his voice, using it as an anchor to bring her back from her panic. To help her eyes focus on something other than fear and chaos and fuzziness. Soon, the edges of objects formed, and after several breaths she could see him. *John.*

The planes on his face were tight and drawn, his brow furrowed as he studied her. Lack of sleep rested in the dark circles beneath his eyes.

When she smiled at him, his countenance relaxed and he smiled back. "There we are. Do you see me? Recognize me?"

She nodded, noting every handsome inch of him. The mere sight of him a balm to her spirit. With him here, she and Cil and Mrs. Dobbs were safe. Abe could not overpower him. Not this man, a pillar of strength, intelligence, and resolve.

Not this man she trusted perhaps more than she trusted her very self. And for reasons she didn't fully understand.

An idea bloomed. If there were a man alive who could solve her parents' case, it was John Brodie. And perhaps once this present case was closed, she would ask him for his help so she could find peace. So they could all find peace before she was forced to let her memories and this cottage go.

"Well, I'm glad to see you have some of your strength back." He shifted on his feet. "Seems you fell asleep again prior to my arrival. After I sent Mrs. Dobbs home, you went into a delusion. I think you believed Abe to be here again. You're safe though. I'm here."

The concern resting in his eyes warmed her. "I hope I didn't do or say anything too horrid. Seems I'm not quite myself yet."

He helped her into a sitting position. She couldn't resist leaning into his warm, strong grasp.

"I've heard far worse. Gave me a chuckle, seeing you so fiery." Laughter danced about his eyes as he settled into the chair beside the bed.

Just then, Cil stirred.

"Perhaps you could help me get up, Mr. Brodie," Lucy whispered. "I'd like to hear of your progress in the case, yet I've no wish to wake Cil."

He nodded. "If you agree to call me by my given name. John. Only when we are alone of course."

Warmth heated her cheeks. How she longed to, but she paused a beat before answering. "Yes. As long as you call me Lucy."

"Agreed." He flashed a bright, winning smile.

"Now, John, will you help me?"

"Of course."

~ ~ ~

John grasped her hand and gently pulled her to her feet. She toppled into his side, landing hard against his chest. *Bollocks.* His body responded at the feel of her. In only a thin night-rail and dressing gown, she pressed upon every part of him as his imagination lit like dry tinder. What would it be like to hold her? Kiss her?

This is a horrid idea.

He couldn't move, nor did he wish to. Clearly, neither did she, and in time his body relaxed. Her soft sigh tickled against his neck. John held his breath.

Breathe.

He blinked and handed her a woolen shawl with which to cover herself. Settling her back against his side, he wrapped his arm around her waist to support her as they walked out of the bedroom toward the glowing warmth of the hearth. The feel of her strong yet petite frame against him filled an emptiness he'd never noticed until now. He took slow steps and enjoyed the wholeness of the moments for as long as they would last.

Easing her into the chair, he warmed his hands by the fire to help them recover from the loss of her. Despite the whisper of space between them, it seemed too great when all he longed to do was hold her, protect her. And to never let her go.

He faced the licking flames of the fire.

And save her.

Worry spiked his pulse. He'd solved cases and he'd chased criminals, but he'd never been attached to the families or the victims. He could distance himself from it and see all the clues from a carefully detached perspective. On this case, he'd lost all of those things. He was too attached, too concerned, his perspective twisted in knots. Especially when he knew he had caused Lucy's past suffering and possibly the most recent attack.

Was someone punishing him by hurting her?

John shoved down the anger brewing in his gut. It was time to try to work on the case. He had to, no matter his guilt. No matter his attraction to her. She deserved his best efforts. So did the victims and their families. His emotions and his feelings for her would have to wait.

Studying her face, he smiled. "You seem better. Despite your confusion earlier, you've more color and spirit to be sure. The rest has helped, I think."

She frowned in response. "I wish I could say such for you. You seem tired. Worn through." She dropped her eyes to her lap and her fingers twisted the loose yarn from the shawl wrapped about her.

"Nothing for you to worry over."

She shook her head and lifted her gaze to him. "That is a lie to be sure. I can hear it in the timbre of your voice."

He balked. "Oh?"

Could she read the turn of his phrases and the pitch of his voice? Did this woman, of whom he'd been acquainted only a week, know him better than anyone in this world? Better than he knew himself? The idea of it excited and terrified him all at once.

"Yes."

"What else can you read from my words?"

"I think you would like my help but fear to ask for it. I am feeling better, and if I could help, I would improve even more quickly. I am poor in the area of patience and waiting. When I am busy, my mind and spirit are more at ease."

The fire popped as if in punctuation of her point.

"Much like myself, I'm afraid." He leaned against the mantel near the hearth and stuffed his hands in his trouser pockets.

"Then you understand." She smiled and the gift of it warmed him like hot tea on a cold day.

He nodded. Where did he begin? How much did he dare tell?

"What progress have you and Mr. Travers made?" she asked.

"Lots of interviews and poking about. A few leads. Fewer than I'd like. More things have gone missing from homes about town. However, no one has seen Abe, not in days. He visited with Miss Clara the day before the attack, and I believe he visited with his friend, a Bobby Dunn, at the tavern for supper, although I can't prove it. Not yet. Mr. Dunn has traveled out of town, it seems, and can't be reached anytime soon. I believe Abe broke in here a handful of hours later that evening, although no one has a guess as to what drove him to it."

Lucy shivered. John started to move toward her but checked himself. He could not comfort her, not as he wished to. Not here. Not like this.

Not ever.

"In my fits of sleep and rest," she said, "my mind has been turning over what happened. And what I don't understand is why he left it unfinished. Why did he leave Cil and me alive? He could have easily done us both in rather than merely knocking us aside. His singular focus seemed to be Miriam. He only attacked us because we stood in his way."

"Perhaps he lost his courage to kill you. You were friends since childhood."

"As was Miriam . . ." Lucy paused and furrowed her brow. "Although Cil and I never had any sort of attachment to him. Not in the way Miriam and Becca had. He had cared for both of them. Deeply. At one time, I believed one of them would marry him."

Curiosity sparking, John stepped away from the mantel and approached her. "Both of them?"

"I hadn't actually thought of it before now. He had courted Becca when we were in our teens, and Miriam for a short while in our early twenties." She nibbled her lower lip. "There was a time we all joked he did not know his own mind as to whom he adored more. So, they each gave up on him, not wanting to have a man so uncertain of his affections."

John rubbed the back of his neck. "Perhaps his affections turned to something far darker. As if he did not wish them to engage their hearts elsewhere, if they did not love him?" He'd seen the darker side of love and adoration in murder before. Abe could be the killer after all, and these murders a simple affair of spurned love.

His gut churned.

Fool.

He knew it was no simple affair. Not with the clues left

at his door. None of which he truly understood. Not yet, anyhow.

First, he needed to find Abe.

"Where would he have gone as a child if he was upset? Secret places to hide and such."

Lucy shook her head and met his gaze. "That's just it. When he argued with his parents or needed to get away a spell, he would go to the woods or come here. He found comfort in our home. And he was welcome here. Always."

She dropped her gaze and stared at her hands. Her smooth, capable fingers mesmerized him. As did all of her.

"Time unwinds parts of us," he mused. "Sometimes for the better, other times for the worse."

Sighing, she gazed into the fire. "And perhaps sometimes forever."

John clenched his fists at his side. *Lord above*, he longed to reach for her. Hold her. Do something other than talk to her and try to use his words to comfort her. But he couldn't. He didn't trust himself. And she deserved better.

"John," she began, "I know this is not the proper time, and I apologize for it. But I cannot bear to not ask it a moment longer." She met his gaze and her rocking chair steadied.

He stepped closer, his heart thundering in his chest. The fact she would ask him for help and feel some trust in him made his spirits lift. Finally, he could do something to make amends for what his brother had done. For what *he* had not done so long ago.

"You may ask me anything."

"It is an almost certainty my cottage will be Mr. Fiske's in a few weeks' time. I can run from the truth no longer. Nor can I endure the thought of leaving here not knowing what became of my parents. Of not knowing who killed them."

John froze. The very air seemed to choke him. His ears buzzed.

Her violet eyes fixed on him with certainty. *And trust.*

His stomach dropped.

"And *you* are the most capable man I know. A constable at that. Could you look into their case and see if you can discover the truth of who killed them? It would allow me to leave here in peace, for I will have put their souls to rest."

He would lose her forever once he uttered the truth. He would be lost and broken without her. He knew that now.

John gulped and sealed his fate. "Of course, Lucy. Of course."

Chapter 17
The Break-In

"You did *what*?" Travers asked as he paced alongside John on the walk back to town.

"Least I could do after all that's happened." John stared out into the distance at the tops of the evergreens bowing to the left and right with each angry slash of wind. The late afternoon hinted at more snow to come. They'd have scarcely enough time to get home before the next storm burst loose. With the doctor watching the ladies tonight, they could finally get a night's sleep before checking back in on them tomorrow morn.

As if John could sleep. His mind swirled with possibilities and clues. With guilt. And the dread of knowing once he told Lucy what he knew about her parents' death, she'd never speak to him again.

He'd be behind bars. Assisting a murderer had its price.

Since he didn't wish to imagine going back to a world without her, the prison sentence would matter little to him.

"Hell of a thing to do, Brodie." Travers interrupted the silence and spat on the ground. He nested his chin further into his wool scarf. As the wind whipped around them, he reached up to keep hold of his hat.

Mother Nature would be releasing some winter wrath in short order. John increased his stride, which Travers matched.

"How will you ever be able to keep such a promise to her?" Travers asked. "Do you not have enough worries to

settle out, with two women dead and a killer on the loose?"
He shook his head.

John didn't meet his gaze. Guilt would reflect off him
like sun on new frost. "I will keep it. I'm a man of my word."

"That's what I'm afraid of. Drive yourself to the grave
or get yourself killed. You're still a stranger here. Being a
constable won't help your case with these folks. They don't
trust you."

So why do you, Augustus? But John dared not speak it
aloud.

He shoved his hands in his coat pockets. "You think me
unaware of any of this?"

"No, which puzzles me. You are already in a twist with
the magistrate, pressured to solve one case, and you add on
another. You're no fool, so why?"

Yet, John *was* a fool when it came to her. To Lucy.
Always. Sleet began to fall, bounding off him like the truth
of Travers' words. They continued on.

"Ah, I see," Travers murmured.

John slowed and glanced over to him. "Did I miss
something?"

His companion chuckled and shook his head. "No, but I
did. She's a beautiful woman, and you're quite suited to her
temperament. You need explain no further. You *can't* say no
to her."

John sighed and rolled his eyes. "So transparent, am I?"

"Only to a man who's been smitten before. Best be
mindful of her. The woman has lost more than most of us.
And despite her independence and strength, she's vulnerable
after the attack. Don't take advantage." Travers' gaze settled
heavily on John.

"It is that sort of hurt I wish to protect her from."

Even if it's from me.

"Well, I guess we had better get some rest before we

tackle two cases," Travers smiled as they entered the edges of town.

John nodded. "I'll be heading up tomorrow around nine to check in on them. Feel free to join me."

"I will. Otherwise Ena would never let me hear the end of it."

John tipped his hat and carried on. As he neared his office door, gooseflesh rose along his skin. His heartbeat increased. The door gaped open. *Bloody hell.* Would he not be offered a moment's rest? He rushed to the door and peered inside.

"Lord above," he murmured, removing his hat and placing it on one of the remaining hooks still clinging precariously to the office wall.

Loose papers, scattered files, and half-open books lay strewn over the wooden floor. All of the evidence from the two cases he'd left out on his desk had been tossed down as well, scattered about like rubbish. As were the shattered remains of the glass holders and their contents. Even the sleigh bells, once snug on the back of the door, sat dull and silent in the corner.

Grabbing the bully club—left over from his London days as a detective—from his bottom desk drawer, John advanced slowly through the remaining room in a deliberate and watchful stance. Club at the ready for a full, heady swing, his pulse thundered in his ears. A musky, animal-like odor assailed him. Perhaps from a person who'd been out of doors, unable to seek out a bath.

Someone like Abe.

Had the bastard pillaged his office? Why? Hadn't he gotten what he'd wanted by taking Miriam? Destroying evidence would do him no good. The man had been seen. Lucy could identify him with ease. Why would he linger about town and do this? Why not scatter in the wind and disappear?

If the dumb bastard dared remain here, John would pummel him where he hid.

Glass crunched beneath his feet with every step, the broken watch and chain he'd found near the lake among it. He yanked the coat closet door open. Nothing. He released his breath and finished his search of the office. Except for the damage about him, it sat empty.

He eyed the partially lit staircase leading to his tiny bedchamber. Inching carefully up the first wooden step, John listened. Nothing. No one. Another step and a pause. Still nothing. He dared two steps in a row. Impatience spurred him on. Three more steps and he would be at the landing. Did the intruder dare wait at the top of the stairs?

John took another step, tightening his grip on the club as he climbed, the weight of it a familiar friend and comfort. He scanned the budding darkness. His leg muscle bunched and he clenched his teeth, silently holding his breath until the pain passed. Two more steps and he'd be at the landing. He paused.

Nothing.

Then he smelled it. The stark, strong stench of blood. His heart thundered in alarm. He hurried up the last two steps and scanned the room. Bedding and a few personal items lay scattered on the mattress or cast to the floor. The single charcoal sketch of his family lay smashed on the ground with its wooden frame and glass crushed.

Turning and peering at the wall behind him, he sucked in his breath.

The bully stick fell to his side.

In bold uneven red letters, the word "murderer" stared back at him.

In blood.

He only hoped it wasn't human, yet how would he know?

The killer was growing restless. Careless. Irrational. Angry.

Desperate.

The very worst kind of killer.

To break in during the day when anyone could have heard? It made no sense. And despite John's desire to investigate this crime, how could he? He couldn't explain the writing on the wall. Nor did *he* understand it. He was no murderer. Sure, he had protected one, his own brother long ago, but he'd never killed anyone outside of his time as a soldier or under due cause as an officer of the law.

Perhaps such a distinction didn't matter to this man.

But again, how would he ever know?

John sat on the edge of the bed. What was going on? Was he so close to the truth, he couldn't see it?

"Lord above." Glass crunched below. "Brodie?"

Travers.

John rose from the bed. "Coming down."

He took the stairs slowly. His bully club still rested at his side. Once he hit the landing, Travers studied him.

"What the hell happened in here?"

"Seems we're making someone angry. Or nervous, perhaps. Bastard broke in and tossed the place. Destroyed what sparse evidence we did have."

Travers set a bowl covered with a dishtowel on John's now empty desk. "Well, I can see that with my own eyes. Why?"

John shrugged and rubbed the back of his neck as fatigue crushed him. He couldn't solve this case alone. He couldn't protect Lucy alone. He'd take the risk and ask for help as he should have long ago when his brother killed the Wycliffes. He'd not lie and hide.

Not this time.

Deception only made matters worse. And more shame he couldn't bear. Nor could he endure any further loss of life.

"And the upstairs?"

"Same as here. He also left me a message."

"A message?" Travers closed the front door and crossed his arms against his chest, as if to anchor himself. No doubt John's body language betrayed his emotion.

"In blood."

Travers scrubbed a hand down his face. "And what did it say?"

"Murderer."

His friend stilled. A muscle ticked in his jaw. "Show me. *Now.*"

John arched a brow in alarm at the change in Travers' tone. "Why such a reaction?"

"Show me."

John started up the stairs. Travers followed, his anger evident in the thud of his boots behind him. Was he missing something, *again*? Irritation riddled him.

Reaching the landing, John stepped aside. Travers entered the room, stared over the chaos of clutter, and froze when he spied the dark letters on the wall. Moments ticked by as they stood in bleak silence.

It made John want to shout at the top of his lungs. Experience commanded him to wait. He had no other choice.

Finally, Travers turned.

"This is the reason no other Constables have taken this post."

"What?"

Travers sighed. "After Old Man Codger died, another man came, before Junior took on the post. He was driven away by similar means. Threats. Dead birds and the like left on the doorstep here. Codger Junior came on, but then abandoned his post as well. For similar reasons, I imagine. Fled to Scotland, so they say."

"Although gossip insinuates he went mad and lives in the woods."

"Then you *are* current on some of the stories."

"Yes. However, *this* one," John gestured to the wall,

"was conveniently omitted. No one has wanted to share with me about why this post had been so abandoned. Not the magistrate. Nor Miss Wycliffe."

"Do you blame them? Would you have come to such a place? With low pay, little to do, and threats to your safety on top of it all?"

John stood silent. If not for his wretched past, he knew the answer was no.

"That's what I thought." Travers neared the wall and sniffed, then cringed. "I'll gather some lye, and we can start scrubbing this off before it becomes even more wretched in here."

"I appreciate it."

"I'd brought you a warm dish. Assumed you hadn't eaten. Not sure you want it now with all this, but it's on your desk. Seems my daughter has inherited her mother's fine skills in the kitchen." Travers beamed with pride.

John couldn't help but smile. "Then I'll be sure to have some. Thank her for me."

Travers nodded and disappeared down the stairs. When the door rattled shut, John released a long, heavy sigh and scanned the room further. The missing pieces of this case grated along his skin. He closed his eyes.

Look at what's no' there, ye bastard.

The raspy-thick Scottish brogue of his old partner rang in John's ears. He missed him. Another man taken too soon from this world.

John opened his eyes and studied each portion of the room slowly. The intruder had taken time, it seemed, in selecting what to damage. Mostly John's personal effects. No larger pieces such as chairs or lanterns had been smashed or tossed. They had sought out what mattered to him and him alone, unlike the chaos of below. Why?

Walking about the room, he collected the busted frame, the few books of poetry and literature he owned, and set them back in their home on the rickety nightstand. Setting down the lantern, he paused again. Something was missing. He had his books, his framed sketch . . .

His heart dropped.

The box.

The small tin box his parents had given him long ago was gone. Yanking the bedclothes off the mattress and stooping to look under the nightstand and bed frame, he searched for it. Nothing. So, the person had taken another prize, it seemed.

But why?

The box had no real value outside of the tiny trinkets and memories it contained for him alone. A medal from his Royal Navy service, a silver St. Christopher's medal from his Nana, and a ring with his family's crest on it. The very crest that had disowned him, which he resented. His reminders of a past now gone.

The loss should have bothered him more. It didn't. The box and its contents served as mementos of mistakes more than anything else, as he never viewed it with joy or reverence. Perhaps the bastard had done him a favor.

Throwing the bedclothes back onto the sagging mattress, he heard something clatter to the floor.

When the object ceased rolling, John froze. A horrid chill sent gooseflesh along his skin. Shock consumed him.

Of all the things he'd found at a crime scene, he'd never seen this.

Walking slowly to it, he couldn't tear his gaze away. He'd seen one once after the war, but only then. And seeing it now on its own, staring back at him, sent every hair on his body on end.

He squatted, ignoring the slice of pain shooting along his thigh. Reaching out with a trembling hand, he picked it up, the cool weight of it a surprise in his palm.

Giving it one last glance, he sucked in his breath and tucked it in his trouser pocket.

Chapter 18
Pressure

A knock sounded at the door, and Lucy started. Pressing a hand to her chest, she almost laughed aloud. She hadn't been so afraid of her own shadow since she wore pigtails.

You're being ridiculous. Take a deep breath.

The doctor had only been gone a few minutes. Perhaps he'd changed his mind about gathering more medicine and decided to stay with them as he'd originally planned. Or perhaps John or Mr. Travers had forgotten something from earlier in the afternoon. There was no need to be afraid. She wasn't alone. A coil of relief bloomed in her chest as she rose from the rocking chair by the fire.

Pushing back the crisp new white curtain covering the cottage window, a gift from Mrs. Dobbs, Lucy smiled and glanced out. Her smile melted and panic crawled along her skin.

Fiske. Again.

What more could Lucy do to keep him at bay before he felt spurned like an old maid and called in her loan even earlier than planned? She cringed and let the curtain fall back.

"It's Fiske," Lucy hissed to her sister and Mrs. Dobbs. "What do I do?"

Mrs. Dobbs chuckled and stirred the stew cooking over the fire. "Well, he's done seen ye. Let him in, why don't ye. Sooner he's in, then the sooner he's gone."

Lucy couldn't help but laugh along with Cil. The old woman had a point, didn't she?

Pulling back her shoulders, Lucy smoothed her skirts, and opened the door. "Good evening, Mr. Fiske. Your visit is unexpected. Do come in. We were preparing our supper."

The portly man smiled, making his full cheeks even rounder. If only he were as full of kindness. "I won't stay long as I know you are still recovering. I commend myself on the timing of my visit." He sighed and placed a hand on his chest.

"Oh?" she asked, tugging at the strings of her apron.

"Perhaps an unorthodox gift, yet a gift all the same. I've brought a cut of meat for you. Doctor said you both needed to get some strength back after such an event." He regarded Mrs. Dobbs a moment before dropping his eyes from her. "I'm sure you understand, Mrs. Dobbs, I've brought only enough beef for the two of them. To be added to your . . ." He paused, sniffing the air. "Stew, of course." He smiled and placed the wrapped meat in Lucy's hands.

"Thank you, sir. It was kind of you to think of us."

"And perhaps we could have a moment in private, Miss Wycliffe?"

Lucy's heart thundered wildly in her chest. Wishing escape, there seemed no means of putting off their conversation. She nibbled her lip, and then went to grab her coat, hat, and gloves. "Fresh air will do a world of good for me, I'm sure."

And it should keep our conversation brief.

Spitting wind pushed her back as she opened the cottage door. Mr. Fiske grabbed his hat before it blew clear off his balding head.

Very brief. She stifled a smile.

"It shall be a quick exchange, Miss Wycliffe. I don't wish to cause you a setback in your recovery." He closed the door behind him, and they stood on the stoop, his presence so close she commanded herself to hold her ground and not step back.

He settled himself and took a breath. "No doubt you know my intentions for you remain as they have over the course of the last few months, Miss Wycliffe. If you would agree to my proposal, we could wed within the fortnight and all of these worries you have pressed upon you now would melt away. I am a man of means as you know, and I am not unkind. I would allow your sister and child to stay on at their cottage until she found other means to support herself, and all of the many things you have denied yourself for so long, such as a family, security, and good standing among society, will be given to you freely."

Freely?

By selling her very soul and happiness to the devil? By chaining herself to Fiske forever?

She'd prefer a beggarly death.

"I fear I cannot marry you, Mr. Fiske. However, I am flattered by your constancy and kindness."

His eyes flared in irritation, and he frowned. "Then your note will be due by the end of the month. If you cannot secure the balance, you will be cast out."

She gritted her teeth. "But I'm allowed more time, sir."

"Actually, I may call in your loan whenever I wish, and I wish to see it repaid in full in five days. If you don't have it, you will be cast out. Am I clear?"

"Cast out even in a snowstorm, sir?"

"Yes. Even then. I am a man of business, and I have buyers waiting to secure this as soon as it becomes available." He lifted his eyebrows.

Lucy laughed aloud. "Buyers? For this cottage? In Clun? You lie."

Stepping closer to her, he grasped her elbow. *Hard.* Pain seared up her arm as she struggled to free herself. He merely increased the pressure of his hold. "I can also tear it to the bloody ground, if I wish. It matters not to me. I hold no attachments to it." He released his hold so abruptly, she fought to maintain her balance.

Her lungs and throat burned with every jagged breath. Fear made her limbs tingle. What had she done? Five days marked the end of the month. She'd never have near enough to save the cottage. And he would throw her out into the cold during the dead of winter.

Horrid little man.

She could find another place to go, and so could Cil and Norah Jane, but Lucy didn't want to leave. Not yet. She had to know what had happened to her parents and who had taken Miriam. And discover the killer walking among them. She blinked back the tears that burned her eyes in the biting wind. She wouldn't cry. Not today. Far too many other things needed her full attention.

~ ~ ~

A hard knock sounded on the door of the office.

Closing his eyes, John gnashed his teeth and let his head loll back. "Bollocks."

Who is it now?

He was in no mood to deal with anyone. He'd scarcely been able to be civil to Travers as they worked to scrub the stains from his bedroom wall. The whole building now reeked of lye, yet he preferred it to the stale stench of blood. He rose from the desk he still worked to set to rights and counted to calm himself. As he reached thirty-one, he glanced out the door window.

Magistrate Kieran.

He should have counted to a thousand.

Ignoring his instinct, he scowled, clutched the doorknob, and yanked it open. Self-preservation no longer coursed along his veins. Kieran could fire him with the flick of his wrist; a truth John no longer cared a whit about. He was angry. Tired. Frustrated. All he wanted was time to solve this case. The murdered women deserved resolution and peace. So did Lucy.

"I'm pleased to see you awake and at work, Constable, despite the late hour." Kieran sniffed and leaned against his walking stick. His black hansom, with driver and horses, had stopped at the bridge. John had no idea how he hadn't heard the man's approach. Few men about Clun traveled in such blatant excess or at such a late hour. It screamed of his level of distraction and disregard, which only annoyed him further.

"What can I do for you, sir?" John strained for civility. His leg throbbed with pain and his mind was coiled tight as a spring.

Kieran leaned to his left, peering over John's shoulder. "Quite untidy. Although I know some people work best in chaos and disorder. And the smell . . ." He scrunched up his nose.

John imagined ripping the walking stick from Kieran's hand and clubbing him in the head with it. He leaned against the door frame instead. "Seems someone burgled it while I was out, searching for something. I'm trying to right it back to the order you mention. It is what I prefer."

"Oh? Bad luck. Any news on the case?"

"Nothing new to report, sir. I will be sure to update you when I have a development." He shifted his weight on his feet and the object in his trouser pocket slid along his thigh, becoming colder by the minute.

A reminder time worked her magical hands against him.

"Disappointing. My wife has put all of the arrangements for my daughter's party in motion. It will be an event not to be missed. Well, except by those uninvited, of course. I'll expect a conclusive end to all of this, prior to then." He readjusted his hat. "Carry on."

"Will do, sir." John didn't wait for a reply. He shut the door firmly. After he locked it, he kicked some glass further into the room. "Pompous ass."

How could he possibly solve this in less than two weeks? What clues he'd had were now destroyed. The killer, or someone who hated the law and what he represented, threatened him at every turn. And there was so much he didn't know or understand about Clun and its people. How could he determine the killer if he couldn't piece together a firm picture of why the man killed? What could those two women have possibly done to deserve such a death?

He stilled and stared at the clues scattered about the floor.

"What if they didn't do anything to deserve it?" he said aloud.

He scrubbed his hand down his face and paced the room. What if they *were* random? Merely killed to serve a purpose, but little else.

If they didn't deserve it and there was no motive, then why? What was this case truly about?

Chapter 19
Nightfall

John tried to work. He'd even taken off his coat to settle in at his desk after removing the shards of glass and chaos of papers once strewn about his floor. Concentration eluded him, and he'd vibrated with energy for a full quarter hour before he gave into his gut impulse to go out in the snowy, shadowy night, and journey back to the Wycliffes' cottage. It was a fool thing to do, travel by night alone with a killer on the loose, but recklessness fueled him as if he'd drunk a bottle of whiskey.

With every step, the object he'd discovered in his room banged heavily against his bad leg, a needed reminder of the importance of solving this case sooner rather than later. The killer grew more dangerous every hour, and what he'd do next was a mystery.

And John needed to get a step ahead of the man. He'd not order another grave dug. He refused. Unless it was for the killer. Then, he would help dig such a grave himself. He smirked. With a bloody teaspoon if need be.

The snow swirled around him, and he tugged the brim of his hat down low as he nestled his chin into the high flipped up collar of his wool coat. The walk to Lucy's home had become second nature. He could as easily recognize the shape of the road and the crests of the bare tree limbs, as he would have the buildings back near his old station close to Hyde Park. He'd only been here a short while, yet he felt he belonged in Clun as much now as in boyhood, long ago. But he was no longer a boy, was he? What he did here now was far from a childish game. The lives of those around him were at stake, and he'd be wise to remember it.

The cold air burned his throat and lungs as he sucked it in, and the smell of smoke from a chimney greeted him. He smiled. A faint glow from the hearth and a single candle burned within the cottage, throwing a whisper of illumination through the window and onto his downy path. He shouldn't have been so relieved by the sight of it, but he was.

His steps faltered in the snow as he eased up the last few steps to the door, and he almost stopped and turned back. Would she think him daft to intrude at such a late hour? What remained of the moon shone high. What *was* he even doing here?

What a lie.

He knew the reason; he couldn't wait until morning, for the proprieties of the day. Questions burned and banked along his gut. Nor could he stay away for fear of their safety. Her safety. Lucy's safety.

John hesitated on the doorstep. Shifting on his feet, he tried to peer into the cottage. The makeshift curtain blocked his view. Should he knock?

Before he could decide, the curtain whipped back. John started and stepped back. Lucy pressed a hand to her chest and smiled, one which he could not fail to return, despite the worry churning along in his sour gut. Her pleasure at seeing him banished all of his doubt and the air from his lungs.

The door eased open gently. "Has something happened?" Lucy whispered. She stepped outside without a coat into the cold and rubbed her arms. She pulled the door closed behind her.

Blast.

Why had he come? They were fine without him. His presence would only thrust them back into worry and unease. "Travers and I adjusted our plan. We decided to stagger our stays, so one of us could be with you at all times until the man is found." Even to his own ears it sounded weak. Idiotic, even. The object in his pocket had grown colder and stung his leg. A reminder there was a reason. A huge reason he'd come.

Fear.

~ ~ ~

"Well then, come in." Lucy forced a smile. Her pulse throbbed double time. John was troubled, which worried her. Lines pulled down the corner of his mouth and his body was tight, his stance rigid. Until he told her what plagued him, she'd make him some tea. It might even calm her own weary nerves.

"Cil and Mrs. Dobbs retired hours ago, yet sleep eludes me. As perhaps it does you. Tea? I've just made a pot."

"Yes. Thank you." He removed his coat and hat and added them to the hooks on the wall. "I apologize for the hour. I don't wish to wake them."

"They are heavy sleepers, and I've closed the bedroom door, so as to block the candlelight. Do not worry yourself." She gestured for him to sit by the fire, which he did.

"Where is Doctor Sykes?"

"Left for more medicine. We told him he needn't return until the morn. We felt safe enough with the three of us."

He frowned at her.

Did he see through my lie?

She felt anything but safe.

"Are you unwell?" he asked. "I worry you haven't been resting since the attack." He leaned forward in his chair, studying her, awaiting an answer.

Did she dare tell him the truth?

She poured the tea and brought him a cup. When he accepted it from her, their hands touched. His fingers skimmed along her own, igniting tiny pinpricks over her skin. How long she reveled in it before she pulled away, she didn't know. She flushed and turned to get her own cup of tea in an attempt to remember herself.

"Tell me why you are troubled. Please." The soft tones of his voice tugged at her resolve, the added *please* crushing any additional resistance.

To be able to tell someone—other than her sister—her burden would be a relief, wouldn't it?

Lucy clutched the warm mug in her hand. "Mr. Fiske came to see me today. Brought me a package of meat to add to our stew. It was quite delicious."

John settled back into his chair. "Mr. Fiske, the banker?"

"Yes. Concerned for our recovery, he said. And since he, along with everyone else, is well aware of what we lack financially . . ." She dropped her gaze and traced a fingertip along the rim of her cup. Her stomach curdled with shame. "He also proposed to me. And then reminded me of the note coming due. As if I needed any additional reminders." She muttered the last few words into her tea.

"Sorry, did you say he *proposed* to you?" John stared at her, openmouthed. His dark gaze penetrated her very being.

"Yes. This is his third attempt. And I know it would ease our burden to accept his offer. Yet, I find I cannot give up my life, what I do, and my happiness only to keep this cottage. I do not love him, and I would wither under his control." She sighed and shifted in her chair. Admitting this to him pained her. As if it were a betrayal, a weakness she was hiding from him. And perhaps it was.

"I know it is not my place, but you . . ." He faltered. "You deserve the best of men. A man who will treasure your gifts." He looked away and took a long sip of his tea.

If only you would be that man.

They sat in silence so long, her skin itched. He was preoccupied with something. The case, perhaps? She ventured a guess to ease the tightness in the air.

"Are you here about the case? Has something new happened?" She offered a weak smile. "You seem . . ." She paused. "Not quite yourself."

John sighed and his shoulders drooped forward. "Yes, there has been a development, and I'm unused to working alone. I know Travers has agreed to help, but he doesn't have your degree of understanding of the body and attention to detail. And since you have lived here all of your life, you also know every bit of information I could ever want to know about Clun and its people. Are you well enough for me to ask you more questions? I worry the killer is still too far ahead of me, and I wish to catch him before . . ."

"Before someone else is hurt?"

"Yes, precisely."

Some other unspoken question rested behind the smooth darkness of his eyes, but he wouldn't speak it. Not yet. And part of her said to wait. In time, he would unwind the entire truth to her of what plagued him and haunted him this eve. Until then, she just nodded.

"The killer broke into my office and upstairs room today. Destroyed much of the evidence we had collected and tossed the place in search of something."

Shocked, Lucy brought her rocking chair to a sudden halt. "Are you well? Was anyone hurt? Did anyone see anything?"

He smiled and chuckled at her rapid-fire questions. "Yes, I am well. And no one was hurt, nor did anyone hear or see anything, despite it happening during the day, or early evening before I arrived." He hesitated a moment. "The lock remained undamaged, and I know I secured it before I left."

"So, someone had a key or broke in with some skill?" She nibbled on her lower lip.

"My thoughts exactly." He took a sip of tea and continued with a smile. "You have a keen mind for inquiry work."

Heat and pride warmed her skin. John was the first man to praise and acknowledge her intelligence since she was a girl. Her father had said she was quick and bright, and he'd always wished for her to pursue a passion, no matter what it was.

Become something, he'd said. *Be something you desire to be, long to be. Let the world, let society be hanged if they don't like it. You, my girl, deserve the world.*

Loss cut a pain through her chest, hot and hard, the agony as new as the night she'd found him here, dead and sprawled out beside her mother, his last act an attempt to protect her, it seemed. Even now Lucy could remember how his fingers had clawed marks into the wood, reaching out to her mother desperately.

She gasped for breath.

"I'm sorry if I've upset you," John muttered, urgency ringing his voice as he sat at the edge of his chair.

At his watchful, heavy stare, Lucy stood, moving to the fire, turning her back to him. She could not face him and say the truth for fear of his response. What if he did not understand? Thought her unnatural as so many already did? She didn't know if she could endure his rebuff of her desires, her longings.

"No, it's me. Old ghosts from long ago. I appreciate your words. No man, other than my father, has ever complimented me on my mind." She picked at the edge of the peeling wood of the mantel before finally turning to face him. "Most men find what I do odd and wish me to abandon it. Even Cil and Miss Clara have warned I am throwing away my chance at a family by rejecting Mr. Fiske. Of being a dutiful wife and blessed mother. What I do, what I long to do, what I am so frightfully skilled at, is *this.*"

She gestured with both hands at the room, the only home she'd ever known. "Preparing bodies for the next world. Giving families peace. And now that I've had a taste of what it would be like to be an inquiry agent, a detective, even as my role as an assistant to you, I am even more reluctant to relinquish. Even when the hounds like Fiske charge at me threateningly." She laughed and took a shaky breath. "I wonder if I am mad."

John set his tea on the floor, and approached, his expression full of emotion. He stood so close, so achingly close, yet not touching her. Could he hear her heart vibrating in her chest? Feel the longing that made her bones ache at the sight of him?

They stood and stared into one another's eyes for long moments, and he reached for her hand. The warm, rough texture of his fingers, the strength of them around her own, sent a thousand sparks through her.

"You are not mad," he murmured. "You astound me in every way, Miss Wycliffe, and there are moments when I think . . ." He paused and swallowed, stepping closer until the heat from his body pressed against her and warmed her. "When I believe, you, Lucy, are the most amazing woman, the most beautiful and real creature I have ever known."

The world fell away, except for him. She couldn't speak. Had she imagined the words falling from his lips? Did he admire her, care for her, as a woman outside of her role as his assistant? Could a gentleman such as he dare to feel admiration for her, a woman of no means and rather unusual skills?

His other hand rose and skimmed along her cheek, cupping her chin. Her lips parted and her heart raged within her chest. He leaned in and kissed her, gently, so gently her lips ached with wanting more. She had been kissed once before, a sloppy, rather wet affair, but *this* . . .

This kiss scored heat down to her toes. Her body grew hot with desire.

She'd not known it could ever be like this. She leaned into him and kissed him back. He pressed against her and deepened the kiss, caressing and kneading the back of her neck with his fingers. How long they were like this, intertwined and in their own world, she didn't know.

When he finally released her, he rested his forehead against her own.

"I'm sorry. I forget myself, Lucy. You seem to have loosened a knot in me that cannot be retied." His breath puffed warm and delicious upon her cheeks. His fingers traveled along her hair, to rest upon her neck.

She smiled, enjoying the feel of him. "Please don't apologize, John. I am happy to forget and be lost in such a place." And she meant it. This man understood her, appreciated her, and longed for her exactly as she longed for understanding, for appreciation and love. He was a miracle amongst all of the chaos and death around her.

He pulled back and studied her, his hands still resting on her shoulders. Curiosity swam in his eyes. "To be lost in a place with me? This battered remnant of a man with so very little to offer you?" He shook his head. "I must be imagining your words from fatigue."

She gripped his forearms. "Any woman would be pleased with your affections. You are a good, decent man who wishes to bring good to the world and soothe people from the greatest tragedies of their lives. You seek truth and find it, no matter the cost. What woman would not wish to bind themselves to a man like that?"

"You make me wish to be such a man, but I am not him. Not yet."

"Oh?" She released her grip, and he stepped away, returning to his chair. Following his lead, she retook her seat. "Well, I will wait for you until you are, John Brodie. I find I am a very patient woman. And you . . ." She commenced rocking in her chair. "I find you will be worth waiting for."

Chapter 20
The Interviews

"I'm relieved to see you agreed to travel with me to these interviews this morn." John risked a glance at Lucy as they walked. Her arm rested in the crook of his own, the same as every other day as he led her along the familiar road to Miss Clara's. Except it was a new day. Things were different. He had kissed her, and she had kissed him back. The words they had shared wove a new thread between them. A thread he feared might fray under the strain of the future. And truth be told, he *was* a rogue for kissing her last night despite how much he'd enjoyed it.

"Perhaps I need remind you I am no wilting primrose, sir. As I said yesterday, I will wait for you to recognize the man you are. The man I have seen you to be. Despite the kiss, our working relationship remains unchanged to me. We have a killer to catch and poor Miriam to find and put to rest." She nudged him in the side. "And you will get close to nowhere without my help with the locals. Despite how odd some may think me, I am still a local which puts me higher than an outsider. Especially a man as yourself from London."

He smiled. Lucy surprised him every moment with her mind, her candor, her ability to speak the truth and her emotions without reservation. He wished to be so at ease with himself. One day, perhaps he would be.

With her.

If she ever forgives me for the truth I haven't yet revealed.

He sighed, not wishing to tell her, ever. Even though he knew down to his core he had to. She, of all people in this world, deserved the truth and the peace to go along with it. He only needed to be brave enough to tell her. And brave enough to accept whatever consequences came of it. His stomach hardened at the thought of losing her.

A consequence he didn't wish to face.

"Who all are we interviewing today, Constable?" Lucy smiled at him, interrupting his own malaise. When kicked a chunk of snow and it flew up in a fluffy, powdery cloud before cascading to the ground, her carefree action made him smile.

"We'll speak to Miss Clara first," he replied. "Based on what she provides us, we'll know where to go next to seek out Abe. He is the key to this and to finding Miriam. Allowing her to be buried properly to provide some peace for her family is first on my list. Then, we can find the bastard and string him up for what he's done."

"I worry he is no longer the man we seek."

"I'm surprised to hear you still have doubts, even though he attacked you." John perused her closely. "Why? You must have good reason."

"As I told you before, he is not that sort of creature. He never has been. He is perhaps odd and awkward and not totally at ease with the ways of society, but so am I. Having known him all of my life, I cannot imagine him hurting either of them."

Nor had I expected my brother capable of it, either.

But there he had stood with weapon in hand, bludgeoned bodies beneath.

People were capable of the worst of things. Even people one loved. John knew this to be true with every fiber of his being. Lucy still found hope and goodness in everyone, a trait he admired.

A trait he had lost long ago.

"I understand your doubt. I do." He cleared his throat. "He is someone you love and care for. But I ask you to remember the fear and horror you felt the day he attacked you and your sister in your home." John tugged her to a stop and turned her to face him. Wisps of her hair drifted across her face, and he resisted the urge to tuck them away behind her ear. "Would you ever want anyone else to feel or experience the same? Your sympathy and compassion for him cannot override your reason when you work a case. Otherwise, it can hinder you to the truth. No matter how dark, ugly, and uncomfortable it may be."

She dropped her gaze and nodded. "I know." A trace of sadness rested in the downturned corners of her eyes when she raised them to his. "I hate to give up on people. I know what it feels like. I will try to be more objective as Miriam deserves. So does Becca. Best we keep moving," she offered and added a shiver.

John bent his head as the wind raged, and pressed his chin into the collar of his coat. "Seems this cold is meant to last." The old snow crunched beneath his boots. The low temperatures last night had frozen any slush and water the mere bit of sun yesterday had dared melt.

"Mrs. Dobbs says it will warm in the next two days. Says she feels it in her aching bones." Lucy edged closer to him as another gust of wind blew. "Does your leg trouble you when the weather changes?"

If another man had asked, he would have bristled, yet her questions didn't prick the same way. Concern rested in her lilting tones, not sympathy. That sort of care and concern, he longed for even if he didn't deserve it.

"Yes. I do my best to ignore it. I know I'm fortunate to be alive after my time overseas. Other men were not so lucky."

She nodded. "Several of the older men of Clun had fought and had trouble, especially in their later years, with their memories, as well as their injuries."

"Not uncommon, I'm afraid."

"Father used to try to help them. He'd talk with them for hours, attempting to ease their burdens. It often helped little, but he always tried. He was relentless in that way. Always on the quest for a solution no matter the issue."

John chuckled. "Sounds like you may have inherited your resolve from him."

She smiled. "Thank you. I'll take the compliment. I do enjoy a good puzzle to be solved."

"Keep that in mind as we interview Miss Clara." He gestured toward the dark cottage looming before them. It offered no semblance of life except for the smoke puffing from her chimney. "Some of the questions may seem unkind to you. Remember, they are only meant to get to the truth of it."

She stiffened against him. "I'll try, although the way you state what must be done makes me cringe within."

She released his arm and cold loss flooded him. Clearing her throat, she knocked on the wooden door. When there was no response she knocked again, much louder this time. "Miss Clara," Lucy called. "We know you are here. I see the smoke from your chimney. We have some questions for you."

When there was still no sound within, she grimaced and added one last plea. "Please. For Miriam."

Footfalls echoed and grew louder as they reached the door, followed by a pause.

"That Constable with you?" the old woman asked.

"Yes. It's his job to find Miriam, remember?"

Another long pause ensued, and John garnered his patience. No amount of force would work on Miss Clara, nor would it help her willingness to tell him the truth. He studied the grain of the wood and noted the weathering, but by all other accounts her cottage stood in good repair. No doubt due to the help of others, Abe being one of them. She would be reluctant to say a word against the man.

Perhaps John could appeal to her equal bits of loyalty toward the women she'd known since they were girls.

"Well, remind him I'm an old woman, and I can't afford to have him block my heat like last time. Otherwise, he'll have another death to deal with."

"I hear you, Miss Clara. I'll take care with where I stand." John couldn't help but smile as he responded. He understood Lucy's devotion to the old woman, as difficult as she might be. Her mettle was enviable. No doubt a reason she'd survived this long alone.

"And mind yer boots."

"Yes, ma'am." Parroting Lucy's actions, John tapped the snow from the bottom of his boots. The door squeaked open, and he followed her inside.

Today, the heat of the cottage was a blessing, and he appreciated how it hit him instantly, as if he stood before an open stove. He began to remove his hat, scarf, and gloves. Several books and items were scattered out of place. The disorder plucked his interest.

Lucy caught his stare and shrugged. Her furrowed brow, the quirked corner of her mouth, showed her puzzlement as well. Despite being blind, Miss Clara's house had been tidy upon their last visit. What had changed?

"How have you been?" Lucy ventured as she added her coat, scarf, and gloves next to his on the hooks along the wall.

Miss Clara sat in her chair and began rocking back and forth. No knitting rested in her lap, and she worried her hands upon the shawl wrapped around her rounded shoulders. Something had her world on end, however small her world was. John stepped aside, allowing Lucy to take the other lone chair in the room. He nodded for her to continue.

"You seem troubled." Lucy's words tumbled out in a hurry.

Miss Clara's rocking stopped. She stared into the fire, crackling hot and bright before them. "Abe is gone. Haven't seen him for days. No' since the day after he broke into yer cottage."

"Does he often disappear for days at a time?" John asked.

"No' without telling me, he doesn't. Something's no' right. My gut tells me so." She sniffed and frowned. Her eyes darted back and forth.

"Did he tell you something? About the women, about Miriam?" Lucy's questions held emotion and desperation.

"No," she answered. "But I smelled her on him."

John froze. "What do you mean? How could you *smell* her on him?"

She began rocking again, in a quick, restless pace. "It's how I know who's here in my home. I can smell them. I know Miriam's smell, just as I know yers, Lucy. And, Abe . . ." She paused with a gulp. Her voice trembled in the air. "And he smelled like her. As if she were here in this very room. He'd been with her. Somehow."

Understanding dawned on John, and he tucked his hands in his trouser pockets. His fingers brushed against the cool object still housed there. "And when you asked him such, he became angry? Is that why many of your belongings are tousled about and not where they usually are?"

Miss Clara wiped at a tear on her cheek and nodded. "Batted about in here like a caged bird until I ordered him to leave. He kept saying I didn't understand what was happening, what was *still* happening. Said he didn't kill either of them. Something about having to save Miriam from the tomb of the earth and keep her safe. Nonsense, all of it."

Lucy stared at her openmouthed. No doubt Miss Clara's words had shocked her as they had him. Why would the man confess to stealing a woman's body, yet not killing her? It made little sense. Hell, it made no sense. Not to his mind.

But he was not a killer, was he?

"Do you know where he might have gone? Does he have

places he hides when he needs to? Places he could be alone. With her, perhaps?" John's questions belied his desperation.

"He kept muttering on about her needing to be in a place fitting for her beauty. Where she could see the stars. Where they could be together finally after all these years. He's gone mad, I tell you. The sickness of the mind has seized him, like it has others in this town."

"Others?" John's curiosity pricked to a fine point. "Who else has had such a sickness?"

"'Tis no secret them Codgers have some of it in their blood. It's what I think happened to Junior. His mother thinks she's fooling us with her talk of her son running away up north to Scotland. Nonsense. They've no cousins there for him to be visiting. And the Magistrate. His tree has branches that have been severed off and disowned. But the blood's still there. It's always there. Bad blood, I tell you."

"Does Abe have any other friends he might seek out?" Lucy asked.

"You know, as well as I, he only worked and visited the bunch of you when he could, then kept to himself. Liked the woods, the sky, and silence mostly."

The old woman stared off into the darkness. Her hands rested in her lap. She'd unleashed her burden and seemed at peace now. If only John felt the same. Dread roared in his chest. Not only did he not know where to look for Abe, he had no idea what the man would do next.

Or if he was even the killer at all.

Chapter 21
Assembling Clues

"I'm sorry our chats with the Lusks and Cunninghams didn't yield much of interest," Lucy murmured as she walked alongside John back to her cottage.

"Sometimes what we don't find is as useful as what we do." John squinted into the sky. "Perhaps the sun will shine light on more clues just as she has warmed us along our journey."

"Quite a romantic at times, aren't you?" Lucy smiled at him. Happiness danced in her eyes, and it nearly stole his breath. He'd never seen such joy on her face before. It slayed him to his core.

"Perhaps I should wax poetic more often if it brings a smile to your lips."

"I hope you will." She snuggled closer to him as they walked, and he took a shuddering breath. How would he ever tell her the truth about him? He shoved the ugly reality aside and reveled in the feel of her joy and warmth next to him.

He'd enjoy it while it lasted.

"Perhaps you'd like to join me and Travers as we analyze what few clues we have? We've plans to meet at my office within the hour."

"I wish I could, but I've left Cil with Mrs. Dobbs too long as it is. I love the old woman, but she can talk you into submission given the chance. She has more stories than I scarce imagined possible. However, I am forever indebted to her for her help. As I am for yours. Not only are you working this case but also the case of my parents. It helps put me at ease and at peace with letting go of the cottage."

He frowned. "So, you've given up the fight to keep it? I'm surprised. Doesn't seem like you." He stared straight ahead. He dared not meet her gaze or he'd give himself away with his guilt.

"This morn when I woke, I felt so peaceful with the thought of letting this place, these bad memories go. It's time. I've allowed myself to be trapped by the fear of losing the cottage. As if I would lose my parents once more along with it, but I won't. They are in my heart, not a place. It just took me a near death encounter to realize it."

"Where will you live? What will you do?"

"I don't know, and despite the panic I should feel about it, I don't. Perhaps it has something to do with you, and your confidence in me and my abilities. I am grateful for it."

He couldn't speak as his body continued moving toward her cottage.

What did he say? What *could* he say?

They walked on in silence, and he escorted her to the cottage door. Her sister waved at them from the front window. She opened the door before Lucy could knock.

"So glad to see you, sister. Please join us." She nodded and reached for Lucy's hand, tugging her inside, her enthusiasm at seeing her a reflection of Lucy's prediction. John smothered a smile when he heard Mrs. Dobbs' voice lilting in the background in a stream of unending words.

Lucy's sister smiled weakly and dropped her voice. "She's scarce taken a breath since you've left."

"I'll leave you then, Miss Wycliffe. Travers will come by before nightfall to stay with you. Until tomorrow." John tipped his hat but his words sounded hollow and empty. Panic ate at him. Was Lucy changing her life for him? Did she think their kiss meant something more?

Lucy glanced back at him and smiled. His heart sank to his toes.

Only this morning, he'd hoped she'd seen his kiss and intentions with affectionate meaning. Yet worry now consumed him. What if his actions or inactions ruined her life?

Again.

He sighed and turned down the walking path back to the road. At least the sun finally shone. The warmth and light should clear his head. Shoving aside his worries about Lucy's future, he quickened his pace, ignoring the strain on his leg. He needed to start puzzling this case together before something else far more dreadful happened.

Like another murder.

~ ~ ~

Travers joined John only a few minutes after he'd reached his office. Thankfully he hadn't been burgled again since he'd left for the day. He'd even checked his bedroom chamber upstairs, and it appeared untouched. For now.

"Tell me you discovered Abe's whereabouts," Travers demanded as he closed the front door behind him. The clanging bells fell silent as his friend rounded the corner. When he met John's gaze, he frowned. "By that look, I'd say you didn't."

John gestured for Travers to take the chair on the other side of his office desk. "I didn't. However, there were some interesting bits."

Travers settled himself and nodded. "Go on."

"Miss Clara had seen him the day after he broke into the Wycliffe cottage. She said she could smell Miriam on him."

Travers blinked, rubbing his beard. "Ah, say again?"

"Seems Miss Clara can identify the people she knows by their smell. As a way of keeping herself safe, I imagine.

Said she could smell Miriam on him, and he admitted he'd taken her from the cottage, yet he denied killing her. Or Miss Lusk."

"Jesus." Travers leaned back heavily in his chair. "So he stole her, but claims he didn't kill her?"

"It seems so."

"Is he disturbed in the mind?"

"Perhaps. I've not met the man. You have. What's your read on him?"

Travers shrugged. "Seemed normal to me. Quiet. Kept to himself but came in when he needed odds and ends for himself or Miss Clara. Was she well when you visited her?"

"She was clearly shaken. Claimed she'd questioned him about Miriam, and he became upset, tossed some of her things about, and left. She doesn't know where he went." John scratched his head. "Or where Miriam is."

"What's the fool going to do with a body if he doesn't wish to bury it?"

"I fear he may use the weather to attempt to preserve her."

Travers squinted at him. "And do what with her?"

"Seems he had deep affection for the girl. Her death may have unraveled him, caused a break in his mind. Perhaps he wishes to keep her in a place where he, and he alone, can be with her. Worship her, in a sense." John stood and walked over to the map of Clun hanging behind his desk. "Where would he be able to do such a thing?"

Travers rose and muttered something about Joseph and Mary as he made his way to stand beside John. "There's abandoned buildings here and there on some of the farms, but no place of worship like a church if that's what you mean." Travers rubbed his chin.

"Those don't seem special enough. The man has gone to some considerable trouble. He'd planned Miriam's abduction and had to have a place in mind before he took her from the cottage. Plus, something had to have triggered him to act now, if he'd never had such an episode before."

"That we know of," Travers added quickly.

John turned to him. "Have you had other strange disappearances before?"

"Only the Constable before you, and you know all about that one. And you know about the murder of Lucy's parents. Other than those two, I can't remember any other missing folk or gruesome crimes. Perhaps you should talk to Ena. She's lived here a long while. And she seems to know all of the happenings in this town even if she wasn't here when it happened. Woman is full of stories."

"A great idea, Travers. First thing tomorrow, I'll stop in and speak with her."

"You may regret such a decision."

"If it helps me find Abe, it will be worth every minute."

"You're a good man, Brodie." Travers clapped him along the back.

John nodded. "Not as good as I wish to be."

Chapter 22
The Truth

A shot ripped through John's leg. The hot burning stench of his own flesh and blood and the sour acid on his tongue gagged him as he hit the ground. Shouting and gunfire continued. Chaos and confusion surrounded him as a bullet whizzed by him and drove deep into the dirt. A spray of earth kicked up near his face. He blinked and started to crawl with what strength he had left. If only he could get to the downed tree for some cover.

~ ~ ~

Knocking shook John from a deep, heavy slumber and from the shores of a battle fought long ago. His heart thundered in his chest; his shirt stuck to his skin, soaked in sweat. What time was it? Had he overslept? He blinked against the sunlight filling his room. *Blast.* He had.

He clambered out of bed. Too quickly. His bad leg gave way, and he landed with a thud on the cold floor.

Seemed the day would not be quite what he'd planned.

"Brodie?" Travers' loud tones shattered the silence from outside.

"Bloody hell," John cursed, and rubbed his leg. He grimaced as the muscle strained beneath his flesh.

"So you're awake. I'll wait." Travers' laugh only added to John's irritation.

His mind whirled with the remnants of his dream as he struggled to catch his breath and slow his heartbeat. And get off the floor. Running a hand along his damp hair, he rested on the hardwood. Would he ever rid himself of the memory? It was long ago, like his memory of Lucy's parents, yet his soul seemed unwilling and incapable of letting go of those most horrid moments of his past. The mind was nasty that way.

Just like fate.

He anchored himself up, leaning heavily on his arm. Lucy's sweet face and bell of laughter rang in his head and a pit opened in his stomach. How much longer could he avoid telling her the truth? Yet, whenever he thought of confessing, the coward in him nudged it away, covering the truth back up with shame as thick and suffocating as black tar.

If only his past could wander about and fall straight down, disappearing in a nearby peat bog like some lost, unsuspecting being. There it would never be found, but it would be preserved, wouldn't it? Found one day by some other stranger. Someone not so emotionally attached. Someone who could look upon it with objectivity. It would become a horrid tale for them to unravel, not him.

That's it!

John bolted upright and almost tripped on his own feet. He stripped off his damp shirt, shrugged on a fresh one along with his trousers, and splashed water on his face. He hurried down the stairs as best he could and scurried about the office until he found a pair of clean hose and his boots where he'd left them near the door. Pulling them on, he chastised his own mental slowness.

Why had he not thought of it before?

With laces dragging on the floor behind him, he yanked open the door and waved Travers in.

"Pull down the bloody map, Travers. I've been an idiot," he exclaimed as he tucked his shirt in his trousers. "A blasted idiot." He hopped on his good leg over to the desk, tying his laces as Travers unpinned the map from the wall and anchored it on the desk with two empty mugs.

"What's gotten into you?" Travers asked.

"Show me where the peat bogs are around here."

"Peat bogs?"

"*Yes*, the peat bogs. The first time Miss Wycliffe and I met with Miss Clara, we had her smell the dirt sample we'd found on Miss Cunningham. She'd said it was peat. I'd thought the same when I first smelled it, but we never hunted for a bog because of the attack on the Wycliffes. Maybe Abe killed her there and has taken her back to the same place. Perhaps Miss Cunningham had seen something there she shouldn't have, something about Abe no one knew, and she'd fled. Run for her very life to escape him, and he'd killed her." He stared at the map. "What better way to preserve a body than to place it in a peat bog where it will never decay."

He glanced up. Travers stared back at him as if gobsmacked. "It's brilliant." He cringed. "And horrific."

"If I hadn't been sidetracked by the attack at the Wycliffes and Miss Cunningham being stolen, I'd have thought of it properly. I would have come to it earlier." John scrubbed his hand down his face. "I've been a fool."

"You are no fool." Travers leaned over the map, skimming his finger across the surface. "It would have to be here. In between the Mill and Lake Summerland."

"How far is it exactly?" John edged closer and attempted to match the scale to what he knew of Clun.

"It would be more than a mile and a half."

Could the poor girl have run so far? With no coat and wearing slippers?

He remembered Lucy's comments about her dress being rather clean despite the mud. He stared at the map in silence. "We're missing something. If she'd somehow run that distance in the cold, with no coat, in such thin shoes, she would have been a mess and covered in mud. She would have *looked* as if she had run that far."

John opened the side drawer in his desk and pulled out his pocket ledger. Scanning his notes, he paused when he found the right page and read it more closely. "Just what I remembered. She was too clean for such a journey."

Travers's shoulders drooped. "What if he killed her at the peat bog and then carried her to the lake, so she would seem undisturbed?"

A chill made John's arm hair stand on end. "He could have. Why would the murderer move her from the perfect spot to hide her? To a place where she would surely be found?"

"Mistake? Perhaps he changed his mind. The man's crazy. There may be no reason at all."

"Perhaps."

Yet John doubted it. The killer's movements were too controlled and contrived. The break-ins, the threatening notes, and deliberate clues left for John to find. The killer wanted them to chase him and engage.

He blinked. The killer wanted, *needed* for them to engage with him.

"That's it." John shrugged on his coat. "He had to leave her where she would be found, so the game could begin. He needs us to play along and engage with him. It's what the break-ins, the clues, what all of it has been about."

"What?"

"We are part of his play. We must engage. It is when we withdraw that he becomes angry and does something else to bring us back in. Grab your coat and hat. We're leaving."

"Don't you want to bring a shovel? Or two? So we can dig up the bog."

John shook his head. "I don't think she'll be there. He's not done yet."

Travers frowned. "Then where are we going? And what about Ena?"

"There is something else we need to catch him with. And we'll stop in to see your mother-in-law and the Wycliffes on the way back."

Travers snorted. "You're as crazy as he is."

"I hope so. Otherwise we may never catch him."

~ ~ ~

Lucy's heart skipped when she spied John and Mr. Travers approaching the cottage with the late afternoon sun setting behind them. She'd been glancing out the window every few minutes, hoping to see them. She longed for progress on the case.

Their cheeks were rosy with exertion, and Lucy rushed to open the door for them as they approached. Perhaps they'd found just the clue they'd all hoped for.

"You both seem spent. And half frozen."

Mr. Travers entered first and nodded. "Yes to both. Been at the bog most of the day."

"The bog?" Lucy's heart fluttered as John smiled at her. His usually crisp cravat was askew and dirt smudges marked his chin. It only added a new charm to his usual controlled and pristine self.

The men removed their outerwear and approached the hearth to warm themselves.

"Yes," John answered. "I realized today we'd never followed up on what Miss Clara had said during our first visit, about the dirt from Miss Cunningham's nails and shoes smelling of peat. So today we spent time exploring the peat bog between the Mill and Lake Summerland."

"When he says *explore*, he means we climbed over and under more rocks, boulders, and heaps of stinking rotten earth than I ever care to discuss again."

Cil laughed. "You must have found something. Constable Brodie's smile is almost giddy."

How Lucy hated to think she would ruin such a day for him. But the relief she'd felt at the sight of him and Mr. Travers disappeared into thin air, and the tightness she'd fought against all day, after finding what she had outside the front door this morning, returned. She clasped her hands tightly in front of her and tried to join in their mirth, but her heart wouldn't allow it for long.

John studied her, his smile faltering for a moment before he regained his bearings. He'd no doubt noticed her expression, and the fact put her at ease. She knew he would commiserate with her later. Relief pressed in softly once more.

"An odd find to be sure. A clue, I think." John pulled a small ribbon choker from his pocket. The dainty flower charm that hung from the muddy yellow ribbon stole Lucy's breath. She recognized it immediately. It was Miriam's.

She'd always favored yellow.

One of the first things Lucy had told John about her friend. He'd somehow remembered.

"It is hers." Lucy croaked a confirmation to John's unspoken question. "Miriam's."

John nodded and handed it to her. "I thought so based on what you'd said about her and what she wore that day."

She fingered it carefully as she studied the muddy charm. It seemed to wink at her in the afternoon light. To think this had once been upon her dear friend's fair neck during the last moments of her life. Grief gripped her and closed her throat.

"It means she was there," John added. "Somehow, some way, she had been there, close to the time of her death."

"Does this bring us closer to finding Abe somehow?" Mrs. Dobbs asked as she set aside her knitting on the table where she sat.

Lucy wondered the same. Had they found him? Would they ever? Her gaze drifted to the shelf where she'd hidden her find from this morning, and she longed to talk to John about them. Longed to enlist his help further, but she'd have to wait. She couldn't risk upsetting Cil. She'd never told her sister she'd asked John to help with solving their parents' murders. Nor had she told her that losing the cottage was imminent. Her sister would be headed back to see her daughter and stay with her in-laws tomorrow. She would be safer there, but how Lucy would miss her.

"Lucy?" Cil's voice pulled Lucy back to the present. "Did you not hear Mr. Travers' question?"

Heat rose to Lucy's cheeks. "No. I'm sorry. I was elsewhere."

John's brow furrowed. Concern rested in his eyes.

Lucy glanced to Mr. Travers to escape John's gaze. "I apologize. What did you ask of me?"

"Was the bog a place Miss Cunningham had been before regularly? Alone or with anyone else?"

"No. Miriam always thought her dog had disappeared in the bog. I can't imagine what might have ever brought her back there. Especially dressed as she was and at night. It can be quite dangerous if one isn't careful."

"As we feared," John answered. "We cannot figure why she would have been there either. Yet she must have been, as her necklace was there and the mud we'd found on her shoe and under her fingernails seems a match."

Lucy squared her shoulders and gripped the necklace in her hand. She had to know but feared to ask. "Where was the necklace, exactly? Were there signs of . . . of a struggle of some kind?"

Travers dropped his gaze, and Lucy feared the worst.

"We also found a coat," John began. "Ripped at the sleeves, near the necklace along the bog. She fought hard to save herself based on how the ground and moss were disturbed. I'm sorry."

Cil stifled a sob. Lucy wished she hadn't asked. Not only had she upset her sister, but horrid images flashed one after another in her mind, of poor Miriam struggling and fighting for her own escape. For her very life. Lucy squeezed her eyes shut.

Then logic burst past her emotion, and she blinked her eyes open. "So why did he not leave her there? No one would have ever found her. He would have been able to hide his crime."

"Perhaps you and Miss Wycliffe should discuss this without your sister and Mrs. Dobbs present?" Mr. Travers inquired gently.

"Yes. Of course. You're quite right. Ladies, I apologize. We can discuss this later." John tucked his hands in his trouser pockets.

"Nay," Mrs. Dobbs chimed in. "We'll just step out a while for some fresh air. Join us, Augustus." The old woman rose from her chair and wrapped her arm around Cil who sniffed and wiped her face. Mr. Travers nodded to John and followed the women outside before closing the door tightly behind him.

Lucy's pulse quickened, and she edged closer to where John stood by the fire. "So, why did Abe not leave her there after he killed her?"

"I'm not sure Abe is our killer. The killer has gone out of his way to engage us. Me in particular in this crime."

"I don't think I understand what you mean." The fire crackled around them as Lucy gazed at him. "You in particular?"

"I didn't tell you everything, Lucy. He's left me notes, messages, and clues throughout this whole affair. He even burgled my office and room above stairs. Stolen things to keep me a part of his game. He *wants* us to be involved. Needs us to be. If he'd left her there, we may never have found her at the bog. He wanted me to find her. To chase him."

Was the killer now doing the same to her? The necklace, the ring left by her cottage door? "Why would he be so desperate to engage you? Or me?"

She stepped closer to him. So close she could feel the warmth radiating from his body and spy the dark new stubble on his cheeks from the lack of a shave. How she longed to touch him and be comforted by it, but she clenched her hands by her side instead. She had to focus on the case.

Becca and Miriam deserved justice.

"I don't know . . ." he began and faltered. "Wait, why did you say *me*? Has the killer communicated with you in some way?" He grasped her shoulders. Urgency resonated off him.

"Why, yes. Just today. This morning. He left something." She crossed her arms against her chest. "I—I went to the door to let Apricot out, and there they were, in the snow on the stoop outside, waiting for me. I don't know what they mean, but it shook me."

"Tell me what you found. Show me," he whispered. "You could be in danger, and I can't abide the thought of it. I care for you. Deeply." He skimmed his hand down her face and cupped her cheek. Desire flared bright and hot in his eyes.

Her stomach warmed, and she covered his hand with her own. "As I do you, John."

She smiled at him and reluctantly stepped away, letting her hand trail over his fingers as she did so. She walked to the mantel over the hearth and removed the items she'd found and hidden behind the framed sketch.

The only sketch she had of her parents. Her heart squeezed.

He watched her movements. Time seemed to slow and ache in the few steps she took, back to him. She opened his clenched fist and pressed the necklace and ring into his palm. "He left me these, and when I recognized the necklace, I could scarce breathe."

John tilted his palm to the hearth for more light. As he did so, he froze.

"Do you recognize the ring then?" she asked.

"Yes, yes," he sputtered, nodding. "It is, it *was* my younger brother's. Stolen from my room the day of the burglary."

She couldn't tear her gaze from him. The way he stared at the necklace and fingered the slim silver chain so carefully. Just as she had. As if he knew it. Recognized it. But how?

"And the necklace?" Her voice wavered in the air. Her body quivered in anticipation. And fear. There was something he wasn't telling her. Her gut cried out in alarm.

He stilled and met her gaze. "Yes. I've seen it before." Lines crinkled around the corners of his eyes, his mouth drawn.

Did her heart stop? Did she imagine his answer?

"How? It disappeared that night. The night my parents died." She searched his eyes. Fear crept along her skin. A fear she didn't understand. Or want to. "Was it referenced in one of Codger's old files?"

"No."

"Then how?"

His silence screamed back at her.

"Answer me." She wouldn't back down. She couldn't. "How do you know *that* necklace?"

He met her gaze and held it. "I saw her wearing it. The night she died."

Lucy gasped. Her chest constricted. She panted for breath, yet no air would fill her lungs.

Is this what death feels like? A cold hand squeezing all from you in a single moment?

She clutched for the chair. He came to her in a slow, blurry movement.

"Lucy?" His voice echoed around her. "Take a deep breath. Breathe. Breathe." He supported her under her elbow.

She blinked and focused on his shoes. The way she'd met him that morning. *Mr. Shiny Boots.* A gentleman. A war hero. A Constable. *Perfection.* All crisp angles and control. But this? This she didn't understand. Couldn't understand. Like his mud splattered boots now. And the idea that he had been here on the night of her parents' deaths. She could not reconcile these two different men.

One of them was a liar. But which one?

"How?" She didn't understand. Nor did she want to. *Him. Here?* In this very home on the night of her parents' murder? A horrid question leapt from her lips. "Did you kill them?"

"No." He paused. "My brother did."

Chapter 23
The Separation

Every part of John grew taut with waiting. With the anticipation of a deathly, final blow. The dreadful, eerie silence choked his breath. Once again he was a sailor on the shores listening for the first shot, unaware he would take the blow until the sound of the bullet crashed into the bone of his leg with a loud, hollow crack.

The silence following had been exactly like this. So he waited. Waited for the final blow to hit.

"You jest. You must think me a fool to fall for such nonsense." Lucy finally splintered the silence into pieces of time . . . one before he'd confessed the truth, and one, after. He could see how she struggled to process the words, a conflict resting in the slight tremor of her waving hand and the quiver of her bottom lip.

If only he could escape the past, but he couldn't. It perched, fat and heavy like a stuffed pig, between them.

"I would give my life for it to be but a jest." He locked eyes on her until she met his gaze. He needed to look into her eyes, into her soul for this next part. "I found my brother standing over your parents. And your mother, she—"

"Do *not* speak of her," Lucy rasped, between gritted teeth. Grabbing a wooden bowl next to her, she lobbed it in the air at him. He ducked to avoid a direct blow to his head. It cracked against the wall behind him and clattered dully to the floor.

John held her glare. She seemed a wild, feral creature. Yet such a beauty, with her dark eyes, hands fisted at her sides. This woman hated him. And that hate rested on him like a black, heavy anvil.

Can I blame her?

He'd hidden the deepest, harshest truth from her to protect himself, not her. The truth would free her in the end. It would also end the idea of *them*. His chest constricted as he admitted the very reason he'd denied telling her for so long. He didn't want to lose her and the future he wanted for them.

A fantasy, to be sure.

"Has this been a game to you?" she asked in wavering tones. She gestured between them with a hand that clenched and pressed against her chest. "Some further pain to affix to me?"

"No." He stepped toward her, but she recoiled. Her reaction stole the breath from him, and he paused. "And as strange, as unfathomable as it may seem, after only mere days of knowing you, I believe . . . I know, Lucy, that I love you."

She said nothing, even as her eyes welled.

Only military discipline kept him still. He longed to rush to her and pull her in his arms, make her understand; yet he knew there were no words to alter what he'd done into anything other than what they were—

Despicable.

He was the basest and most selfish of men. A better man would have left her once he'd sensed such a heady attraction. But he'd waded into it until it lapped about his neck. That was what love did to a man.

He'd forfeited all reason.

To her.

For her.

And now he'd lost her.

~ ~ ~

Rage churned in Lucy's gut. Along with sickness. The two battled and waged inside her against the loss and sorrow budding in her chest. She loved this man above all others.

And he was a pretender.

He had lied to her as a man might lie to a mistress or a fool. And she had held on to every syllable, word, and line as if they were tethers to this world. Perhaps they were. Now that he'd told her the truth of what he was and what his brother had done, she felt as if she were falling into a pit of blackness and despair. She had been cut from her anchor, from her understanding of the world, and been crushed by it.

Was she melting into nothingness in the rain as a pile of snow turns to a slush and disappears into the soil? Glancing at her skin, she was surprised to see she was not. She was still here. As was he.

Lucy sucked in a breath and wiped the sleeve of her dress across her face to blot away her tears. She would weather this as she had all the other disappointments of her life. Straightening her shoulders, she drew a breath of courage and began the long walk past him to the door. A mere handful of steps, but a journey today. One she hoped she could complete. Taking the first step, she didn't crumble, so she continued her course.

The closer she came to him, the sharper the pull to him like a tide to the moon. And how she longed to slide forward, into his arms for comfort, but she couldn't be the weak, lovestruck fool she had once been. How could she ever trust a man who would keep such truth from her?

Her pride wouldn't allow her to drop her eyes from his gaze. He would know the rage and brokenness he had fashioned by his choices. Pausing before him, she held his stare and let the unease she felt soften and settle between them. When she couldn't bear a moment more, she thrust the door open.

"Leave," she commanded. The strength of her voice proved an unexpected surprise to her own ears.

To his credit, he didn't balk or attempt a last explanation or plea. He gathered his coat, gloves, and hat, donning them as he headed to the door.

At the threshold, he stopped, and there he remained, staring deeply into her eyes which welled traitorously with her affection for him. A tear fell along her cheek; she blinked furiously to keep the others at bay.

"I was a young man when I protected him," he began in soft, resolute tones. "I clung to what sparse family I had left, and I cast aside all care for you and your sister. And for that, I have suffered. As I should have." A muscle flexed in his jaw and he cleared his throat. "I never meant to hurt you. Especially not again. As little as it means to you now, I am sorry. For keeping such a secret. For not telling you a thousand times when I could have. With every part of my being, I beg for your forgiveness, even though I know I don't deserve it."

Her breath hitched, trying to hold back a sob.

And then, he was gone.

Chapter 24
The Castle

After he had disappeared around the bend in the road, Lucy fled into the cool night air to a place that had given her comfort in the past when she needed to be alone.

The castle.

Cold winds whirled gently around her skirts as she walked quickly through town and across the bridge. Nodding to a few townsfolk, she increased her pace and climbed the motte leading to the ruins of Clun Castle. The grass crunched beneath her feet in the harsh freeze. A few lone, bare trees shook in the wind, as eager for spring as she.

However, spring hid far away. Winter loomed, causing her to nestle further into her cloak, hungry for warmth. The chill of disappointment and loss aching deep in her bones, experience told her the feeling would far outlast the gooseflesh running along her skin. While spring would come in a few months, this chill of deceit would last far beyond.

And to think she'd all but given her heart to him. *John.* The liar. The deceiver. The pretender. She gnashed her teeth as anger began to replace her sorrow. If he'd only told her. The thought made her pause.

Would an early confession have even mattered?

She would have only pushed him away sooner, wouldn't she? Or would she have forgiven him?

How did one forgive the man who had, for so long, denied her not only the truth, but her parents' justice? All the while he served as a soldier, a man of the law, a servant to his people.

She snorted. All while being an accomplice to protect a double murderer.

Bastard.

Entering the damp, dark confines of the ruins, she exhaled harshly, though leaning against the cold and hard, solid wall of the place calmed her. It had survived hundreds of years, hadn't it? It hadn't fallen. Not yet. Not entirely.

Just as she would not fall. She would not crumble yet.

Figuring a way through all of this was imperative. Despite how she longed to, she would not tell anyone of John's confession. Not Cil. Not Travers. Not Mrs. Dobbs. Nothing would be gained of it but more heartache for her sister. And herself.

She would grieve the truth of it now and move on. However, she would command his resignation at the end of this case. The people of Clun deserved a better man than him as a protector of their town. And once he left she could move forward, but how? To where?

Fiske would call in her loan soon. Her rebuff of his advances and further refusal of marriage made such an outcome inevitable. Cil and Norah Jane would be on their way to Obley.

Where will I go?

Without the cottage, she'd also have to relinquish her work as layer-out for Clun. Another pang of loss chided her. Did she even remember a time before she was a layer-out?

That life seemed ages ago, and without a profession, what would she do for money? She cherished it despite everything. Currently she had purpose and meaning. Without it, heaven only knew her future or where she would go.

Her heart thudded in her chest. As the wind whipped up her cloak, she continued deeper into the ruins.

Within the interior of the Great Tower, she could escape from the wind. The light was fading quickly as evening neared. She'd have to leave soon or Cil would worry and ask questions, the last thing Lucy wanted. Huddled against the cold weathered stone, she hid, partially protected from the elements despite the missing roof. Glancing up she could see the moon rising slowly, fighting for a break in the clouds.

How many times had she and Miriam come here and unburdened themselves in the quiet solitude of these ruins? So many moments they had shared since they were mere girls, and all of those moments had been borne because they'd had one another. Who would she talk to now? Who would listen to her and help her find her way past this sorrow?

"Miriam, what should I do?" Lucy asked aloud. "I know you'd already have three other solutions worked out in your mind to help me." Wiping a tear from her cheek, Lucy chuckled. And Becca would have been her shoulder to cry on. She always carried an extra linen handkerchief in her dress pocket for such occasions. Lucy would have soaked it this day, if Becca had but only been here—

But she wasn't. Nor would she ever be, again.

I am alone.

So alone, her heart twisted and pulled in her chest. Longing and loss filled her lungs, threatening to starve her for air. Sliding down the wall, she gave in fully to her despair, pulling her legs to her chest. Resting her forehead upon her knees, she wept until she fell asleep.

She woke in a shiver and noted the high moon overhead. Her limbs ached from the cold, and flakes of snow cascaded down from the open roof around her. How long she'd been there she didn't know. If she had to guess, it was late enough she would have given her sister a fright.

Thistles.

She stood and stretched with a groan. Rubbing her gloved hands against her legs, she warmed them enough to move. Hoping to exit more quickly, she stepped toward the back entrance, heading to one of the small branches of the river behind the castle.

Rounding the corner, she gasped and froze.

Miriam.

In a shaft of moonlight with snowflakes cascading and twirling down around her, her friend rested prone and in repose. She looked exactly as Lucy had left her the night before her burial. The night before she had been taken.

Lucy tried to summon the courage to move or scream. But she just stared. Shock rooted her to the ground. Abe had brought Miriam here. To a place she had loved. It all made sense now. They had all loved this castle since they were children.

Tears burned. She blinked them away, needing to get help for Miriam.

As much as she didn't want to, she pushed off the ground and ran toward town.

And to John.

~ ~ ~

Lucy burst through the Constable office door and skidded into the entryway. She'd had no time to wipe the snow from her boots, and she clung to the wood of the door as she panted for breath.

"Miss Wycliffe." Mr. Travers smiled at her. "It is a true relief to see you well. You gave us a fright when you didn't return from your walk. I had to promise your sister and Mrs. Dobbs I wouldn't return to the cottage without you."

"John? Mr. Brodie, is he—"

At that moment, John rushed haphazardly down from his bedroom with his shirt untucked and gaping open at the neck. When he met her gaze, he froze and stared at her.

"I am here," he answered.

Such simple words landed heavy upon her heart, and she struggled for composure. It no longer mattered how she hated him and raged at him for what he had done to her.

This was for Miriam. Her friend deserved a burial and final rest.

She pressed down her feelings. "Miriam," she panted. "I've found her. I need help to retrieve her before he returns."

"Found her?" Mr. Travers' jaw fell slack.

"On my walk. I went to the ruins. I fell asleep and when I woke and started to leave by the Great Tower, she was there." Her eyes betrayed her, filling once more with emotion. "There in the snow and moonlight. She was beautiful."

A tremble entered her voice, and the emotion in John's gaze undid her. She covered her mouth and sobbed. She could take no more this day.

Mr. Travers turned to John. "Best I see to Miss Cunningham. Join me when you can."

"Take my gun, Travers." John descended the stairs and reached Lucy's side but didn't touch her until the door had closed behind Mr. Travers and the room had fallen quiet once more.

"I am so happy you are well. And here with me. I've no right to after all I've done. But I am. And that you found Miss Cunningham." He pulled her to him, into a strong, warm embrace, which she should have resisted, but she couldn't. She was in ruins. She hiccupped against his chest.

She sobbed into his shoulder until she'd soaked the thin material of his shirt with her tears. When she'd cried herself out once more, she pulled back.

"When I was there," she hiccupped, "I decided something." She wiped her face and met his gaze. "I will never tell anyone what you've told me, and you will leave here once this case is done. Resign from your position and never return. You will tell no one. Not Cil. Not Travers. It is all over." She stepped out of his embrace. "As are we."

A muscle ticked in his jaw and his Adam's apple bobbed in his throat. "As you wish, Lucy. I can ask for nothing after what I've done. I will tell no one, and I promise you I will leave after this case is solved." He stepped closer. "But you must agree to listen to my warnings despite how much you may hate me. Whoever this is, he is dangerous. Now more so than ever."

She nodded. His agreement soothed her, and her breathing became more even. Things between them had shifted back into only work, a far safer space for her to reside in. "And now, we must help Mr. Travers with Miriam."

Uncertainty rested in his eyes, yet he shrugged on his coat, and followed her out the door. It seemed whatever personal affections between them were done. Finished. Neatly concluded and wrapped up like a resolved case file, and now they had agreed to return to being colleagues. As he pushed the door open, John concluded their affair by abandoning her given name. "Miss Wycliffe." He gestured to her. "After you."

Her steps faltered, but she replied in kind. "Thank you, Mr. Brodie."

~ ~ ~

John walked her home in silence and at a distance.

Lucy missed the warmth of his offered arm and their easy banter, but those were memories best left in the past. Miriam had been collected and placed at the church where she would await her burial tomorrow. Mr. Travers had gone ahead to let the Cunninghams know Miriam had been recovered.

As she pushed open the cottage door of her home, all Lucy felt was weary, when she should have been relieved. Weary of loss. Weary of disappointment. Weary of life. When Mrs. Dobbs pulled her into a fierce hug and Cil fussed over her arrival, Lucy battled against the urge to crumble at their feet. Instead she hugged them and sent John—*Mr. Brodie*, she reminded herself—on his way.

He merely nodded and bid all a good evening. He made no mention of stopping in tomorrow or the next. She supposed he'd left it to her to decide, which disappointed her. His agreeableness irked her, worse than wool upon her bare skin.

Mrs. Dobbs tugged off Lucy's coat and gloves, while Cil removed her hat.

"Come by the fire and warm yerself," Mrs. Dobbs commanded. "What happened to ye, child?"

"I went for a walk in the castle ruins, fell asleep, and when I realized the lateness of the hour, I began to exit out the back, when I saw her. Miriam." Lucy stared into the fire.

Cil gasped. "Was she . . .?"

"She looked as perfect and as peaceful as the night I finished preparing her for her burial. Snow fell about her face and moonlight shone on her. Abe had posed her as if she could see out of the tower and watch the stars."

"Lord above," Mrs. Dobbs muttered and sat down hard in the kitchen chair.

"I know," Lucy replied. "If I hadn't seen it with my own eyes, I would never have believed it. She'll be buried tomorrow."

Cil nibbled her lip as she grasped Lucy's hand in her own. "I'll be traveling back to Obley tomorrow. I've been meaning to tell you, yet there never seemed a good time. I must see Norah Jane and begin what preparations I can to get us settled there."

Lucy smiled. "I understand. I'll miss you both, but your happiness means the world to me."

"As does yours to me." Cil winked at her. "And I am forever hopeful Mr. Brodie will make you happy."

Lucy feigned a smile. She would pretend for now. She'd not ruin her sister's joy. "Time will tell, will it not?"

Mrs. Dobbs chimed in behind them. "It always does, dear. It always does."

Chapter 25
The Hunt

When the funeral concluded, Lucy could scarcely keep her eyes open. She covered a yawn with the back of her hand and rose from the pew as the organ sounded. She'd slept little the previous night. Yesterday's events had taken a toll on her, but at least Miriam was at peace now.

One part of the case had been solved. Unfortunately, they'd yet to find Abe. And without him, they were no closer to solving the double murder than they were when Mr. Brodie first walked into her cottage.

But that hadn't been his first day in the cottage, had it? How had he masked his emotions when he'd entered the room again after so many years and after what he'd witnessed there?

She peered at him across the pews as he spoke with the Cunninghams. Fatigue rested in his weary eyes. His shoulders appeared high and tight. No doubt his leg most likely plagued him as well, since the cold and wind had refused to relent and now promised to bring the coldest January yet to Clun.

Perhaps he managed with the cool detachment he showed her now. He approached and tipped his head in greeting.

Her stomach knotted.

"Seems you are one step closer to being able to send me from this place," he said.

She should have been relieved he seemed so willing to leave her and Clun, yet she wasn't. It irked her further. She should hate the man, but she hadn't quite managed it yet.

"Yes, sir." It was all she could trust herself to say.

"If continuing on as my assistant is too difficult, just say the word. I will release you from any further duty. And I can pay the wages I owe you."

She sighed. He was so bloody nice. And she needed whatever income she could gather before being thrust out of her home. She had no choice but to continue on a while longer. She owed it to her friends and to herself, didn't she?

"No. I wish to see this to the end. No matter what other surprises it brings." She stiffened her spine. Perhaps a nasty barb to have thrown, but instead of being rankled, he smiled.

Smiled, of all things.

"If that's true, we've got clues to study back at the office. Now that you are privy to all the details of this case, I know you'll have some more insight into who else we should be considering as our main suspects."

"Then, what are we waiting for?"

~ ~ ~

At first, Lucy had been surprised that John—she'd long given up on trying to call him *Mr. Brodie* in her mind or out loud—didn't invite Mr. Travers to join them in their discussion of the case. But once she heard some of the finer details of what the killer had been taunting him with, it became apparent as to why. If he told Mr. Travers about the clues the killer had left, he'd have to reveal the nasty truth about his past.

Something he'd promised her he'd never do.

Unfortunately, it made their gathering rather more intimate than Lucy would have liked. She did her best to remain as professional as possible. Her sister would have laughed at her failings. She missed Cil desperately already. They'd said their goodbyes only this morn, and Cil's in-laws would have gathered her up by now to make it home to Obley by nightfall.

Lucy shoved her thoughts aside and focused on the evidence before her. "Do you think he knows what your brother has done?" She couldn't say *murder*.

John rubbed the back of his neck and untied his cravat. "He has to know. Otherwise, there's no point in him leaving the necklace and signet ring at your doorstep or those five-jacks and 'murderer' scrawled on my walls. He knows and he's threatening me with it. And torturing you with it." His gaze dropped away. "I'm sorry."

He studied the map of Clun sprawled out on the desk. During the last hour, they had marked every potential point of significance since the case had begun.

"So where could he be staying where he could get to all of these places with ease?" John ran his fingers over the map. "Within an easy walk, I would think. He'd need to hide as well. And stay warm somewhere, somehow."

When she sidled closer, he stepped back as if he'd been startled. She pretended not to notice and scanned the bold black X marks they had added to the map. "There's a gap here in the woods where he could hide and still be within a walk."

"Are there any houses or buildings out there? Abandoned or otherwise?"

Lucy studied the map closer. "There *was* a hunting shed or something of that sort way back in the woods, if I remember correctly. My father and I sheltered there once when we were trapped in a downpour." She shook her head. "Even back then, it was in shambles. More a heap of rotting wood and falling rocks than anything else. Most likely even worse off by now."

"It might be the perfect place." He glanced outside. "It's too late today. Tomorrow we can search for it. I'll ask Travers to join us. Can I walk you back? And I can stay with you for protection, in a professional capacity, of course. Until the killer's been captured, if you wish."

Yes. Please stay.

But her lips betrayed her heart. "A walk back would be fine, but you don't need to stay as our watchman. Mrs. Dobbs will be with me. I've grown quite fond of her company."

He nodded. Did disappointment ripple across his features?

"And one more item I wanted your opinion on." He pulled an object from his trouser pocket and placed it on the desk. "This was left in my room after it was burgled. Odd, don't you think?"

Lucy stared in curiosity as it rolled closer to her. "A glass eye?" She reached out to touch it.

John shrugged. "Seen one in my time in the service. Expensive, from what the man told me. And I thought it odd for it to have been removed from whomever it belonged to. Grotesque, even."

"Quite beautiful work, though. And the shade of the blue iris is somehow familiar." She paused and pursed her lips.

The click-clack of hooves and carriage wheels on cobblestone sounded. John opened the door as a young man brought his team and wagon to a stop and approached the office.

"Good afternoon, sir." The man pulled his cap from his head. A farmer, if his worn clothes and sun-weathered face in January were of any indication. "Came from Obley to fetch Mrs. Newberry. Her in-laws are keen to have her join them this eve, but I couldn't find her at the cottage. Mrs. Dobbs asked me to come here to inquire if she'd stopped in."

Lucy's heart skidded in her chest. "No, she's not here. We've been here for hours, and she hasn't stopped by. She wasn't at the cottage?"

Her mind whirled in circles, trying but making little sense of what the man said.

The young man shrugged. "Mrs. Dobbs said the cottage was empty when she returned from the funeral. She thought perhaps Mrs. Newberry had come to wish you a final farewell."

"Did you try her old home down the road from the cottage?"

"I did before I came here. Just in case she'd forgotten something. No one inside."

Lucy couldn't breathe. She stared dumbly at the man.

John placed her coat around her shoulders and pressed her hat and gloves into her hands before clasping one in his own. "Take us to the cottage," he ordered the young man. "Quickly."

Exiting the office, John ran across the cobblestones and pounded on the door to Travers' store. The door flashed open and although Lucy couldn't hear the words the men exchanged, by Travers' frown and hasty departure, Lucy knew John was equally worried about Cil not being accounted for.

All this time, they had feared Lucy the target, but the killer might have had another Wycliffe in his sights.

Lucy smothered a sob.

Her sister, Cil.

Chapter 26
The Search

"Whatever you're thinking, Lucy, don't," John ordered. He swung his lantern high and to the left as they spread out and began their harried search of the area around her cottage. Darkness entombed them and the biting cold stung her cheeks. Time was not on their side.

"I wasn't thinking anything," Lucy snapped as she swung her walking stick out in an arc, searching for any clues that would help their search. She lied of course, yet it irritated her that he knew her so well. She did imagine the worst.

That Cil might be dead. Lucy's pulse sprinted.

And he was right. Lucy had to stop the negative, horrid twirl of her thoughts and focus. She needed a clear, sharp mind to find Cil and catch this killer.

It's what my sister deserves.

John shook his head. "Well, then. Continue on. Once we've completed this cursory search, Travers will have gathered more men to help as we move deeper into the woods. We'll find her."

"I know," she answered, in softer tones. "And I'm grateful for your help. More than you know."

"I do. And we're all here to help you. We all care for your sister." He paused. "And you."

"Except for the man who has taken her. What does he care?" When she swung her stick just out of the scope of the ring of her lantern's light, it hit something hard. She froze. The sound of it was eerily familiar. The feel of wood connecting with flesh and bone.

She knew before John would cast his light on it. A body rested there. Her years as a layer-out had tuned her ear, her very being, to understanding the human form, especially in death. But she couldn't look. She dared not. Trembles overtook her as sickness threatened. Gooseflesh scampered up her arm even as sweat beaded her upper lip.

Had the air thickened? She could scarce breathe.

What if her sister lay there? *Still. Dead.* Her only family left in this world. Lucy would not survive such a discovery. It would rip her from this earth.

"John," she begged, her voice a tremble in the air. "Something's . . . *someone's* there. To my right." She squeezed her eyes shut. "I cannot bear to look. If it's her . . ."

"Stay still," he answered, in a soothing, firm tone. "Wait. Wait for me." He jogged over to her side and moved past her. Lucy held her breath while blood pounded against her ears. She felt the heat of his lantern near her face as he shone a light where she'd just searched.

"Lord above," he whispered, followed by a sigh. "It's not your sister. It's a man. He's dead. Stabbed. Bled to death it seems. Tried to crawl for help from the looks of it. Perhaps you can identify him?"

She glanced down and pressed a hand to her chest. "It is Abe."

Relief seized her, followed closely by shame. She shouldn't be happy someone else was dead. Cupping her mouth with her hand, she tried to mask her emotion, by seizing one ragged breath after another.

Cil was still alive. They would find her. They would. Lucy chanted it in her mind like a prayer.

But first, she needed to regain her wits and look for clues. Beginning with Abe. She stooped to get a better look at what had become of her friend.

"He seemed to be crawling *from* the woods to your

cottage of all places." John shone his lantern into the black pit of the forest. "Where the hell did he come from?"

Lucy squinted. "I'm not sure, but he suffered. He lost a tremendous amount of blood based on the dark crimson stains on his shirt and trousers."

Just as Miriam and Becca had suffered. It turned Lucy's stomach.

Had Abe, their good friend, really murdered them? If so, who had killed *him*? And why?

A glimmer of silver caught the glow from her lantern, and she shifted to get a closer look.

"He's clutching something in his hand, John. Do you see it?"

He knelt next to her.

She set down her lantern to pry open Abe's fingers. "He's still warm and easy to move. He didn't die long ago, and I—" The sight of the bracelet stole her breath. She fell back on the ground, landing hard. Her limbs tingled. Her throat dried.

"What is it?" John shone his light closer.

"This is Cil's. Her husband gifted it to her on their wedding day. She is never without it. Never."

She shook her head. "I cannot bear it. If she is dead . . ."

John grasped her shoulders. "Don't. Don't assume the worst. Someone ended his life. Perhaps she killed him in her escape."

He was right. Cil could be alive. Lucy could not, would not, believe otherwise; she couldn't bear it.

She frowned at him. "But my sister is incapable of killing, as I am. She could not have done this to him."

He sighed. "If she didn't, Abe may have died trying to protect her or perhaps he created an opportunity for her escape from the real killer."

"And if it didn't succeed? If the man who killed Abe has her, what then?"

"Then we work together, and we find them." John's resolve and determination shone in his even timbre and demeanor. He believed Cil was alive. So would she. He stood, and Lucy accepted his offered hand and settled into his side, leaning heavily on him. She needed his strength as he needed her forgiveness.

In this moment where all she wanted was her sister back in her arms, she wondered if she wouldn't have done anything to have done so. Lied, cheated, stolen, and perhaps even killed to keep her sister safe, just as John had protected his brother to keep him alive and away from the hangman's noose.

Suddenly, the very black and white world she resided in was becoming very, very gray.

~ ~ ~

"I believe all of the answers we seek rest out there in the woods." John spoke with Mr. Travers a distance away from her, discussing locations on the map.

Lucy's hands shook as she attempted to fasten her sister's bracelet around her own wrist. Unable to manage the fine clasp and riddled with frustration, she tucked it in her dress pocket. This waiting addled her usually-keen mind. Why could they not set out already?

Because we have no plan, and the killer is ahead of us.

Far ahead of them. But how? She closed her eyes and tried to piece together what she'd seen from earlier in the night.

"Got several men here at the ready, divided in pairs. Show me the grid where you want them to start and I'll send them out." Mr. Travers' voice rang even and steady like John's. How could they be so cool, so calm? It unnerved her. She was edges and barbs and ready to claw out the eyes of the killer. If she—

Of course!

She'd been a fool.

She ran over to John and Mr. Travers as they continued to study the map. "I've remembered," she panted, clutching John's forearm. "The glass eye. It was Old Man Codger's. As was the pocket watch you found smashed at the lake."

John stilled and blinked at her.

"That's why they seemed familiar. I'd seen them before. He was my first preparation many years back. He died months after my parents' murder." She dropped her gaze from John and stepped back. For a moment, she'd forgotten herself.

Mr. Travers broke the silence first. "You found a glass eye? Codger's eye?"

"Yes. Killer left it in my rooms after tossing the office below." John pulled it from his pocket. In the glow of the lantern light, the glass glinted.

"Jesus," Mr. Travers muttered, running a hand down his face. "When were you planning to tell me about it?"

"Couldn't figure out how it related. Until now." John offered a smile. "Thank you, Miss Wycliffe." He shoved the eye back in his trouser pocket. "The killer has to know of both crimes and somehow be intimately connected to them."

"But Old Man Codger's death was no crime. It was natural and caused by a weak heart. He was found in the woods, frozen through. No murder or foul play to speak of." Lucy couldn't figure out how all of it related to Becca and Miriam.

"Was he well-acquainted with the Lusks and the Cunninghams? Have any difficulties with them or their daughters?" Frowning, John rubbed the stubble along his chin.

"No." Mr. Travers shrugged. "Can't see the connection yet."

"Best we continue to focus on the search. Have the men spread out ten paces and move together toward the shed.

Miss Wycliffe and I will swing wide and come around from the back side, and report back to you what we see."

"Just the two of you?"

"I've my revolver." John adjusted his weapon resting in the back of his belt loop.

"No place for a woman to be, John, you know that." Travers dropped his voice.

John shook his head. "I also know Miss Wycliffe well enough to know she won't sit at the cottage and do needlepoint as she waits."

"John—" Travers began.

"You're a capable assistant, Miss Wycliffe, and you know this area far better than I." He handed her the hidden blade from the ankle of his boot. "And I trust you. With my life. Will you aid me in the search?"

John's gaze and his outstretched hand signaled his absolute and unyielding faith and confidence in her. Lucy's heart filled with emotion. "Thank you," she whispered. "As I do you, sir."

Nodding, she accepted his knife, thankful he understood how important it was for her to be there, to help, and to save her sister.

His features softened and he gifted her a small smile. Was it from relief? Hope? She couldn't tell, but she was glad she'd said it. If something happened, she wanted him to know that, despite his lies, she appreciated his belief in her. His confidence in her exceeded her own, making her feel she could indeed do anything.

Like save my sister. Live a better life. Embrace something other than the sorrow of the past.

"You and Miss Wycliffe go on, then." Travers glanced between the two of them. "I know she's troubled about her sister's disappearance. As we all are."

"He's right, I am troubled. And ready to resume our search." Lucy's patience dwindled into nothingness. Search party be damned. Her sister was out there in the cold. Alone. Without her. Without anyone.

Except possibly a coldblooded, deranged killer. She stamped down the thought.

"We'll see you at the shed." Mr. Travers shook John's hand. "Be careful."

John turned to Lucy. "Ready?"

Her heart tripped over itself. She met his gaze and nodded.

They started their journey to the spot where she remembered the abandoned hunting shack once stood. Clouds blocked much of the moonlight and fog thickened about them. Lucy gripped her lantern and walking stick, a weapon light enough for her to yield and inflict some injury, if needed.

The knife would be her second option, an intimate weapon she'd only use if she somehow got close to the killer. And how she hoped to have such an opportunity. This man, who'd most likely killed two, perhaps three, of her friends and who now might have her sister, deserved punishment. And she longed to dole some out on him before it was all over, an act she wouldn't have thought herself capable of a month ago. So much had happened since then.

Her life had changed. *She* had changed.

Only the animals disturbed the silence of their progress along the snow-covered meadows beside the old Mill, whose dark form rose atop even the highest of evergreens and trees. Lanterns cast a stark, icy glow before them, offering guidance for a mere arm's length ahead.

They had enough oil to last them the whole night if needed, but Lucy hoped they would find Cil sooner than that, much sooner. And that somehow the fog would lift, because right now it hampered their progress. The temperature had dropped since they'd left town hours ago, and the cold began to bite and nip along her legs, feet, and face.

What if Cil had even less to keep her warm? Such thoughts did her no good, so Lucy cast them aside. She bolstered her resolve and increased her pace to match John's. His gaze slid over to her briefly before scanning the ground slushing beneath their feet. The ground would be frozen solid again by morning, and she could feel the drop in the air.

John halted, and Lucy did the same.

"Smoke," he murmured. "I smell a fire nearby. Follow me."

If she'd been alone, she would have missed such a clue. *Curses.* She frowned and trailed him a stride behind. As they approached a row of tall evergreens, he stopped and yanked her back. She leaned against his shoulder.

"We've got to leave our torches here," he whispered. "I can see a light coming from the hunting shed. As it's quite open and exposed, we'll be seen immediately if we don't use the dark of night and the budding fog to aid our approach."

"And if he's there? With her?" She grasped his arm. "How can we protect her? What if he does something to her? What if he already has?" She hated the pathetic, pleading tone of her voice and the way it revealed how she felt.

Desperate. Afraid. Out of control.

He set his torch and her own on a boulder. "Perhaps you should wait here. There is no way to ensure we'll find anyone or anything. It could be another trap."

"Or she could be dead." Her shoulders sagged.

"Lucy." He pulled her close. Moonlight glinted off his eyes. "You are the most intelligent and resourceful woman I have ever known. Do not let fear rule you. Push through it as you did long ago. And help me. Help me save your sister." His plea surprised her. "You are strong, but you must believe it. As I do."

He thinks me strong? Capable?

Tears encroached. Lucy blinked them away as she fell into the longing and belief in his gaze. After all she had said and done, he still believed in her. "Yes. Yes, I will." She sniffed and wiped her face. "Tell me what you need of me."

"I will approach from the back, where he won't expect it. If he is there and I can engage him, I want you to grab Cil and run from here. Run from here with all of your might and back to Travers, who will be coming from the other direction. Do not look back. No matter what you hear. Do you understand?"

Lucy swallowed hard. "And what if she is—" Her voice wavered. She cleared her throat. "What if I cannot rouse her and get her out?"

He grasped her shoulders. "Then you still run. Escape. I cannot bear the thought of you being harmed. Promise me, you'll run."

She could only nod once, although her mind screamed no. She wouldn't leave him or Cil there with a murderer. She couldn't.

"Count to sixty after I leave, then start out toward the front. And be careful. Use your knife if needed. Do *not* hesitate."

He pressed a kiss, heavy and full of the future they could have had, to her lips. Loss consumed her when he pulled away and began his careful entry into the clearing past the evergreens. Soon he had disappeared entirely in the fog.

And she was alone. So alone.

She strained to hear. Little besides a few solitary hoots of owls and cries of animals echoed in the darkness. The counting took ages and challenged her against the pounding of her heart in her ears. Once she reached sixty, she pulled the knife from her boot, inhaled deeply, and took her first step out into the fog.

A step into oblivion.

Chapter 27
Oblivion

Bollocks.

John paused and squinted out into the hazy veil of fog surrounding him. The further he'd advanced into the meadow, the thicker the gray had become, the more precarious his situation. John scanned the area. Darkness loomed, a heavy gray-black blanket of nothingness. It reminded him of being out at sea in the fog. No stars, no sky, no ocean. And he felt precisely as he did then.

Lost.

Clenching his jaw, he fought the pain throbbing along his leg as he did his frustration. The killer could be anywhere. He could be right behind him, and John wouldn't know. Lucy could walk straight into a madman and be none the wiser. Why had he allowed her to come here? He was a fool to put her in such danger.

Nothing could be done for it now. She was here. With him. Out in the darkness.

Most likely with a killer.

John took a steadying breath, stopped in his tracks, and listened. He had to focus on what he *could* do to keep her safe; use his senses to find the killer before the man found them. Traces of smoke and wild animals greeted him as he walked. He stretched out his arms and found nothing, but he could hear footfalls. Quiet, careful, evenly paced steps on the ground. Only a subtle crunching gave them away.

Blast.

Was it the killer? Or Lucy?

Or her sister?

Without a lantern, there was no way to know. John closed his eyes and listened until the footfalls ceased. They had been on his left, progressing away from the shed toward the tree line. From exactly where Lucy had come. His heart dropped.

If it was the killer, she walked right within his path.

His mind raced. He didn't dare call out to her and reveal himself. Nor could he attempt to intercept the man without knowing the whereabouts of Mrs. Newberry. If he'd hidden her somewhere else, they'd never find her without the killer's help.

He'd have to continue his advance and trust in Lucy. She would no doubt hear the steps and pause. She was no fool, and he believed in her abilities and wit. He had to allow her to care for herself if he wanted to find this killer and Mrs. Newberry. Changing his plan to intercept Lucy would only endanger her further, and he couldn't risk her safety because of his own fear and love for her.

Step after step, he gained ground and drew closer to the shed. The stench of smoke became stronger, and the tang of oil assailed him. This was no wooden fire. Oil fueled the blaze. Why? Had the dampness in the air made it difficult for the flame to catch? Or had the oil been used to make the fire more intense?

Is it a trap?

He paused and heard steps. Tentative, hesitant steps. Not the confident carefully placed steps of a moment ago.

Someone else was in this meadow.

"Lucy?" Mrs. Newberry's voice trembled weakly over the night air.

John held his breath and sent up a prayer of thanks. Lucy's sister was alive.

Now he merely had to keep her that way.

~ ~ ~

Lucy gasped when she heard her sister's voice drift out of the fog like an apparition. *She's alive.* Clamping a hand on her mouth, Lucy fought tears as well as the urge to scream out to her. To let her know she wasn't alone. That she was here. John was here. And we would save her.

"I'm frightened," Cil whimpered. "I cannot see. Where am I? Where are you?"

Lucy bit her lip. Why could her sister not see? Did the fog blind her? She cringed. Or had she been blinded? Was the glass eye a message that he would harm her, or already had? Worrying her hands, Lucy took one step followed by another toward where she thought her sister had called from.

Snap.

A stick cracked loudly beneath Lucy's boot, and she froze.

Why now?

She shivered. Did she dare press on? Was she safer to move or to stay? She held her breath. Looking up in hopes of gathering her bearings, she noted a trail of smoke twining into the dark sky. The shed. She was closer than she imagined. She could do this. Clutching the knife tightly in her hand, she ventured forward. One foot in front of the other, then another. Two more steps and she could see it. Her shoulders sagged in relief.

The structure vaguely resembled the shed she'd seen long ago. Time had distressed its form, and the frame of it leaned heavily to one side as if it might topple over at any moment. Rocks clung precariously to one another and oblong clumps of wood and mortar emerged at irregular angles. It had a single open space for a window which had been haphazardly covered with brush, but a fire smoked within and offered a sliver of light to view the empty space inside.

Her heart plummeted. She resisted the urge to cry out. Where was Cil? What about John? What did she do now?

Lucy tiptoed away from the rear of the structure. The clouds uncovered bands of stray light from the moon, and she scanned the darkness. Still nothing. She forced herself to take regular, even breaths, but she couldn't prevent the spent air from coiling wildly into the cold darkness as it escaped her lips. Or fear from tightening like a band across her chest.

Something was wrong.

Should she keep waiting for John? Her baby sister was here in this field somewhere. Trembling, Lucy rubbed her hands together.

Think. Think.

A long, sweet starling call went out. Chills ran up Lucy's arms and the hairs on her body stood on end. No starling would be out singing this late. Nor alone in a meadow. She held her breath. And then she heard it.

A low, baritone laugh.

"It's how all this began, isn't it?" the voice taunted. "Some bloody starling. You going out to chase after some stupid wild bird you thought a pet? Foolish girl."

That voice.

It was familiar, yet Lucy couldn't place it. Not yet. She closed her eyes and focused on the voice. On what he said and what he hadn't. Perhaps then she would remember.

"Shy, are we?" Another eerie laugh followed. "Never expected you'd be. After what you see while doing what you do. An abomination to touch the dead like you do. An abomination, I tell you."

He thought *her* an abomination? She fought not to laugh aloud at the irony.

"I struggled for so long," he said. "Trying to cope with it all, but it proved too much for me. Eventually, I gave up."

Why couldn't she place that voice? Frustration consumed her.

Think.

"Angry. Confused. So many voices clamoring around in my head." Another laugh. This one sounded closer.

Could he reach out and clutch her shoulder? Did she dare move? What if she backed right into him?

"So many voices, my dear mother sent me away for a spell. And there, Fate smiled upon me and presented me a solution. A way to avenge my father's death in one neat, tidy plot involving the two of you."

Father's death? Two of us?

"And Abe. Tsk, tsk. Almost ruined everything. So sentimental. Needing to keep Mir from the cold, dark earth. Foolish imp."

She flinched on the word 'imp.' Only one man had ever used that word to describe Abe. It used to be a term of endearment and joking.

Junior.

Her childhood friend. Constable Codger's son. The man who had all but disappeared was alive. Here. In this field.

The man who had killed her friends. Killed Abe. Kidnapped her sister.

Rage swallowed Lucy's self-control. The self-preservation she had a moment ago melted away into the fog. She wanted revenge.

"Junior." His name burst from her lips in a biting snarl she scarce recognized as her own. "You had best run for I will cut you down where you stand." She panted for breath and the knife shook in the air as she stretched it out in front of her. "I dare you to find me, you murderer."

~ ~ ~

John froze, stunned by what he had heard. Constable Codger's son was the murderer? And Lucy had baited him, threatened to kill him? The world tilted on its axis. He struggled for breath.

"Lucy," Cil cried out again.

Blast.

John had to get Mrs. Newberry out of the center of this chaos. And he had to remind Lucy of the plan.

To rescue. Not take revenge.

"Junior," John shouted, desperate to distract the man, so Lucy could get her sister to safety. Would she remember what was important, saving her sister and not avenging her friends? She could seek justice later.

Right now, he needed her to remember the living, to focus on her future and not throw it away to the past.

The way I have, these last ten years of my life.

With his next step, something sharp clamped around his foot, biting into his flesh and muscle like the fangs of a wolf. Pain seized his ankle and shot up his leg. He shouted in agony.

"Shit," he cursed as he collapsed to the ground and groaned. Breathing through the pain, he glanced down and peered at his ankle. He'd stepped into a fox trap. The iron claw cinched his lower leg, tight and grotesque.

What the hell would he do now?

"John? John?" Lucy's voice, climbing to a high pitch, triggered Junior's loud, exaggerated laughter.

Had the direction of the bastard's mirth come from the north?

John rolled to his side. He'd been in *worse* situations. Closing his eyes, he sucked in deep breaths to slow his heart and the bleeding.

Opening his eyes slowly, he stared out into the meadow and saw a pair of boots. Men's boots. Off in the distance.

Bloody hell.

And what irony, for the agony of his situation had just gifted him a new plan and a way to escape. And a way to avoid more blasted traps and surprise Junior.

Leaning on his elbow, he tore a shred of fabric from his shirt. After tying it around his leg above the wound, he bit down on a stick and then wrenched open the trap until he freed his foot. Groaning from the pain, he commanded himself not to pass out as a wave of nausea rose in his stomach and sickness threatened.

He imagined Lucy's face and focused on the memory of her smile and sweet violet eyes until the nausea passed. He could do this. *For her*. Rolling onto his stomach, he sucked in his breath as numbing cold from the wet snow along his leg and ankle eased some of his pain.

Pulling the revolver from his belt loop, he began a slow, deliberate crawl toward where he estimated Junior hid. The bastard wouldn't expect him slithering about on the ground like a snake, which was exactly what John hoped for.

"Landed in a trap, did we, Brodie?" The cur snickered loudly. "No worries. I've still got two to play with before it's all said and done."

"You'll never make it out alive, Junior," Lucy warned. Rage trembled at the ends of her words. "More are coming. Coming for you. You're a dead man."

Junior sighed. "Perhaps. Perhaps not. This fog is working in my favor. They won't know where to shoot."

The man was *truly* mad, but Lucy's spirit and fight drove John on. Crawling through the cold slush, his teeth chattered as he gained ground slowly in the direction of Junior's voice . . . and his boots. The fact the dullard liked to talk would work in John's favor.

"What is it you want?" Lucy bit out.

John shuddered. She was close, which meant she was also close to Junior. And John wanted her as far away as possible before he attempted to fell the man.

"Well, revenge, I suppose. It is timely you're here. At this place. My father loved this shack. Until you all sucked the very marrow from his bones pestering him to solve your parents' murder. An impossible crime to solve. He was obsessed. You all killed him. This town killed him, drove him to the grave. It's why I have to kill you, as many of you, as I can. Eye for an eye, you see?"

John rolled his own eyes heavenward. He didn't know how much longer he could listen to this drivel. Shivering against the cold of his sodden clothes, he gritted his teeth to keep them from chattering even more.

Keep moving, keep moving.

He had to reach the bastard before he lost consciousness from blood loss. And before Junior captured one of them.

It seemed the man had come here to die, which made him all the more dangerous. He'd planned no means of escape.

Or at least none John could see.

"Although I am a touch disappointed in you all." Junior sniffed. "I worried I made the clues too easy and you would mistrust them, but I gave you far too much credit. It took you so long to begin to put some of the clues together, I grew impatient. No challenge at all to fool you, bait you."

Anger stilled John. He saw the man's boots only an arm's length away now, muddy and worn. He licked his lips and slowly pulled back the hammer of his pistol, taking great care to prevent the telling click of it locking into place.

He'd have one chance before he'd used up his element of surprise.

If he missed . . . John buried the thought. He wouldn't miss. His aim would be as true and unwavering as Lucy's spirit. He exhaled, took another breath and held it. Staring down the barrel, he prayed for accuracy—

And pulled the trigger.

Chapter 28
The Arrival

A shot rang out.

Lucy froze. The shot came from behind her. But where? Had John fired it or Junior?

A male groan followed, but whose?

She prayed it wasn't John.

Scanning the darkness around her, she dared not move. Commanding herself to listen, she held her breath.

"You'll regret that, Brodie," Junior growled.

The voice was close, so close. Gooseflesh crawled along her skin. She gripped the knife harder. She had to find Cil.

A cold, strong hand gripped Lucy's ankle and tugged her to the ground. Hard. So hard she couldn't breathe. She gasped for air. None came. She couldn't scream or plead for help, but only stare through the fog into Junior's beady eyes.

He pulled her ever closer.

Frantically she patted the ground as he dragged her along the muddy earth.

Where had her knife gone?

Gasping, she clawed through the snow and mud for her weapon. Wheezing for breath, air finally entered her lungs. The relief of it fed her strength. Kicking and flailing her legs, she pummeled his body. He groaned and his grip on her lessened as she emitted a scream.

"Lucy!" John yelled.

He was alive. And near. Her heart soared with hope.

"Sister?" Cil's shriek echoed in the distance, thankfully clear of immediate danger.

"Stay there," Lucy commanded. "Stay still until John finds you!"

Then Junior landed a blow to her side and she cried out. Kicking out with her foot, she attempted to crawl away, but his hold on her opposite ankle was so strong, so fierce, she could not wrench free of him.

A glint of metal caught her eye. *My blade.* Scrabbling both hands deep into the mud to gain traction, she fought to reach the knife winking at her in the brief moonlight emerging from the clouds above. She stretched even farther, the fingertips of her glove touching the shiny metal.

Before she could grab it, the violent force of Junior's pull on her leg dragged her away from it. Slipping through the slushy mud and snow, she couldn't gain purchase.

In an instant she'd lost what advantage she'd had.

"Say goodbye to this world," Junior mocked as he wrenched her arm and tugged her to him.

Panic screamed along her body. "Get *off* me!" She hit his chest with her fists, raging against his monstrous deeds, the evil he had brought to Clun.

His heavy weight pinned down her legs. Trapping her wrists in a hard grasp, he yanked them over her head.

Fear exploded in her chest like fire. What could she do now?

"Perhaps," Junior panted, "this will be better than I had planned. I've killed his brother, and now you. Killing you will end him. I've seen the way he looks at you, my lovely." He laughed. "That is what they call you now isn't it, Lovely Digits?" His eyes roved along her face. "Maybe, in your own grotesque way, you are. No matter. He will mourn you and I will have my full revenge."

A long blade appeared in his free hand.

She recoiled, struggling with all of her strength. This could not, would not be the end of her. After all she'd survived, she wouldn't die by his hands. Not like this.

Suddenly John's voice seemed to resonate around her like a prayer.

You are strong, but you must believe it. As I do.

She *was* strong, and she did believe in herself. She could do the impossible. She could survive.

"I will *kill* you." Lucy thrashed against him. "Perhaps not in this world, but the next." Provoking him further was a risk she had to take.

For Cil. For herself.

"Oh?" He loomed over her with a smirk.

Mustering all of the gumption and strength she possessed, Lucy headbutted Junior. Hard.

"*Bitch*!" He swayed, his grip loosening. Dazed, she tried to clamber away from him.

Before she could escape, he seized her by the wrist with one hand and slapped her face with the other. She clawed at the arm and hand that gripped her so fiercely, and he landed a fist to her chest, knocking the breath out of her. She kicked him once, twice, and then again with what strength she still had through the dizziness and pain consuming her. She wouldn't give up. She wanted to live.

I deserve to live.

Another shot sounded. Junior cried out and collapsed to the ground, his dead weight pinning her legs. She squirmed beneath him, struggling and panting to free herself.

"Lucy? Lucy?" John shouted.

She shivered at the sound of John's voice, and relief flooded her. "John."

Lucy shoved Junior's bulk away as John crawled to her. Her body shook as he cupped her cheeks in his gloved hands. "What a sight you are. I thought for a moment there, I'd lost you." He brushed muddy hair from her face. "I should have known far better. You are no ordinary woman, Miss Lucy Wycliffe. And I love you."

The sight of the usually controlled, pristine John Brodie covered in muck, full of emotion, tears glittering in his eyes, nearly undid Lucy. She blinked through hot tears. "And I you," she choked out. Despite all the reasons in the world why she shouldn't, she did.

She loved—*adored*—Constable John Brodie.

For a moment he stilled at her words, before pulling her into the tightest embrace she'd experienced in all her life. All of the sorrow of the past dissipated, as if it could not survive such fierce devotion. Such unbridled love.

Letting the past go lifted a weight from her she'd not realized she carried.

"Brodie? Brodie?" Mr. Travers' voice rose strong and loud in the darkness.

John lifted his head, groaning from the pain when he tried to move. "Here. We are here, Travers. Be careful. The bastard set fox traps out."

"Mind the traps, men," Mr. Travers ordered.

"Lucy?"

Cil.

"Yes, sister." Lucy struggled to right herself. "We're all right. Stay still until Mr. Travers finds you. Junior is dead."

As Cil began to sob, Lucy wiped her eyes in relief. She understood her sister's reaction. It mirrored her own. Was it finally over? Had they all really survived a madman? Had Becca, Miriam, and Abe's killer been caught?

Trembling consumed her as John held her, murmuring reassurances.

A few minutes later, the glow of an approaching lantern shone upon them. Lucy squinted up at Mr. Travers.

"Relieved to see both of you alive. And that bastard dead." He turned back to the rest of the search party. "Need a few men to help the Constable here and carry out our murderer."

Local townsmen approached. Two fanned off to gather up the body, while another helped John stand. Lucy accepted Mr. Travers' hand and rose on wobbly legs. He steadied her with an approving nod. "Brave woman, Miss Wycliffe. Not every day a lady dares track a killer into the woods."

She smiled. "I cannot thank you enough, Mr. Travers."

A short distance away, a lantern bobbed. "Found Mrs. Newberry, sir."

Lucy whirled in the direction of the light and the rescuer who held it aloft. Her heart squeezed in her chest. "Is she well?" Her voice cracked.

"Bastard blindfolded her and bound her hands. Seems frightened but unharmed," he assured.

Lucy sighed in relief. "Thank God." She started toward the lantern. "I want to see her."

Mr. Travers caught her by the wrist. "As much as you may wish to, I can't let you charge headlong into a sea of fox traps. Found a handful of them already. Best follow me and let him bring her out safely."

"Yes." Lucy wrung her hands. She wished to see her sister well with her own eyes.

John took her hand in his own and squeezed it briefly before he was guided from the meadow, leaning heavily on one of the search party members. Noting the damage the fox trap had done to the man she loved, Lucy gasped. With every step, he dragged his wounded foot. Her chest tightened as she realized it was the same leg already ravaged by war.

And yet, he had crawled to defend her, to kill Junior, to save them all.

To bring justice to her friends.

"Ready?" Mr. Travers offered his arm to guide her back home.

"Yes, sir. I'm ready to leave this chapter of my life behind."

Chapter 29
Forgiveness

The next day, John and Mr. Travers called on Lucy and Cil as promised. The sun rested along their shoulders as Lucy greeted them on the doorstep of her cottage late in the afternoon. Mrs. Dobbs sat with Cil at the kitchen table.

Lucy's throat closed with emotion at the sight of John. They had much to discuss about the case now that Junior had been caught, not to mention his subsequent demise.

I don't want to.

With the truth, the soft tendril of connection between them all would fracture. Lucy had held secrets, as had John, and secrets created fissures in even the closest of relationships.

Dread crept along her skin as she closed the door behind them. John limped in, leaning heavily on a cane to support his injured foot. He hung back and tugged Lucy close to him for the briefest of moments. "No matter what happens," he whispered, in a puff of air along her ear, "know I love you and I understand. Because of you, my soul is free. There are no more secrets. Not anymore. You have brought a dead man back to life, and I am forever grateful for it." He pressed a warm kiss to her brow before seeking a place to sit.

An ache, deep and full, budded in her chest.

Lord above, hadn't he done the same for her? Brought her back to life? He'd freed her from her guilt from the past and her fear of the future.

She could say nothing, do nothing, but follow him to the table.

They settled into chairs. She chose one next to him, sitting so close she reveled in the heat emanating off his body.

"Thank you for agreeing to meet today," he began. "There are things I wish to tell you all, share with you about Junior Codger and the motives behind his crimes. You deserve to hear the truth of it from me before I resign."

Mr. Travers balked. "Resign? What's gotten into you, John?"

Lucy dropped her gaze. His decision didn't surprise her. He was a man of honor. He'd promised her he would resign even though she'd told him he didn't need to keep such a promise to her after saving all of their lives.

John ran his palms down his trousers, a nervous gesture she now recognized. Lucy slid her hand under the table and laced her fingers with his. Though a bold action she wouldn't have taken a month ago, she was no longer that woman. He had changed her. She squeezed his hand, and his breath hitched.

"Go ahead, John," she urged. She understood the courage it took to let go of shame. He had helped her banish her ghosts, so she would help him as well.

John rested his free hand on the table and traced a grain in the wood before he began. "When I was a boy, my family would visit here in Clun. Mostly in the summers, but occasionally we came in the winter. My mother loved the snow, the quiet, the peace of this place. It was far from the maddening noises of London, so my father indulged her at times. As he did the winter ten years past, almost to this very day."

Cil blinked at him. "You've been here before? Why did you pretend to not know this place when you took on this post?"

"Shame," he replied, simply. "Shame and regret filled every part of me. And I thought if I came back here, I could make amends for what my brother had done, for what I had *not* done a decade ago for you. For your sister. For your parents . . ."

Cil gasped and tears sprang to her eyes. "Our parents?" she sputtered. She stared at Lucy, who fought to hold her gaze. "Do you know who killed them?"

"Yes." Lucy's affirmation held a quiver. John squeezed her hand in reassurance.

"What?" Cil's voice rose in pitch. "You knew? And you kept it from me? Why?"

"I thought it a kindness, sister. Nothing more. I wanted to protect you. And John agreed to leave after the case was closed."

With a glare at John, Mr. Travers reached over and gripped Cil's forearm. The fleeting glance he cast to Lucy made her suspect he had already pieced it all together, faster than Cil. Was he preparing her for what he knew was coming? The horrid, ugly truth of it?

"She's only known a few days, Mrs. Newberry," John assured. "I had not confessed it to her until then. You see, my younger brother Sean murdered your parents that night. He was deranged in the mind. Unwell. By the time I found them, your father had already passed." He gripped Lucy's hand fiercely as if he clung to life itself, then took a breath. "I tried to save your mother, but I was too late."

"You, you bastard!" Cil burst up from her chair. It clattered back against the floor.

Mr. Travers stood quickly and gripped Cil gently by the shoulders. He said nothing, but held her, supporting her. He was a good man who would allow her to say her piece, yet he'd also not let her harm herself or anyone else for the sake of Norah Jane.

Mrs. Dobbs sat in dumb silence, with a hand covering her mouth. For once, she had no words, a feeling Lucy understood.

"A description I deserve," John added. "Please sit, so I can explain it to you as best I can. I want to give the facts. From there, you can do what you wish with them."

Mr. Travers leaned closer and murmured something in Cil's ear. Her face softened and her limbs relaxed. He released her and righted her chair, so she could settle back at the table.

"Once my older brother, Cameron, learned of what had happened, he involved my parents." John cleared his throat. "They ordered me and Cameron to clean up the scene as best we could, and they sent Sean away into a wellness home, a sanatorium of sorts. A place that takes those with an altered mind and secrets them away from society, so family names are not tainted. We were commanded never to speak of it again. To anyone. I entered the Royal Navy to try to escape my guilt and shame, and my parents disowned me. When they died, I tried to convince Cameron to right the situation along with me, to tell the truth, but he refused. Sean later died, by his own hand, I had thought. Self-slaughter, the home had said. Now, it seems likely Junior killed him."

"Why?" Mr. Travers asked.

"Seems Junior met my brother at the home after his mother sent him there for care," John continued. "Struck up a friendship until Sean confessed what he'd done. My guess is it may have caused Junior to have a further break in the mind. Somehow he believed the death of your parents, Mrs. Newberry, caused the death of his father, Old Man Codger."

"Codger Senior *was* obsessed with the case," Mr. Travers admitted. "Chased clues here and there, but never came up with anything substantial. Then, one day he disappeared. Found him frozen to death in the woods. Heart failure, Doc Sykes said."

"Our first prepping," Cil murmured. "I remember."

"Junior must have tried to solve the crime when Kieran named him the new Constable, so he could soothe his father's soul. When he couldn't solve it, he couldn't cope. Blamed the town for his father's death."

"How would you know that?" Cil snapped.

Mr. Travers rested a staying hand on Cil's forearm once more. "Brodie and I went to visit Mrs. Codger this morning. To inform her of Junior's death. She told us all about his struggles since his father passed. These struggles started long before when he was a young man."

"Then how did we not see it?"

"He hid it well, and she helped him. Said he was so obsessed with solving his father's death and the murder of your parents, he stole his glass eye and pocket watch before the burial. Said he felt it allowed his father to watch over his progress on the case. To spur him on." John repositioned himself in his chair.

"Lord above," Mrs. Dobbs muttered and crossed herself.

"Glass eye?" Cil echoed.

"He left it for me to find after he burgled my rooms as well as the office. He left me clues, taunts, to keep me in his game. To keep us all in his game." John glanced to Lucy.

Pride at his honesty inspired her. He kept nothing back, so nor would she. "He left clues here as well at the cottage. The ball, John's ring with his family crest, and Mother's necklace. Signs the two cases were linked, but we could not piece them all together at first. Mostly because we hid the truth from one another. Deception that could have gotten us all killed."

"Because of me," John admitted. "I didn't tell Lucy or Travers of the coin or five-jacks the killer had left at my door. And my silence . . ." He paused and took in a shaky breath. "My silence almost cost you your lives. I'm sorry beyond words for it. The very night Abe broke in your cottage, I thought it was the killer and felt responsible. When I learned Lucy received more clues on her doorstep, I realized I had no choice but to confess to her the meaning of the ring, the necklace, and the ball for the five-jacks. As well as the significance to me being here in Clun."

Silence settled into the room, broken only by the fire crackling behind them in the hearth.

"And when he told me," Lucy added, "it was the night I'd run from this cottage, needing to get away. In my distress, I stumbled across Miriam at Clun Castle. I couldn't leave her, and I had no way to protect her without John. So I rushed back to him at his office and asked him to resign in return for my silence. And he agreed to not tell anyone upon my request. That's why none of you knew. I wanted to keep it a secret."

"To protect me?" Cil's eyes were rimmed red with tears.

"Yes," Lucy whispered. She paused and shook her head. "No, that's not entirely true. It was also to protect me. I've always been ashamed of my part in it. Of not being there that night. For being angry and leaving to find my starling. And then, I fell in love with the very man who had not granted them—or us—peace, all those years ago. I hated myself. I was ashamed. So, I wanted to hide it. Hide *from* it, like I have these past ten years."

John smiled at her. Pride gleamed in his eyes. And she was proud of herself, too. She'd related the whole truth of it, ugly as it was.

She felt so free and alive, she feared her heart would burst from her chest.

"And now, with the case done and you knowing the truth of what happened to your parents, I will be resigning from my post." John straightened to his full height.

"John, there's no need," Mr. Travers argued.

John shook his head. "Augustus, you know there is every need for it. I have broken the law several times over. I can no longer be such a hypocrite. And it is already done. I sent my resignation on by way of your son this morning to Magistrate

Kieran. I urged him to name you as my successor. A title you deserve far more than I, my friend. Your service, your friendship has been invaluable to me. I am grateful for it."

"And you will always have it. As long as I draw breath," Mr. Travers vowed.

John cleared his throat. "That is an unexpected gift. Thank you."

"And your first task, Augustus, will be to forget any mention of Mr. Brodie's involvement in this entire affair." Mrs. Dobbs winked at her son-in-law, and Lucy smiled.

"I think it is a fine idea, Mrs. Dobbs. What say you, sister? Shall we ask Constable Travers to press charges against Mr. Brodie for his involvement or shall we say he has paid his debt by saving our very lives?" Lucy asked.

Cil blinked at her, and Lucy held her breath. Cil had every right to wish a punishment on John for what he'd done, but Lucy hoped without measure she would forgive him and release him from the burden of the past.

Just as she wished to be freed from her own.

"I'd say his debt to us has been paid in full, sister." Cil wiped her eyes. "And I hope we can unburden ourselves from the shadows of their deaths. They would wish us to live in the present and with grand hopes for the future, would they not?"

"Indeed they would, sister," Lucy whispered. "Indeed they would."

Chapter 30
New Beginnings and Old Endings

"You know you didn't have to resign, John." Travers packed up John's old case files and popped them in a box to be sent to Magistrate Kieran.

"I had to. I can't stay on as constable here. Not after what I did. These people deserve a better man. Someone like you, Travers." He smiled.

"Kieran is only pleased with my appointment because it's a thorn on you."

"Perhaps. However, you deserve this post. You are the best of us, you know." John paused and slapped a hand on his friend's shoulder.

Travers dropped his gaze. "I don't know about that, but I appreciate those words coming from you." He sighed. "Where will you go?"

"Well, I have my eye on a place in Wales. I'm hoping I might be able to convince Miss Wycliffe to join me in a new life elsewhere, despite all of my failings. They have a training facility there for women who wish to pursue medicine. I think it would be a fine fit for her if she so chooses."

"And you?" Travers asked. "What will you do with your time?"

"I think I might open up an office for unusual cases. An agency of solutions, you might say."

"So, still a detective?"

"In a sense, I hope. But without all of the bloody rules. I try my best but I seem prone to breaking them."

He stretched out his hand and pulled Travers into a tight embrace. "I'll send word once I've settled in. Then I'll send for what's left here. I hope you can get some help getting this office finally back to rights. Bloody mess in here."

Travers smiled. "Mrs. Newberry has offered to assist me and Ena with the store for a spell here. She's back at the cottage helping her sister pack up before Fiske comes to reclaim it. I've grown quite fond of her company. Hoping I might be able to make some regular visits to call on her in Obley."

John clapped him on the shoulder. "Now, *that* is the best idea I've heard from you yet. I wish you success in your endeavors, Augustus. It's well past time we all let go of the past, don't you think?"

He shook his good friend's hand once more and exited, listening to the sleigh bells clang loudly on the door behind him one last time.

~ ~ ~

Lucy placed the last of her meager belongings in her trunk and let it fall shut. The sun shone through the window and a hint of spring rested in the bright blue sky and warmer air. Taking one last, final look at the cottage she'd lived in all her life, she sighed. Rather than being sad and grief stricken about losing her home as she expected to be this day, contentment greeted her, a welcome and heady surprise.

For once, the past didn't weigh upon her, heavy and thick. The future awaited her on the other side of her door. Her excitement for the unknown felt pleasant—and unexpected.

A knock sounded, and she smiled. The hackney driver was here to help her with her things. Cil had left only an hour ago, eager to set up a spare room for her at her in-laws in Obley. Lucy would stay with her there for a while until she decided where to go next. And the idea, of not knowing exactly where that would be, thrilled her.

Lucy opened the door and her heart fluttered. Of all the boots she expected to see on her doorstep this morn, she'd never thought to see those of Mr. Shiny Boots himself, the former Constable of Clun, Mr. John Brodie.

"John."

He stole her breath. All crisp lines and edges and perfection, his smile bright and full. His hat rested in his hands as he ran his fingertips along the rim. How she would miss such familiarity. How she would miss him. She stifled a sigh.

He gestured to her trunk. "I see you're packed and ready to begin a new adventure."

"Yes. I'm off to Obley for a while. After that, I'm not quite sure."

His eyes softened and uncertainty registered in them. He grimaced, leaning heavily on his cane, and struggled down on one knee.

"John, you're injured, what are you—"

Taking her hand, he asked, "Any chance you'd care to take an adventure with me? As my wife?"

Did she hear him right?

"Are you proposing to me?" she gasped.

He chuckled, though pain edged lines around his mouth. "I am. Perhaps not the most romantic of deliveries as I kneel crippled before you with little to offer, but I couldn't contain the words any longer. You are all I think of and dream of. And the idea of exploring the world, the future with you, steals my breath." He paused. "I love you."

His Adam's apple bobbed as he awaited her answer. She couldn't speak. She couldn't move.

Yet the future she longed for was right there. With him.

"You wish to be with me? Even if I still wish to be a layer-out?"

"I fell in love with every part of who you are. From the

first moment, I was taken with you and enraptured by you entirely, my Lovely Digits."

And like the first day they met, she flushed under his assessment and praise. Her future, *their* future glowed in his gaze. She knelt before him and rested a palm against his chest. He caressed her cheek, cupping her face as his eyes darkened with emotion. He leaned in slowly, his lips hovering over her own, before seizing her own in a deep, gentle kiss. A kiss she wished would never end.

When he pulled back, he rested his forehead against her own. "What say you, Lucy? Shall we carve a new path together?"

She smiled and leaned back to look into his eyes. "Yes, John Brodie, I wish to be your wife and your fellow adventurer. No matter where our journey leads."

THANK YOU for reading LOVELY DIGITS, by Jeanine Englert! If you enjoyed her book, a review at Amazon would be most appreciated.

Jeanine Englert is a teacher by day and writer by night. After years of writing in secret (despite having a master's degree in writing), she joined Romance Writers of America and Georgia Romance Writers in 2013 and has been an active member ever since. She writes Scottish Highland historicals and historical romantic suspense novels. When she isn't wrangling with her characters on the page, she can be found trying to convince her husband to watch her latest Masterpiece or BBC show obsession. She loves to talk about books, writing, her beloved pups, and of course mysteries with other readers on Twitter @JeanineWrites, Facebook, or at her website www.jeaninewrites.com.

Her debut novel, *Lovely Digits*, will be released in 2019 by Soul Mate Publishing. It is a Victorian romantic suspense that won the 2017 Daphne du Maurier Award and was named a 2018 Golden Heart ® Finalist for best unpublished romantic suspense.

CPSIA information can be obtained
at www.ICGtesting.com
Printed in the USA
FFHW011132111019
55481085-61278FF

9 781682 919576